# Jade's Treasure

## ANA KRISTA JOHNSON

CRIMSON
ROMANCE

F+W Media, Inc.

This edition published by
Crimson Romance
an imprint of F+W Media, Inc.
10151 Carver Road, Suite 200
Blue Ash, Ohio 45242
*www.crimsonromance.com*



ISBN 10: 1-4405-7175-9
ISBN 13: 978-1-4405-7175-6
eISBN 10: 1-4405-7174-0
eISBN 13: 978-1-4405-7174-9

*To my parents, Jim and Janet Johnson,*
*who have put up with me the longest!*

# Acknowledgments

Many thanks to my parents and family, The Last Minute Poetry Club (past and present members), Paul Kreiling, Chris Frank, Jake, Zoe, and of course the love of my life, Patrick.

# Chapter 1

*D-o-n-e*. Done. Done. With. Men. Jade hefted the axe above her head again and let the blade fall with a satisfying thwack into a log resting on the old, scarred stump. The stump had served as a chopping block for the Lakehaven Cabins for the past forty years. The year her grandfather had purchased the place the old tree had been struck by lightning, forcing William Sawyer to chop down the beautiful old elm. Jade smiled at the thought of her poppa telling her the story of the thunderstorm—how rare a lightning strike was and how that made it a special stump. This was only one of the many interesting stories surrounding Lakehaven.

She reached for the split wood and threw it onto the growing pile. She tried to focus on the fresh mountain air and the stretch of her shoulders as she grabbed another log for the chopping block, but she couldn't help it—her mind went back to today's mail. Maybe if she imagined Nick's head on the stump or, better yet, Stacy's, she might feel better. The log split cleanly. Her smile flashed wickedly.

They were getting married. She should have expected it, really. Nick had been her fiancé and Stacy her roommate when she'd caught them kissing on campus. Since then, Jade had seen them from time to time—the university was a small community and her dad worked there. When she did run into them, everyone managed to be awkwardly polite. Now, three years later, they sent out a "Save the Date" invite on cream card stock with graceful black script. Nick and Stacy were getting married. They had, no doubt, invited her parents to the *schmoozefest* and felt obligated to include her as well. *Jerks.* Jade felt petty for being angry. A better person would be over it by now. Three years was a long time to hold a grudge.

She shook her head to clear the memory and set herself for the next assault on the log. She had been chopping for about twenty minutes now. She could've had Jeff or Ben do the work, but Jade needed to expend the energy. She blew out a breath, and her bangs lifted off her forehead. Three years passed quickly. She had left the university, run back to Lakehaven, taken some metalworking classes, dated a little. Three years.

A light sheen of perspiration glistened on her forehead, and a small trail of moisture showed through her shirt. Her jacket hung from a nearby tree, forgotten. The exertion of her chore kept her warm enough; the only proof of the early autumn chill was her cheeks, flushed pink. Jade widened her stance and swung the axe in a wide arc above her head and down toward the next log, letting the momentum and weight of the blade split the log cleanly. They were getting married. Crap. She couldn't successfully navigate a date, and they were getting married. Clearly, she lacked the skill set necessary to date. There was no point in trying. Ergo, done with men.

•••

Matthew McLaughlin skillfully maneuvered his SUV around the curved dirt road toward Lakehaven Cabins. He gritted his teeth as the tires skimmed the edge of a hole, dropping the passenger side nearly ten inches lower than his side of the vehicle. He shook his head. The website had made Lakehaven look like a luxury mountain resort—granted, an isolated one—but he had expected pavement at the least.

This path could barely pass for a road. He guessed it had looked much the same four hundred years ago. The terrain was beautifully wild from a romantic's point of view; visions of men on horseback—fur traders, trackers, guides—filled Matt's head. He smiled at his fantasy. He had always been a daydreamer, and hours reading tall tales and legends about Lakehaven were heady fuel for his imagination. A harsh jolt surprised him out of his reverie. Matt had seen some pretty big potholes in Manhattan, but these were obscene.

It was only for a week, then back to civilization. Matt smiled to himself. Calling New York City "civilized" might be a stretch. The fact that you could get food delivery at three in the morning *almost* made up for the concrete jungle mentality. Oh well, one week without late night takeout was hardly roughing it. As if on cue, "Sabotage" by the Beastie Boys blasted out from his cell phone. It was Samantha calling.

Matt flipped open the phone with one hand. "What?"

"Niiiice greeting." Sam's voice dripped with sarcasm.

"Yeah, what?" Matt repeated.

"Can't I just check up on you?"

"Without raising suspicion?"

Sam laughed. "Okay, I kind of told your mom I'd check up on you."

"Sam, you're my manager, not my babysitter."

"For some writers it's the same thing."

"Not this one," Matt said.

Sam sighed. "Yeah, I know. She's your mom. She worries. Unfortunately, she's also my godmother, so I get to relay the message."

"She worries about me finding an appropriate wife, about me being seen in the right places, about me circulating in the correct social circles."

"She just wants you to be happy," Sam said.

Matt took a deep breath and blew it out. "I know, and I am. But it's just not enough anymore. It feels like … something's missing."

"Please tell me this is not going to be one of those rich-successful-famous-writer-whines-about-his-fabulous-life speeches."

Matt laughed at himself. He was doing precisely that. Thankfully, Sam never let him get away with any of that garbage "Okay, you're right. Life is good. Maybe just some time away from that fake social crap will give me some perspective."

"Okay, I get it. Peace and quiet."

"Yeah," Matt agreed softly.

"And this wouldn't happen to have anything to do with some crazy treasure legend?"

Matt grinned. Sometimes Sam knew him too well. "No! Absolutely not. Just tell my mom I'm fine. I'm working."

"Riiight. Okay, can do. As far as she's concerned you're doing great and researching the next book."

"Thanks, Sam. You're the best."

"Don't you forget it." There was a long, comfortable silence on the phone, just Matt breathing and Sam breathing, a moment of easy companionship. Then Sam broke the silence. "Let me know if you need anything else?"

"Just time to think, for now."

Matt could almost hear Sam smiling on the other end of the line. "Check in in a few days, okay?"

"I'll try."

Sam laughed. "No you won't, but I'll call you." Matt chuckled as he shut his phone. Samantha Parker was younger by two years, but it was kind of like having an older sister checking up on him. He slightly resented it, and at the same time, loved the fussing. It was nice to be fussed over, sort of.

He took a deep breath of fresh air through the open windows of his SUV. You didn't get to do that in the city. Matt smiled as he made his way down the dirt road that led to *sanctuary*. It was a beautiful sunny day, cool and crisp with the tang of fall in the air. The sun filtered through the trees lining the drive and dappled the windshield. It was quiet and peaceful and the perfect retreat to give him some space. The city had taken on a claustrophobic feel lately. Matt normally loved the buzz and hum of city life, but recently the success, the social whirl, the obligations had started to close in on him.

He felt like he was living a double life: one as himself, just plain Matt; and the other as his alter ego, the famous M. Riley McLaughlin. Despite career success, notoriety, and his pick of beautiful women, lately neither identity was enough. Or at least not enough of what he *really* needed. Whatever that was. He rolled his eyes at his own pathetic thoughts. At what point had being *the* M. Riley McLaughlin become such a burden?

As Matt navigated the minefield of rocks and potholes, he scanned the road and did his best to avoid any damage they might do to the truck chassis. The road opened out into a parking lot of sorts where he guided the SUV to a nearly silent stop. He noticed a young figure about a hundred yards to his right, wielding an axe with proficient strokes, and clearly at home in this environment. Must be the caretaker. He appreciated the scene: a palette of greens and browns with the lone figure, in jeans and a cream-colored shirt, chopping wood. The image was picturesque and somehow lyrical.

Matt grabbed his laptop case and duffel from the passenger seat before sliding out of the driver's side. He stretched his legs, stiff from the long ride up, and looked around.

The lake stretched out in front of him, a deep olive color surrounded by the brighter shades of the various conifers. Trunks and branches of leafless oaks, elms, and maples made grey-brown hatch marks through the green of pine needles. The still waters of the lake reflected a heavily clouded sky, putting a silver sheen on the water. Matt knew from the website that there were eight cabins and a main house dotting the lake's edge, but they were well hidden. It was extremely isolated and a perfect setting for the novel he was beginning to write. The lack of distraction would help his writing if he could stand the quiet. Living in the city, he was accustomed to a certain level of noise: traffic, yelling, sirens, music.

Somewhere in his consciousness, Matt registered that the rhythmic thud of chopping had stopped. The silence was strange, eerie. He turned toward the caretaker who was removing leather work gloves and slapping them against a slim thigh. Matthew narrowed his eyes as awareness bloomed in his gut: the graceful, small movement of her hands, the delicate curve of her spine, the fluid rolling of her shoulders as she worked the kinks out . . .

In the time it took for her to turn and face him, he knew. *Shit.* He had left the city to get away from distractions, and she was definitely a world-class distraction: slim torso, high breasts, muscled thighs that Matt could easily imagine ... *Okay, back to reality*, Matt thought. He watched her tuck her gloves into the back pocket of her loosely fitting jeans and stop by the tree to pluck her coat from the branches. From this new angle, Matt could see her black ponytail twitching from side to side in rhythm with her gait. Her steps were quick and light as her small frame approached.

• • •

*Oh great*, Jade thought. She watched the tall, lean, and definitely male figure exit a sleek black SUV that had pulled into the Lakehaven parking lot. And just like that, all of the extra energy that she had worked off by chopping wood suddenly sparked back to life. Jade blew a quick breath out and narrowed her eyes. *I'm sooo not interested. This guy has heartbreaker stamped all over him. Not to be trusted. Damn, but he looks good enough to ... oh, whatever.*

He was tall, just over six feet, and broad-shouldered with sandy hair tipped with gold. A hard-muscled chest, evident under his grey t-shirt and black leather jacket, tapered down to narrow hips, then long, lean thighs that had her stomach doing little somersaults.

It was all she could do not to lick her lips. Jade pleaded to the heavens. *God, why me? Why now?* She nibbled on her lower lip nervously. Not interested. She focused on her life mission, which was, at the moment, keeping Lakehaven running smoothly. Great service at a peaceful mountain resort. No drama. *Just be friendly, that's it, friendly and professional.* She dragged her eyes from his gorgeous biceps.

"Sorry, I didn't hear you pull up or I would've stopped sooner. I'm Jade. You must be Mr. Connor. We've been expecting you." She swiped at a fringe of black bangs and wiped a sweaty palm on her jeans before extending her hand toward his.

• • •

Matthew smiled at Jade's use of the fake last name. Samantha always wanted him in the public eye, claimed it made the PR team's job easier. She was firmly in the "all publicity is good publicity" camp. From a business standpoint, he could wholeheartedly agree. From a personal one, it sucked. That was the problem with celebrity. You always brought your work along with you. It followed you like a cloud. It was a running argument between them—Matt preferred his anonymity, and Sam preferred he be high profile. But on this occasion, Sam had reluctantly agreed that they wouldn't be missing out on any great opportunities by going covert in a small, isolated place like Lakehaven.

Jade's handshake was firm, energetic, and warm. Her skin was creamy and tinged with pink; her eyes were green. Matt felt like the wolf coming upon Red Riding Hood, instantly alert and up for the chase. A smile tugged at the corner of his mouth.

"Please, call me Matt. If you could point me in the direction of my cabin, I'll go settle in."

He watched as she donned a chipper smile like a suit of armor. "Nonsense, I'll help you with your things. It's right this way." For some reason, her forced smile bugged him. He got enough fake social interaction in Manhattan. He was hoping for something different here.

Before Matt could protest, she grabbed the bag out of his hand. It had to be heavy for this sprite of a woman. She was only about five feet and some change, but she made no comment, nor did she slow down. Matt's last girlfriend had been five-foot-ten, and she wouldn't even tote her own carry-on luggage. Matt smiled at the petite woman's back. She barreled on toward the lake, talking as she went. She was intriguing—guarded and distant one moment, enthusiastic the next.

"The cabins are all numbered. The main house here is in the middle, number five. It has a kitchen where we lay out a nice continental breakfast every morning if you don't want to fend for yourself. You can also request a boxed lunch to take on a hike or whatever else you need. Meg, our cook, is really quite good. There is also a great room with a fireplace, a game room, and a porch if you feel like socializing with any of the other guests. Beyond the main house to the right are cabins one through four, and here to the left are six through nine." Jade stopped and looked over her shoulder at him. Matt stared back at her, a smile playing at the corners of his mouth.

"What?" she asked.

"I just wondered if you were going to take a breath or turn blue."

"Sorry." Jade blushed, a soft shade of rose staining her pale cheeks.

Matt's smile faded. *No distractions … Yeah, right.* Matt took a step toward Jade and stood close enough that he could feel the heat radiating from her. He frowned at himself; he usually wasn't this pushy.

Jade took a step back and turned on her heel. She tightened her grasp on his suitcase and made her way between the large central house and a cabin with a wooden number six on the door. She then turned left onto a path that wound its way past additional cabins, parallel to the lake. He noticed she didn't turn to see if he was following. Instead, she was focused on maneuvering his large luggage through the underbrush as she veered off the main path onto a smaller one that led back to a wooden door marked with a *seven*.

"Well, here we are, Mr. Connor." Jade put down his case to dig in her pocket and pull out a set of keys.

"Please, call me Matt." Matt stood behind her, looking down at her glossy hair. He was close enough that he could smell the mint of her shampoo mixed with pine. He took a half step forward for a better whiff. At the same moment, Jade's upper body leaned forward to unlock his door.

• • •

So far, so good. Jade was managing to stay professional and completely ignore the inconvenient attraction she felt for this virtual stranger. Everything was perfect until she put his case down, pulled out the key, and leaned in to unlock cabin seven.

Her butt pressed back, brushing against his well-muscled thighs. Jade inhaled sharply and jumped as if she had been burned, then straightened suddenly, overcompensating in her haste. Her momentum carried her backward, and her back met the wall of his chest with a soft thud. She felt his arms come up and around her shoulders before she could spring away. She had gone from opening his door to being wrapped in his arms, a guest's arms, in seconds. *Fast hands.* She felt her body's response, quick and sharp, as a warm flush spread down to her core. Matt's sudden intake of breath betrayed his equally strong reaction.

"Oh! Uh, sorry. Wow, sorry," Jade said. She pasted an awkward smile on her face.

Matt made sure she had her balance before releasing her and taking a controlled step back. If she hadn't been crowded between Matt's body and the door to his cabin, Jade would have sprung away.

"That's the third time you've apologized to me since I arrived." His voice was dry, but when she turned to face him, Jade was sure she saw teasing humor in his eyes.

Jade forced a light laugh. "Hmm, you're right. I take it back, then."

"You're *not* sorry?" He cocked one eyebrow and took a half step forward again.

"I'm sure I will be, very soon." She grumbled and turned to the door to unlock it. She did so stiffly, careful not to repeat her earlier clumsiness, and handed him his key without touching his hand. She stepped off the path to let him enter the cabin. He sat his laptop case down inside the door and turned to reach outside for his other bag just as Jade bent down to retrieve it. She stopped herself right before their hands would have met, and straightened awkwardly. *Good going,* Jade admonished herself. Matt easily swung the heavy bag inside next to his others and directed a devastating smile her way.

"Where can I find you if I … need anything?" The devilish glint in Matt's eyes left no doubt about his intentions, but Jade reined in her reciprocal smile. She was doing her job here. Nothing more.

"From nine to five I'm in the main house or on the grounds." Jade bit her lower lip nervously.

"And after hours?" Matt teased.

Her response was terse. "Check with Ben. He's on nights." She did her best to ignore the stunning smile he gave her before she turned and walked away.

Jade groaned inwardly as she made her way back to her cabin to change out of her sweaty clothes. *How does this always happen to me? I was resolved! I made a sound decision based on really great supporting data. And bam! Mr. Sex-on-a-Stick shows up. This is obviously the universe's idea of a cosmic joke. I might as well be on the second day of a diet with a triple bacon cheeseburger, fries, and a shake laid out before me.* She blew out an exasperated breath that cleared her bangs from her eyes.

Jade let herself into her cabin, hung her parka from the peg by her door, and worked her feet out of her boots. She looked around her cabin, which was not a total disaster—yet. The laundry bag was getting too full, books and jewelry supplies were strewn across the table, and there were some dishes in the sink, but it was nothing a twenty-minute cleaning session couldn't solve. She could always ask the cleaning crew, Maddie and Stu, to stop by, but that felt too indulgent. After all, she was staff now, not a guest. Not just staff, but the management.

Jade shook her head at the thought. How the hell had that happened? Oh yeah, free room and board during the winter months while her aunt and uncle wintered in Florida. She could manage the resort and still have enough time left to design and cast jewelry, and maybe even launch a jewelry business. Best of all, it was not only convenient from a financial standpoint, but a social one too.

Hiding out was easy at Lakehaven. Hiding out was, in fact, the whole point of a mountain retreat. Jade smiled to herself. She was good at retreating. She hummed a bar of Pat Benatar's "Love is a Battlefield." That pretty much summed it up. And if retreating was good, keeping busy was even better; managing Lakehaven provided both. She could do this!

Then she remembered the Kent sisters, Mr. Boyle, and the treasure hunting wackos and thought, *I'm doomed.*

# Chapter 2

Jade showered quickly and dressed casually. The manager's office was on the first floor of the main house, so she headed back in that direction, passing cabin seven on her way. She glanced toward the cabin, but even though it was close, it was barely visible through the trees. All was quiet—no sign of Matthew Connor. She quickened her pace. Some boring paperwork and bill paying would be just the thing to keep her out of trouble.

Two hours later, Jade finally stood up from her desk to stretch and take stock. The office was tidy for a change, the bills were ready to go out, the paperwork was done, and her stomach was empty. Satisfied that she had done all she could here, Jade headed for the kitchen.

Meg Hammond had worked in the Lakehaven kitchen since high school, at first helping Nani Sawyer and Aunt Bertie, and eventually taking over for them. She was, in Jade's opinion, a culinary wizard. Jade insisted the gift was God-given, but Meg always pointed out that sixteen years of practice and a few lessons here and there didn't hurt.

The kitchen was Jade's favorite place in the main house. (The front porch was a close second: screened from bugs, a view of the lake, a porch swing … what was not to love?) Meg's food was great but her company was even better, and she always gave Jade the scoop about what was going on at Lakehaven. The way Jade figured it, spending time in the kitchen was an invaluable source of information and sustenance for a manager.

"Ah, yes, I thought I heard these brownies calling my name!" Jade said to Meg's back. She snatched a brownie from the pan. They were still warm.

"Really, what do they sound like? High and munchkin-y or deep and husky?" Meg replied.

"Deep and husky? Why does every discussion with you go in the same direction? Mmmmmm!" Jade finished on a bite of brownie, frosted of course.

"Speaking of 'deep and husky, mmmm,' did you get an eyeful of our new guest?"

Jade feigned ignorance. "Which new guest would that be?"

"Oh please, I know you checked in Mr. Connor. And if you are breathing, I know you checked him out."

Jade laughed. "Yeah, I saw, I came, he conquered. But he's a guest. I'm not interested and … I'm not interested."

"You said that second thing twice."

"New topic, this one bores us," Jade said in a corny upper crust accent.

"Okay. Did you e-mail those pictures to Francesca?"

Jade was silent, chewing intently on her brownie.

Meg gaped. "You are kidding me. She wants to see your jewelry! She wants to *sell* your jewelry, and you—"

"Maybe. Maybe she wants to sell it. I don't think the line is ready yet."

Meg was shaking her head. "But you'll never know if it is because you won't e-mail the pictures!"

"What if she hates them?"

"Then she has shitty taste, and you find another boutique owner. There must be about, oh, say ten billion boutiques in New York. Trust me, your work is beautiful and people will buy it."

"I don't like this topic anymore, either." Jade chomped into her brownie.

Meg sighed. "Eventually you'll have to stick your neck out and debut your jewelry. So … Mr. McHottie?"

"No."

"No to the jewelry and no to the hottie. I'm sensing a trend."

"Aunt Bertie is counting on me to run Lakehaven efficiently and professionally. I'm pretty sure that doesn't include sleeping with the guests."

"Yeah, and I'm pretty sure the employee manual doesn't say anything about fraternizing."

*Fraternizing?* Jade thought. *There is nothing about that man that makes me think of a brother.* "I am *not* interested. In fact, I might even try a year of celibacy. Did I already eat that whole brownie?"

"Mmm hmm. So, your date was a bust." It wasn't a question.

Jade frowned. The date they were discussing had been a disaster, one in a long line of disasters. "I have a strictly no kiss, no tell policy. Can I have one more brownie?"

Meg handed Jade a brownie. "No, not that one, one from the middle." Meg sighed and picked one from the middle of the pan.

"Jade, your policy is more like a kiss-off policy."

"Bite me." Jade took a particularly vicious bite of brownie to make her point.

"Look, you keep talking about finding the love of your life, but you're in here with me eating brownies like they're the *Last Supper!*"

"A girl's got to eat."

"Well, try varying your diet. I'd recommend adding a little meat."

"Meg, are we still talking about food?"

"No, I'm talking about a six-foot-two side of grade-A."

"I am so not having this conversation! Does your husband know you talk like that?"

"Honey, he loves when I talk like that!"

"Okay, let's say I take your fine advice. What happens when I bite off more than I can chew?"

"Then you tell me all of the delectable details, and we both end up happy!"

"I'm afraid there will be no happy endings for this girl. Look, I've tried all sorts of … dishes. None of them satisfied. I have a very discerning palate."

"I just have a feeling about this. Your next great adventure is around the corner. Take a risk, Jade. You've got to take the bull by the horns, or whichever other body parts you can grab. I know it isn't always easy, but it's worth it. Unless you're *chicken*?"

"Nice try, Meg, but I'm not biting."

"Not biting what?" an amused male voice chimed in from the doorway.

Jade nearly choked on her last bite of brownie. Meg laughed.

"Mr. Connor, welcome to Lakehaven. I see you've found your way to our kitchen." Meg used her most cheerful hostess voice.

"Yes, thank you. Something smells wonderful," he responded.

Great, nice cover. Jade shot a glance at Meg, then turned slowly. The sight of him … God, he was good looking. Jeans, a fisherman's sweater, laughter in his eyes—too unreal. *Okay, stop staring now and say something.*

"Mr. Conner, this is Meg Hammond, our chef extraordinaire."

Matt flashed Meg a million-watt smile that had her grinning. "Great to meet you, Meg." He turned to Jade and took a deliberate step toward her. "Do I have to beg in order to get you to call me Matt?"

"Oh! Uh, no, not at all. No begging necessary."

"I should say not," Meg murmured under her breath.

Jade shot Meg a dirty look, but Meg ignored her. Or, was too busy smiling widely at Matt to see her glare.

Jade glanced at Matt just in time to see him wink at Meg. Apparently, his hearing was keen enough to pick up her comment. She could see him bite the inside of his cheek to keep from laughing. Great. What a typical male, flirting with anything in a skirt. Though technically, Meg was wearing pants.

"Okay then, dinner will be in twenty minutes. Can I get you a beverage in the meantime?" Meg offered.

"That would be great, thanks."

"Jade, could you take the iced tea and show our guest out to the dining room?"

"Sure." Jade forced a smile onto her face while she tried to determine how much of their earlier conversation Matt might have overheard.

Meg interrupted her thoughts. "Just remember what I said, Jade."

"Yeah, which thing you said? The stuff about the 'Last Supper,' or the stuff about the bull?"

"No, the stuff about the chicken."

*What a smartass. Chicken, my butt. I'll show you chicken. I can't believe Meg thinks I'll fall for her juvenile, reverse psychology crap. He's staring at me.* "What?" It came out sharper than she intended.

Matt raised an eyebrow. "You're scowling."

"Sorry."

"You're apologizing again."

Jade sighed. This was not going well. "Right. Not sorry."

"Good. Look, if you don't want to accompany me to the dining room ... "

Oh great, now she was alienating the guests. "No, God no, it's not that. I'm just—oh, ignore me. I'm just a huge geek."

"I like geeks."

"Really? What's the appeal?" She couldn't help the note of sarcasm that crept into her tone.

"They're usually interesting. So what's on the menu tonight? *Chicken?*"

Jade laughed nervously at the misunderstanding and unintended (she hoped) double entendre all in one. She had to give it to Meg. The girl knew how to manipulate a situation. Jade stifled a sigh. Might as well play the gracious hostess and change the subject at the same time. "How do you like Lakehaven so far?"

"Well, it's very … charming. So far."

"Great! We're glad you're enjoying the ambiance. I hope you'll take in all we have to offer."

That got her another raised eyebrow. *Oh, geez. Extract foot from mouth. Ugh.* Jade bit her tongue to get her brain into gear before her mouth did any more damage. Her eyes darted to Matt's mouth. She blushed as she thought of the exact kind of damage her mouth could cause. *No, no no! Damn Meg and her suggestive conversations.* Matt grinned down at her and said nothing. Absolutely nothing. *She had to drag her gaze away from his mouth. Not good.*

Jade led him quickly to the dining room, set down the pitcher of iced tea, and pulled a tall glass from the sideboard. They were alone in the dining room. *Damn, where was everyone?* "You have your pick of tables, Mr. Connor."

"Matt."

Jade bit her bottom lip. Her instinct told her to keep her distance, but she couldn't see how to refuse his request that she use his first name and still maintain the friendly charm that was as much a part of Lakehaven as its view. She wanted nothing more than to make a hasty exit. Jade thought of her cozy cabin. She would rather be there working on the jewelry she had spread out on her dining room table, but her job as the manager of Lakehaven dictated otherwise. She fought back a sigh. "Right, Matt. Well, which will it be?"

"The small one in the corner."

Jade nodded and headed for the corner. "Good place to people watch." Jade set the tea down.

Matt shot her a look of surprise. She guessed he hadn't expected her to understand it, but the corner table happened to be one of her favorite spots in the dining room. Matt pulled a chair out for Jade and gestured toward it gallantly.

*Why couldn't he just leave her alone?* Her brain searched for a good excuse, but all she could come up with was, "I have to shampoo my hair." It was such a ridiculous thought that she smiled. The next thought she had was, "The cat ate my homework"—no, wait, it was "dog." She almost giggled at herself and Matt was smiling back at her, which made her scowl. *Crap, now he would think she was imbalanced or mentally deficient.*

The only thing she could come up with to make it better was to sit with him to prove she was stable. She tried to think up something normal to say. Matt wasn't saying anything either, and they both sat there smiling at each other in silence. Then after a few tense moments, they both spoke at once:

"So what brings you ..."

"How long have you ..."

"... to Lakehaven?"

"... been working here?" The exchange was followed by awkward laughter. *Smooth.* Matt recovered first.

"Actually, I'm here to write."

"Really? My mother was a writer. A poet, actually."

"Do you write?"

Jade laughed. "No, that talent did not get passed down to me. I—" She was almost going to say something about the jewelry designing but stopped. She could feel heat creep up her face. He was watching her intently and that only made the blush worse.

He smiled. "Come on, tell me. You what?"

She waved the question off. "So, what do you write?" She meant to be reticent. Instead, it came out enthused.

"Fiction. Novels."

"I love fiction. So, what? Mysteries, horror, spy novels?" Again with the enthusiasm. For some reason she couldn't help herself.

"Something like that. Action thrillers to be exact."

"Oh, I get it, spooky wooded area. Good setting."

"Yeah, that's the idea. Research."

"You're here for a week."

"Yeah. How long do most people stay?"

"Usually about that—a week or two. Some of the regulars stay much longer, but not usually in the winter. Summer is our busy season. It's beautiful then. Lush, green, alive. Don't get me wrong, it's beautiful now with the leaves turning, but pretty soon everything will get quiet, stark. That's beautiful too, but in a different way."

"You love it here."

"Mmmm. Yeah, I grew up here."

"Good, then I already know something about you." Matt smiled a smile that reached to his eyes.

Jade had been so engaged in the simple conversation that she had forgotten her prime directive: be professional, but keep your distance. Matt was just another relationship disaster waiting to happen. Luckily, the second he turned on a bit of charm, Jade's inner cynic kicked in. Nick had been charming like that, and look how that turned out. "Wow, that is such a line."

Matt shrugged, but if her chilly tone bothered him, he didn't let it show. "Yeah, it was, wasn't it? I wouldn't even let one of my characters get away with that one." Jade gave him a begrudging smile for his honesty. "But it's still true. You're interesting."

Jade deflected his interest. "Nah, not so much." Other guests were starting to enter the dining room. The Andersens, the Jordan family, the Kent sisters. *Perfect, a getaway strategy!* "Well, it's getting busy in here, and I've got work to do. Is there anything else I can do for you?" Jade said as she stood.

"I'll most certainly let you know." Matt grinned.

Despite her determination to feel nothing for him, Jade's heart rate elevated as her face flushed yet again. "Great." *Exit stage left.*

Three hours later, Jade sat on the porch swing, glass of Merlot in hand, looking out at the lake's silvered surface. Dinner had gone well, and all of the guests had raved about Meg's chicken parmigiana. She and Jeff, Lakehaven's grounds and maintenance man, had stacked wood by each cabin. Everyone was tucked in for the night, and Ben, the assistant manager, was on duty for the evening. Jade leaned her head back and closed her eyes, listening to the crickets and the breeze through the pines. She sighed deeply and gently rocked in the swing. It was an absolutely perfect end to the day.

•••

After dinner, Matt took his time unpacking his things and soaking up his surroundings. The cabin was small and cozy. The front door opened onto the living room with a bedroom and bathroom at the back of the cabin and a kitchen to the right. The living room featured an ancient stone fireplace, already stoked with wood and crumpled newspaper, two couches in an L-shape, a coffee table, and a large oak desk against the wall. The desk was perfect for writing; there were no windows on that side of the room, no pictures either. No distractions. Matt set up his laptop and some research materials there. Some related to his current novel, others to the legend of the Cartwright treasure. A letter, allegedly penned by Adam Cartwright, sat on the top of the pile.

*Hudson River Valley Outpost 54*
*September 9, 1615*

*Dear Mother,*

*I have arrived on the new continent. I am sorry it has taken me so long to write. It has been an incredible journey thus far and I have you to thank for providing the wherewithal to embark on such an adventure. I know it can't have been easy to let me go, releasing me from my familial duties and obligations and to an unknown fate. You have my undying gratitude.*

*This new land is staggering in its vastness. Spending so much of my time growing up at our country home, one would think I would be quite at ease in this wilderness, but in fact, it is as foreign as if I were a city dweller. It is both daunting and exhilarating to be so far out of my element. There are areas so remote that one must rely solely on the land and one's own wits. Still, it is worth any risk to be able to explore such pristine environs. There is a sense of timelessness. The land here whispers of events prior even to man's recorded history and watches our gentle footsteps with tolerant composure. It is a fanciful sentiment, to be sure, yet I can find no other way to describe my experience of this strange and alien land.*

*Clearly, there are many ways that I am an outsider here; however, the people that I have met are generous and welcoming. I have great hopes for a successful future. I will share more news soon.*

*Your loving son, Adam*

Matt smiled. The wilderness of Adam Cartwright's time had been perhaps a bit more unspoiled, but Matt could relate to Adam's fish-out-of-water experience. That wasn't the only thing that made Matt smile. The letter seemed to imply that it was the first missive of many, which meant Matt might find more clues to the story behind the Cartwright treasure.

Matt stowed the rest of his stuff hastily in the bedroom, pausing long enough to note the queen-sized bed and see the possibilities there. He shook his head. *God, get a grip, McLaughlin.* He left the bedroom and sat down at the computer to get started on some notes, distraction free.

Three hours later, Matt picked his way along the path from his cabin back toward the main house. It was dark now, and the rugged terrain required careful navigation. The writing hadn't gone well. His thoughts kept getting tangled up in her: the jet hair, those bangs always in her eyes, the slender figure perpetually in motion, the energy and intensity that she radiated. It was only through sheer will and discipline that he had gotten any work done at all. It seemed like a good idea to take a walk and explore a little of Lakehaven.

He took in the cool air, scented with pine, and the faint lapping of lake water on the damp shore. He heard the sound of his own footsteps crunching through dead leaves and branches. Crickets chirping and a sliver of moon completed the scene. It all got filed away in his memory for writing. The breeze in the treetops made an ancient rhythmic sound like the ebb and flow of ocean waves.

Matt was jarred out of his reverie by the ring of his cell phone. It was Samantha.

"Yeah?"

"Could you, for once, answer your phone with the manners your dear mother taught you?"

Matt smiled. It was Samantha's life's mission to reform him, and his life's mission to thwart her. "Is that really what you called about?"

Matt could hear Samantha's sigh over the phone, even with the mountain reception. "No, of course not. Would it kill you to call me and let me know you made it there safely?"

"Kill me? No, but it would definitely cramp my carefree, spontaneous artist's spirit.

"Spontaneous?! Fuck you, McLaughlin."

Matt laughed. "Hey, that reminds me, thank you for booking me under the alias."

"I'll expect some sort of favor in return for that and for keeping your whereabouts secret."

"I don't doubt it. Do you really think anyone will be following my whereabouts that closely?"

"Maybe, maybe not. Never hurts to be a little paranoid."

Matt grinned into the phone. "Spoken like a true New Yorker."

"Born and bred, baby, and don't you forget it."

"As if you'd let me. Can you call Allison and have her e-mail me the maps and research on my desk? I'm actually going to see if I can match the map to any landmarks around here."

"Please, you don't actually believe that treasure exists?"

He knew Sam couldn't see him, but shrugged out of habit. "Most legends have some basis in fact. I'm intrigued to see how closely the topography matches the maps. Besides, who can resist treasure hunting? It'll be an adventure."

"Someone once told me that if anyone says, 'It'll be an adventure,' you should get out of the car immediately and by any means necessary."

"Probably good advice."

"Which you won't follow," Sam said, laughing.

"Of course not." And with that, Matt flipped the phone shut.

• • •

Matthew stood at the door to Jade's screened porch, watching her. The wiser part of him thought to leave her alone here. He should go back to his cabin and get some sleep. It had been a long drive from the city, and he wanted to get a good chunk of work done tomorrow. She looked so peaceful there alone. The wiser part of him lost.

"Mind some company?"

Jade shivered the slightest bit, and Matt wondered if she was cold. He waited for her invitation before he sat down.

She opened her eyes just barely and nodded her assent. "Be my guest."

"I already am." There were two Adirondack chairs on the porch placed opposite the swing where Jade sat. She stopped the swing, and Matt took it as a sign. He sat with her.

She sighed and opened her eyes to look at him. "Good point. Get any writing done?"

In the low porch light, her eyes looked mostly grey, but he was close enough that he could see a hint of the green he had noticed earlier. "Not much yet."

Jade's forehead wrinkled. "Oh? Writer's block?"

"Mmm, not exactly." He didn't bother to tell her what exactly had stopped him from getting work done.

She sat up straighter in her seat, causing the swing to rock forward. "Is there anything wrong with your cabin?"

"No, no, it's nothing like that. The cabin is great, really. It's just the … scenery is distracting."

She relaxed again, sinking into the swing. "Yeah, it's spectacular, isn't it?" They sat together, soaking in the hushed night.

He leaned back in the swing, tipping her back with him. His arm was already stretched across the back and rested behind her neck. She either didn't notice or didn't object, so he left it there. Silken strands of black hair brushed against his forearm. God, it felt good. He angled his head just close enough to smell her mint-scented hair. Close enough to kiss her. "Breathtaking is the word I would use."

She shrugged. "You're the writer."

Matthew laughed. In the city, whenever any woman found out who he was, he ended up dodging advances and none-too-subtle phone calls for weeks. Now he was the one with the obvious come-ons, and she didn't even notice. Payback was a bitch. Of course, Jade only knew him as Matt Connor. He wondered if it would make a difference to her if she knew who he really was. Screw that. He wanted her to want him for himself, not for his celebrity or his bank account. It was great to just be Matt, but beyond the solitude and anonymity, Lakehaven was turning out to have an allure all its own.

Matt spoke into the silence. "I'm wondering if you can act as a guide. I want to hike the lake trail, get familiar with the terrain. Part of my research."

Jade frowned. "I thought you'd be tied up at your computer the whole time."

Matt grinned. The phrase "tied up" opened up a whole new avenue of daydreaming. He shifted in the seat to see her face better. Big mistake. Her face was only a breath away from his, and her eyes glittered silvery green in the moonlight. He drank in her face for a long moment. Her eyes locked in on his and held.

"Nope."

"Oh."

"So . . .?" When Jade didn't answer he repeated himself. "A hike?"

"Yes, I mean, no, I mean we've got some great guides who could take you. On a hike."

"What about you?" Matt's voice was solemn, but his eyes twinkled with mischief. She seemed flustered, and it pleased him to catch her off balance.

"Oh, I've been on hundreds of hikes. Maybe thousands," Jade responded obtusely.

"Great, tomorrow morning then?"

"What? Wait, I don't think … "

Jade looked panicked, and Matt pushed his advantage. "You can come by my cabin around ten."

"Oh, uh, I've got a really full day tomorrow. Lots to do. I'm very busy." Matt raised an eyebrow and nailed her with a stare. "Really, I'm sure you'd much rather hike with … um … " Jade made a twirly motion with her hand as if to conjure up the perfect hiking guide for Matt. Matt just continued to stare at her. She had a sudden look of triumph in her eyes a second before she blurted out "Jeff!" She beamed a smile in Matt's direction.

Matt felt a pang of … something, surely not jealousy, and wondered who Jeff was. "Jeff?" He shifted toward the end of the swing.

Jade was nodding enthusiastically. "He's a great guide. He works on the grounds mostly, but he'd probably rather hike with you than clear brush around the cabins. He's usually trying to get out of doing it anyway! And he knows the lake as well as anyone."

Matt nodded. "Sooo … he's an employee, then?"

Jade tilted her head side to side. "Yeah, sort of."

Matt lifted an eyebrow. "Sort of?"

"Let's just say we pay him, and sometimes he works. He's a bit … flaky."

"That doesn't exactly sound like a great way to run a business."

Jade sighed. "Probably true, but Lakehaven is more than just a business. It's a family. He's been here since he was a kid. We grew up together. The guests know him and like him. He's a bit like a scruffy stray that you get attached to."

Matt's eyes narrowed, and he crossed his arms across his chest. "This doesn't exactly inspire my trust in him as a guide. I'll be asking questions for research and—"

Jade cut him off. "No! I swear he's the best. You'll be in good hands." The look in her eyes was almost pleading.

Matt wanted to laugh. Usually he had women throwing themselves at him, but here she was, this pixie of a woman, practically begging him to hike with scruffy Jeff. It was not exactly what he had in mind, but he could tell she was reluctant to go with him. It was an odd feeling not to be pursued. He was used to drawing flocks of women, not for who he really was, but because of his public persona. He had forgotten what it was like to get to be just himself and maybe have to woo someone. It had been a long time. Still, he was pretty sure he remembered how.

*Okay then, hiking with scruffy Jeff.* He moved closer to her on the bench, their faces just inches apart. Her eyes were wide, waiting for his answer. He let his gaze wander. He lingered at her lush lips, then traveled up to her high cheekbones, cute nose, and finally met her stare. Then Matt smiled. He knew by now that he had a killer smile and how to use it. It was a disarming weapon whether used on the press, on a date, or sometimes even on Sam when he wanted his way. In this case, he set it to stun, then whispered, "Okay." Without another word, he left.

He walked back to his cabin under the sharp silver glow of moonlight and focused on listening to the crunch of rocks and twigs under his feet. He had wanted to kiss her. It had been a close thing there at the end. God, those lips, that hair, those eyes. He ran his hand through his hair, leaving it sticking up in places. He forced himself to take in the crisp mountain air in slow, even breaths. *Shit.* He smiled to himself. *I don't think I'll ever be able to smell pine and mint again without getting a hard-on.*

•••

Jade held her breath until she heard the screen door bang against the doorframe, then she let it out with a *whoosh*. For a moment, she had thought he was going to kiss her. Which would have been bad. He was hard enough to resist when he was just being nice, but if he tried to actually pursue her, she would be in big trouble.

God, this was crazy. Despite all of her good intentions and judgment, she had wanted to take him hiking more than anything. It was pure survival training that had saved her.

She frowned. What was it about him that she couldn't resist? A part of her, that elemental female energy, was aware of him on a very primal level. Jade chalked it up to hormones—just some chemical thing. Yeah, it was that and a few bad dates. And a few celibate … oh well, never mind. Not a problem. She went over the interaction, trying to figure it out.

Something in her had known he was there before he walked through the door. He had entered the porch silently, but she had sensed him there, even with her eyes closed. Maybe it was his body heat or a trace of his soap scent. Jeez, he even smelled sexy.

It was strange. She hadn't wanted him to sit next to her on the porch swing, but she had stopped swinging as he entered, hoping he would choose one of the Adirondack chairs across from her and hoping he wouldn't. He hadn't. She had liked the hardness of his thigh as it brushed against hers.

Thank God he had agreed to the hike with Jeff. Jade sighed. Of course, now she had to call Jeff to let him know that he was going hiking with Matt. Jade sighed again. Just when life seemed easy, something, or someone, came along to complicate things.

• • •

Jade was having a fabulously uneventful night of sleep until Jeff called at five-thirty in the morning to say he wouldn't be in that day. "Patsy" wouldn't start, and he couldn't get the right part to fix her until later that morning. Patsy was his truck; she was more rust than steel and always breaking down. Jade rolled over, looked at the clock, and groaned. There was really no one else to take Matt on a hike, and it was too early to call his cabin and cancel. She thought about rescheduling and decided it wouldn't look good. Lakehaven didn't really need bad reviews. They did a steady business, and if she had anything to say about it, it would stay that way. She pulled the covers over her head and tried to fall asleep again but couldn't.

Jade called Ben in the main house. He would leave a message for Matt, letting him know that Jade would be taking Jeff's place. With that obligation met, she yanked the covers up over her head and fell into a fitful sleep. She dreamt Nick was a zombie, and when she chopped his head off with an axe, it popped back up, this time with Matt Connor's face.

# Chapter 3

Jade woke up at 7:00 A.M. after hitting the snooze bar five times. She wasn't a morning person. She wasn't even a late morning or a noon person. It was only through sheer determination that she was fully dressed and stumbling toward the main house—specifically toward the coffee maker in the main house—by 7:15. Meg wasn't due until 9:00 A.M. after she dropped her kids off at school, but through the miracle of modern technology, the coffee maker was set to brew at 7:00 A.M. every morning. Jade considered this one of man's greatest achievements.

There was already an array of baked goods carefully laid out on trays in the dining room. Jade simply added the cream cheese, butter, and cream, and, voila! Breakfast was served. Jade let Ben know that she was on shift, and he could go home. Mornings were easy on the lake. Many of the guests slept in late and there was little to do.

When Meg arrived, Jade was in the kitchen with the newspaper, drinking coffee.

"So, how did last night go?" Meg nearly sang as she began preparations for boxed lunches and the night's dinner.

"Dinner was great."

"I know it was great, I cooked it. Did you see Matt Connor?"

"Yes, he ate."

"Aaaand?"

"He wants a guided hike at ten o'clock. I guess we'll need a boxed lunch." Jade blushed.

"Yes!" Meg grinned and danced around the kitchen.

"Give me a break! It's just a hike, you dork!" Jade scowled and buried her nose deeper in the newspaper.

Meg laughed and pulled supplies from the refrigerator. "Wow, grouchy. You must still be on your first cup of coffee. So, are you taking him up to the point?"

"Are you kidding? I have no idea what kind of shape he's in. I don't want to kill him!"

"He looks in pretty good shape to me. He must belong to one of those hardcore gyms in the city."

"Yeah, well, I'll probably just take him up the lake trail. The scenery's good and the grade is gentle."

"Yeah, you'll want him to save his strength," Meg laughed.

Jade rolled her eyes but declined a reply. She knew better than to engage Meg in an argument. After all, Meg was making their lunch.

Jade wasted time checking on the dining room and grounds for a half-hour before heading to Matt Connor's cabin. She swung through the kitchen, ignoring Meg's looks long enough to grab the boxed lunches and stuff them in her backpack.

Though she told herself it was just a hike, her heartbeat quickened as she approached his cabin. She rapped sharply on his door and waited. No answer. She waited until she couldn't stand it anymore and knocked again. She waited. Jade was about to knock a third time when the door swung open. Matt stood in the doorway, hair akimbo, chest bare, jeans slung low on his hips—extremely low—so low that it would be very hard to hide any sort of underwear below that waistband. He stared at Jade for a moment, clearly perplexed.

Jade frowned. "Um, didn't Ben call you?" Matt shook his head at her and she made a mental note to talk to Ben. "Jeff couldn't make it."

Matt seemed to take that in but didn't ask any further questions. He nodded, turned, and walked back into his cabin. Without invitation, Jade followed. She just couldn't help herself. Matt didn't object. In fact, he seemed to know she would follow. He walked back through the living room and into his bedroom. Jade followed. He grabbed a t-shirt out of his drawer and pulled it over his head, talking through the fabric. "Sorry, I slept in a bit." Jade's eyes were glued to the hem of his t-shirt as it slid down over his abdomen. He pulled a pair of black boxer-briefs out of the dresser drawer and looked into her eyes. "I'll just be a second," Matt said. Jade blushed as he went into the bathroom. That left Jade standing in the bedroom for two minutes, staring at the tangle of sheets and blankets on the bed. They still looked warm. And rumpled.

Matt emerged, face damp but still unshaven. Without a word, he went back to the dresser, grabbed a pair of socks, and headed for the front door. He pulled on the socks and shoved his feet into a pair of well-worn hiking boots. That was a surprise. Jade had expected top-of-the-line, brand new, stiff-as-a-board boots from the city boy. These were top-notch but had been broken in at least five years ago. They were as beat up as Jade's.

"All right, I'm ready to go."

"Are you sure? Don't you want coffee? Breakfast? Anything? You're barely awake!"

"Nope, I'm good. Let's roll." Matt grabbed the strap on Jade's daypack with remarkably fast reflexes for someone who had been fast asleep five minutes ago. He swung it around onto his shoulders and headed out the front door, leaving Jade staring after him.

Matt strode out of the cabin and turned left at the trail without a word or backward glance. They passed cabin eight, but he paused in front of the last cabin before the trail inclined to the right.

"Yours?" He indicated her cabin with a nod.

"Yep."

Matt stared at the cabin intently for a few moments, making Jade nervous. Perhaps he had x-ray vision and could see her mess. Jade shifted her weight uncomfortably. He smiled, turned back to the trail, and started walking.

It was a perfect day. The air was cool and crisp. The scenery had the sharp focus and vivid color that reminded Jade why fall was her favorite season. She took a deep breath of mountain air. Matt led the way easily, as if he had been coming here as long as Jade had. They walked for ten minutes in relative silence.

"How do you know where you're going?" Jade looked up the trail at Matt's world-class backside. Damn, that was a great view.

"I checked a trail map. I always do my research."

"So … you don't exactly need me as a guide."

"Not true. There are certain things that I can research on paper, and other things I like to find out first hand."

"Okay, like what?" Jade was half listening to Matt, half listening to the voice in her head that was wondering how his tight butt would feel naked and "first hand."

"Well, as a writer there are sensory experiences you write about that only ring true if you've actually experienced them. Hence the adage: 'Write what you know.'"

"That makes sense." She'd like a "sensory experience" of that butt . . .

*Cut it out! Think clean thoughts!*

"I can read about the terrain and environment, but I can't hear it or smell it."

"Uh-huh." Jade thought about the subtle smell of Matt's soap.

"Not that I need a guide for that either. But I did want your input on some of the local lore."

"Mmm." Jade gave up on the conversation and instead thought about what it would be like to run her hands down his muscular thighs and back up again … to that butt.

•••

Though Jade seemed to be in great shape and was most certainly used to hiking at this altitude, her breathing had become quick and shallow. Matt was keeping his pace casual, but sometimes he forgot that with his long legs, one of his strides might be two of Jade's. He slowed his pace and glanced over his shoulder to make sure she was all right. Jade nearly ran right into him. He caught her shifting her gaze upward at the last minute.

"What are you doing back there?" Matt grinned, widening his eyes innocently and crossing his arms in front of his chest in mock indignation.

The look on Jade's face was perfect. She blushed furiously while her mouth opened and shut again like a fish. Panic flashed in her eyes as her brain frantically searched for a lie.

"Uh." She took a deep breath. "Okay, I'm going with honesty here. I was checking out your butt. I mean, it's quite frankly amazing. And I mean, after all, I'm a healthy woman with … I mean, you can hardly blame me … I couldn't quite help myself. God, I'm sorry … that sounds so rude. Please don't hold it against me."

Matt waited a beat for her brain to catch up to what her mouth had just blurted out. Then he burst out laughing.

"Oh shit. I'm sorry." She blushed an even brighter shade of red, if that was possible.

Matt could barely get words out between his laughter. "No … apologizing … It's great! … Ogle my ass … all you want … but … are you sure … you don't want me to … hold … *it* … against you?"

"It's not funny! Oh, God." Jade started to laugh too.

Matt was laughing so hard he finally had to sit down right in the middle of the trail. He rolled onto his back and wiped tears from his eyes. Jade laughed harder, and she flopped down next to Matt. Five minutes later, they were still there trying to catch their breath. Then Jade broke out in giggles again. It was a full ten minutes before either one could regain composure.

They lay there on the trail in silence with the warm sun on their faces. Matt could see flashes of light behind his closed lids and hear the breeze play through the branches of the sparse remaining dried leaves. He could feel and hear Jade breathing next to him, and he felt deeply content. If only time could freeze . . .

Jade broke the silence first. "I really am sorry. That was ... inappropriate." Her voice was soft.

Matt rolled over on his side to face her. He reached over to brush her bangs out of her eyes. Eyes the color of sea glass. Her breathing was still uneven and quick.

"I had this idea that I would back off for a while. Give you some space. Just be friendly. I figured you would appreciate having some time to make up your mind about me." Matt's voice was deep and gentle.

Jade turned her head to look at him. "Very wise move."

Matt's gaze dropped to her mouth. "Yeah, wisdom isn't really my strong point." He rolled himself over her, meaning to lean down and just barely touch his lips to hers. But Jade leaned into the kiss, into him, at the same time.

The kiss started slow. His body pressed down onto hers as he deepened the kiss. But then she was reaching for him. Her hands thrust into the hair at the nape of his neck, and she just sparked. Her hips lifted off the ground and pressed into him. Jade made an urgent sound against his mouth, and he almost lost it right there. *Holy God, this feels good.*

Maybe. Back. Off. Just ease up a little bit. Yes, that would be a good idea. But no fucking way it was going to happen. He had spent half the night tossing and turning and dreaming of doing exactly this. Of her lying there with her mouth on his, her soft breasts pressing up into his chest and her hips grinding against him, a hint of what could be or of more to come. God, but it was so much better than he had dreamt. And they still had their clothes on. That really needed to be remedied. He reached one hand between them and slipped it up under her shirt. Ahh, yes! Skin. Her flesh was silken soft beneath his hand as he spread his fingers wide and low across her stomach.

*More,* Matt thought through the haze of feeling her, wanting her. There was only one word for her: un-fucking-believable. Or, perfect. Perfect would do, too. "Oh God, Jade. You're just so . . ."

Then, beyond the sound of blood pounding in his ears, he heard something else. There was a light crunch of footsteps and the low sound of voices approaching them from the trail below. *Oh, shit. What crappy timing.* Matt took another deep breath as he pulled away from Jade. He looked at her, laid out beneath him, her black hair fanned out around her head, cheeks flushed and her eyes half closed. *Shit again!* He almost laughed with the absurdity of their situation.

Jade's eyes fluttered open as Matt pulled away from her, confusion in her gaze. He smiled down at her and tugged her shirt back into place, then rolled to his feet and glanced down the trail. Matt could tell the moment she heard the approaching hikers by the way her eyes widened in surprise. She scrambled up to a seated position and took his hand as he stood and reached for her. She shook her head and frantically tried to brush the dirt off her clothes.

When the hikers reached them, Matt was surreptitiously pulling leaves out of Jade's hair. And biting his lip to keep from laughing. *Oh well, never a dull moment.* Which was ironic, since he had come to Lakehaven for exactly that—a week of doldrums. So much for expectations.

•••

The hikers turned out to be none other than the Kent sisters, both in their seventies and spunky as hell. Adele was tall and spindly with a scrawny neck and oversized feet. The rumor was that the

Olive Oyl character from the Popeye cartoons was fashioned in Adele's likeness. Her age and the timing made it impossible for the myth to be true, but the rumor persisted. Her sister, Beatrice, was smaller, with a dancer's grace. In her day, she'd been quite the beauty and supposedly the lover of Joseph Pilates, creator of the famed exercise method. The two were arguing as they approached.

"That is absolutely untrue, you bean-headed dolt!" Adele shouted.

"Oh look, Jade and that young man are out … enjoying nature!" Beatrice grinned up at Matt.

"Oh, perfect. I wonder if you two wouldn't settle a dispute we're having."

"Sure, what kind of dispute?" Matt asked good-naturedly.

Jade stared at the ground in front of her while she drew circles in the dirt with the toe of her boot.

"This is quite important, you understand," Beatrice began.

Adele nodded vigorously. "We've got a wager going."

Beatrice rubbed her hands together—the international Dick Dastardly sign for greed. "Yep, big money riding on this one. None of that penny-ante stuff."

"Really! Big money?" Jade's head whipped up, eyes wide. "But Adele, you never paid Beatrice after the last bet."

"Oh, don't you worry about that," Adele said. "This is my chance to win back my losses."

"Don't be ridiculous, you'll lose this one just like the last," Beatrice gloated.

"Well, why don't we let Matt be the judge of that?"

"Yes indeed, why don't we?"

"Fine." Adele crossed her arms over her chest.

"Fine." Beatrice mirrored the motion. The two stood in stony silence for the space of a few heartbeats. Matt finally interrupted the stalemate.

"What is it you need me to settle?"

"Do zombies eat flesh or drink blood?" Adele asked eagerly.

"Excuse me?"

"I told you he wouldn't know," Beatrice gloated once again.

"He didn't say he didn't know. He just didn't understand the question," Adele snapped.

"Okay, the question is: Do zombies eat flesh or drink blood? This is our wager. I think—"

"No, no, no! Don't influence him by telling which way you bet. You always do that: try to manipulate things by throwing your womanly wiles around and getting some unsuspecting sex-hound to vote your way. It doesn't matter which way we've wagered. He just needs to answer the question. Assuming you have an answer." Adele smiled at Matt.

"That is so unfair! I can't help the way I look, so don't assume I'm using my overt femininity to unduly influence the outcome. I was merely trying to clarify the situation." Adele slowly swiveled her head toward her protesting sister and raised her eyebrows. Beatrice huffed. "Fine. Please answer the question." Beatrice smiled up at Matt and shamelessly batted her eyelashes. Matt cleared his throat.

"Well, I'm not sure this is a definitive answer; however, in the *Odyssey*, Homer references bringing forth 'Shades' by cutting the throats of two sheep and letting the blood run into a trench … "

"Ah, see, there you are. Homer! One can hardly argue with that," Beatrice crowed.

"Homer! What nonsense. He was a writer! All they do is make things up. I do not concede."

Matt ran his hand across the back of his neck and shook his head slowly. "But those aren't zombies."

"Aha!" Adele gestured vigorously, and Jade had to back up to avoid getting poked in the eye.

Matt squinted in thought. "The Vodun religion asserts that the blood of animals or humans swiped across the mouth of a newly deceased corpse will raise the corpse while binding its will to the animating priest or priestess."

All three women shuddered at the gruesome image.

"However, some literature suggests that if the priest or priestess is not sufficiently powerful enough to bind the will of the raised dead, then the zombie will uncontrollably devour flesh."

"Well," Adele harrumphed. "This was terribly inconclusive. I will need a second opinion." She turned and headed up the trail.

"You always want a second opinion. You never just trust people. That's your primary flaw—a basic mistrust of your fellow human beings," Bea chastised as she followed in her sister's wake.

"Maybe it's your primary flaw. Just too trusting."

"Oh, here we go again with the character analysis. You can't ever just lose gracefully. Always have to get a dig in."

"You started with the character assassination. I said I would concede with a second opinion. Is that unreasonable? Why can't it ever be enough with you? You always want to make it about . . ." Adele's words faded as the two marched off up the trail, bickering as they went. Matt and Jade just stood there in the blooming silence. A breeze danced through brittle leaves and lifted Jade's bangs from her forehead. The scuttering sound of a small animal whispered through the underbrush nearby.

"Are they always like that?" Matt asked.

Jade grinned. "Really? Homer?"

• • •

The hike back to Lakehaven was less eventful, with Jade playing guide and Matt listening intently. She was determined to keep her distance after that kiss—that mind-blowing, amazing kiss that she was most certainly *not* thinking about. Instead, she focused on all of the reasons it was a bad idea. One: He was a man. Enough said. Two: He was a sophisticated city dweller and therefore her complete opposite. Three: He was pretty great and she was sure to mess things up anyway. Four—there was probably a four, but who was counting?

"All of this land used to be home to the Mahican, or their real name, the Muheconneok, meaning 'from the waters that are never still.' As with much of this country, most of the names that were originally used are still used today. Matt quirked his lips, biting back a full smile. For some reason it irritated her. "What? Is that funny?"

"No, no, I'm just smiling. Is that okay with you?"

"Yes, but are you smiling *at* me, or are you smiling *with* me?" Jade stopped walking for a moment and crossed her arms in front of her chest.

Matt smiled in return. "I was just thinking how much you sound like a history professor." He reached over and pulled a leaf from Jade's hair.

She jerked away and reached her hand back to smooth the hair at the back of her head. "Probably comes from my dad."

"Doctor Joel Sawyer." Matt stood staring at her hair.

Jade turned to head back down the trail. "You've heard of him?" Jade was thoroughly surprised. Her dad was top in his field, but it was a very obscure and unglamorous area of expertise. Not many people were familiar with it.

"I did some research ahead of time."

"On Renaissance art?"

"No, the Cartwright treasure."

*Crap!* Every time someone brought up the myth of the treasure, it stirred up trouble. People seemed to get a little crazy in the name of striking it rich. It wasn't just tourists either. The locals were as likely to go hunting for it as anyone else. The tale of the Cartwright treasure was part of the local lore. Many of the families in this area told and retold the story, not only to their offspring, but just as often to the out-of-towners, mostly, over a beer at

Fitch's Tavern. The details changed depending on who told the tale, but the basic framework remained the same.

Almost four hundred years ago, Adam Cartwright left his wealthy family in England to come to America. He became a fur trapper and fell in love with an Indian princess named Alsoomse. He gave the tribe his fortune in jewels and gold as a bride price, but it brought great misfortune to the tribe. This misfortune included the death of Adam Cartwright. His bride was consumed with grief. The tribal council voted to rid themselves of the cursed treasure. They held a purification ceremony and then buried the gold and gems, returning that which came from the earth to the earth. Only one piece of treasure was not buried with the rest: a ring given to Alsoomse by Adam as a wedding gift. She wore it always.

"Don't tell me you believe in that old tale?" Jade scoffed.

Matt smiled. "It's a poignant story."

Jade smacked her hand on her forehead. "Oh no, you're a romantic!"

One corner of Matt's world-class smile crept up. "I'm not saying it's true, but what if I am? Is that really so terrible?"

"Dear God! It's worse than I thought! You're a romantic *and* deluded. You probably dot your 'i's with little hearts! You need help." She was shaking her head with disdain, and it set her hair swinging behind her.

"Hmm, cynical. I smell a past breakup. Something particularly ugly."

Jade's spine stiffened. "Butt out."

"Sorry." Matt shrugged. "Not trying to be rude."

"Mmm, then it must come naturally to you. Look, I'm not cynical, just a realist. Stories are just that: fiction, make-believe."

"Yes, but the really good ones, the ones that stick with us, usually have some ring of truth to them."

"Like the Cartwright legend?" She was hiking up ahead, keeping space between them and doing her best not to roll her eyes at him.

"Yeah, I think that parts of it are true. I don't know about the treasure, but I think that there was a man who fell in love with the wrong woman. Two completely different worlds … "

"Or a woman who fell in love with the wrong man," Jade interrupted.

Matt stared at her for a moment. "Right, a woman who fell in love with the wrong man, and it ended badly. And the story was told again and again, maybe with certain parts changed, dramatized … "

"Romanticized," Jade sneered.

Matt laughed, "God, what did he do to you?"

She stopped in her tracks and turned to glare. Daggers.

Matt raised both hands in surrender. "Okay, *romanticized*, but for whatever the reason, the story still lives today. I mean, it intrigued your father enough to write about it, and it isn't even his field."

"He used to say it made him dare to dream."

"Sounds like he's a romantic."

Jade sighed heavily, lifting the bangs off her forehead. "Both he and my mom."

"Maybe we were switched at birth. My parents were nothing but practical and perhaps a bit … "

"Cynical?"

"Aloof."

"Oh."

"Don't look so concerned. I had a great upbringing. My parents weren't mean or even indifferent. They cared deeply about us, and they were involved. They just weren't in the least bit fanciful or quirky. They were more practical, goal-oriented."

"Yes. Goal-oriented. Very good. I approve." Jade nodded and continued down the trail.

"See, switched at birth."

She walked farther down the trail, her eyes landing on various details: wisps of clouds, crags in rocks. The curve of a vine winding up a tree trunk caught her attention and she stopped walking. Matt nearly bumped into her. She blushed, embarrassed. "It's the vine, there. See how it's gently curled around the tree, like an embrace? It caught my eye—I sometimes design jewelry and . . ." She didn't know what else to say about something she was so passionate about. It felt too vulnerable.

Matt was staring. At her. Intently. One second they had been talking, and the next thing she knew, it felt like the air had been sucked out of the room. If they had been in a room. A whole friggin' mountainside of air, and Jade could barely catch her breath. Plus, her heart felt like it would beat out of her chest. Just say something, anything, to break the spell. She just knew that two hours from now she'd have a killer line that would break the silence flawlessly, making her sound witty and clever and sophisticated and … *oh fuck it*. "I think my dad still has some of his Cartwright research here. In the office."

* * *

Talking with Jade was easy, like talking with a friend. Yeah, a friend with high breasts, a sweet ass, and pants that he wanted to get into. *Badly*.

But mentioning the dad was a sure way to get his mind off fucking her. Good conversational save. Thank you, Jade.

It was so easy, just talking with her. Even surly, she was fun to talk to. In Matt's experience, conversations were fraught with landmines. You treaded carefully or you pissed people off, and caution was not Matt's strong point. The few close friends he had were not the types to be easily pissed off. Matt had little tolerance for pandering and coddling. It was probably why the string of dates that his mother kept pushing at him never seemed to work out. Conversation with them was work on par with solving the problems of world hunger, global warming, and world peace. Simultaneously.

"Really?" he said. "I'd love to take a look. If you don't think he'll mind."

"I don't see why he would. I'll call him just to check. If he doesn't mind, you can have at it."

Hmm. "Have at it" was an unfortunate turn of phrase that brought Matt's mind back to its previous train of thought. Her, him, *coitus stupendous*. He was about two seconds away from mentally undressing her. Not good. Maintain eye contact. God, her eyes were green. Sea green. *What the hell had they been talking about?* Oh, yeah, Joel Sawyer's research notes. It would be great to get a look at them. The notes.

"Uh, great." *See, he could hold up his end of a rational conversation.*

"Okay, good," Jade lobbed back at him.

"Thanks."

"No problem. So, I'll, uh, call him and then … let you know."

"I'd appreciate that." *Fuck.* This conversation had flat-lined, and he had no one to blame but his libido: *Frank.* Frank the libido. It was all that guy's fault. 'Cause it certainly wasn't Matt's fault. No way. Matt had a modicum of self-control. Yesterday.

They had managed to hike their way back to Lakehaven's main lawn (right past his own cabin), and he could either pretend he meant to go to the main house or turn back to his cabin and look like an ass. Oh, what the hell, that ship had already sailed anyway. "Well, thanks for the hike."

"Sure. No problem. I'll let you know about those notes."

Matt just smiled and turned away, his hand waving a salute as he crossed the lawn back the way they had just come. It was interesting. They had both managed to avoid talking about the kiss.

# Chapter 4

Jade went straight to the kitchen for a cup of coffee. A fresh pot was on (bless Meg), and Stu and Maddie, the Lakehaven cleaning crew, were seated at the table in the corner, each with their own steaming mug. Jade poured herself a cup and perched on a stool by the counter in the center of the room. Meg worked steadily at the butcher-block island rolling pastry dough into large sheets. Scruffy Jeff bounded into the room from outside. He reminded Jade of an ill-behaved dog—loveable, but always into something he shouldn't be. He had gotten his truck working and had finally made it to work, late. That wasn't anything new.

He dropped his tool belt on the steps before swinging the door shut. "I suppose you're all wondering why I asked you here," he joked. "That's not some weird, flavored coffee is it?"

"Good God, no. This is a civilized kitchen. You're probably smelling the almond in the pastry I'm making," Meg said.

"Phew, you had me worried there." Jeff poured himself a cup.

"Hey, I happen to like those flavored coffees. Hazelnut is the best," Maddie piped in. Jade and Jeff swung their gazes around toward Maddie.

"What? It's good! You just don't appreciate gourmet." She got three sets of raised eyebrows in response. "Stu, you think it's good, right?" Stu just grunted in reply. "He drinks hazelnut coffee all the time at home." Stu and Maddie had been married for decades. He no longer bothered to argue with her; he just shrugged.

"Okay, before we get any more frightening factoids about the drinking habits of Stu, I'm changing the subject. The Jordans in cabin four want to know if they can get more towels and an extra pillow," Jeff informed Maddie.

"What, are they showering every hour on the hour? I just brought them eight towels this morning!" Maddie did not look happy.

"It's the kids. Extra napkins at the dinner table, extra towels in the room. You should see how many loads of laundry I do at home," Meg said.

"Maddie, when Ben gets in for his shift let him know to plan for extra laundry for the duration of the Jordans' stay," Jade requested. "Also, I'm doing all of the orders this week, so if we're low on anything, let me know by Wednesday."

"Yeah, I meant to tell you, we're low on morale, but it's nothing a good party and a case of Sierra Nevada pale ale can't solve," Jeff quipped.

Meg laughed. "The last time you planned a 'morale-boosting event' you spent the next day barfing in the bushes while you were supposed to be trimming them."

"Hey, I got them trimmed … eventually."

"Yeah, but they looked like Godzilla had gnawed on them," said Jade.

Maddie jumped in. "And they smelled even worse!"

"It took them three weeks to look normal again," Stu mumbled.

"Okay everyone, if you're going to stay in the kitchen then at least help me cook while you're here," Meg said. Suddenly the conversation stopped and everyone looked at Meg. Stu shifted uncomfortably in his seat, and Maddie grabbed his coffee mug along with hers and moved toward the dishwasher to put the mugs in. Jeff mumbled about clearing some brush off the path in front of cabin three and began to move toward the back door.

Jade laughed and winked at Meg. "That works every time.

Meg quirked an eyebrow. "The Kent sisters came in earlier. They were very chatty."

Jade tried not to blush but failed. "Yeah, well, when are they not?"

"They were making a bet."

"Again, when are they not?"

"About whether Mr. Connor had kissed you or not."

"Oh." Jade slid her gaze away from Meg and then to the clock on the wall. "Wow, will you look at the time? I must have a hundred things to do in my office."

She could hear Meg calling after her: "Chicken!"

When Jade got to her office, she sat heavily in the chair and blew out a deep breath that lifted her bangs off her forehead. She swiveled in the chair and faced her desk. A smile played across her face, followed by a frown. What a mess. Kissing Matt had been stupendously erotic and monumentally stupid for numerous reasons. One, he was a guest. Two, he was here for a week and only for research. Three, he was incredibly charming and too suave. And four, and this was the kicker, he was a man, and therefore not to be trusted. He had "devastating heartbreaker" written all over him. He was trouble with a capital "T," a big league player who probably had his pick of hot women—sophisticated, worldly, sexy, man-eating women who would take one look down their rhinoplastied noses at Jade and laugh—tinkling, brittle laughter. There was only one plan of action that seemed wise: avoid at all costs.

As Jade stared at her desk lost in thought, something seemed off. More than just her mood turned sour. The papers on the desk seemed out of place. Weird. She was pretty sure that they had been stacked and lined up with the corner of the desk, but they seemed like they had been moved slightly. She reached for the phone and that too was sitting at a slightly different angle, just a little less easy for her to pick up. Maybe someone had come in to use the phone, or maybe Maddie had come in to dust. She'd have to ask her about it later. She slid the phone forward, picked up the handset, and dialed her father.

"Hello?"

"Hi, Dad. It's me."

"Jade, what's wrong?"

"Nothing."

"Oh, okay. Why the phone call?"

*Jeez, can't a girl just call her father?* "I have a quick question."

"Okay, shoot."

"I ... There's a writer here. He's doing research on the Cartwright treasure. He wants to look at some of your papers. Would it be okay if I showed him your work?"

"A writer?"

"Yeah, a novelist. Wants to include some of the research you've done. Do you need details?"

"No, no that's not necessary. I'm just ... surprised, I guess."

"Why?"

"I just thought that I was the only person even remotely interested in that old story anymore."

"Apparently not. He says it's an intriguing tale."

"A *he*, huh?" She could almost see her Dad wiggling his eyebrows at her the way he used to anytime she talked about a boy. Any boy, any time.

Jade sighed. "Yes, Dad, a *he*."

"Is there something else going on?"

"No, nothing. He's a guest, and I just thought I'd be helpful."

"If it seems okay with you, Jade; I trust your judgment."

Jade paused a moment to think. Did she trust Matt? Maybe not with her heart, but there was something about him, something genuine.

"Jade? Are you still there?"

"Yeah, Dad, I'm here. I do trust him. I barely know him, but I trust him somehow."

"That's good enough for me, Jade. You're good with people. You always had a way of knowing ... "

Jade flinched at her father's statement. He was so sure of her, so confident. When had she lost that in herself? Probably about the time she and Nick broke up. *Shit. Water under the bridge. Don't go there.* Still, she missed that self-assuredness, that ease and certainty. "Thanks, Dad."

"Just telling it like I see it. If he turns out to be a good guy, maybe he could escort you to my banquet."

*Oh, crap.* She had almost forgotten about her dad's retirement dinner at the university. Her dad had been teaching there for twenty-five years, and even Jade had attended classes there. For awhile.

Jade leaned back in the chair and rolled her eyes at the ceiling. "Yeah, sure, Dad."

"Good. How's the jewelry coming?"

"Uh, good."

"Okay. If you need anything else, let me know."

"I will."

"Love you, Pumpkin."

"Love you too, Dad."

Jade hung up the phone and went to the filing cabinet where her mother and father kept their work. Every manila folder was carefully labeled. Each poem, each academic paper, each short story was lovingly catalogued with a name and date. She found the folder labeled Cartwright. It was from eight years ago, the summer Jade was seventeen. It really wasn't that long ago, but she had been naïve and hopeful. It seemed like a lifetime ago.

*Hudson River Valley*

*April 7, 1616*

*Dear Mother,*

*I do not know when I will be able to post this. It may be many weeks until I arrive some place that can deliver this to you, but I sit here in this wilderness and I wish to share my thoughts with you. I am camped out about two days travel south of a scheduled meeting with a colleague and potential business partner. I should be on my way soon, but I am reluctant to leave here. I have met a woman, Alsoomse, and it is hard to pull myself away from where she is.*

*So I sit at the side of the river, watching eddies curl around the rocks and thinking of a girl with black hair, flashing green eyes, and high spirit.*

*Her name means "independent" in her language and it suits her well. It suits me well for that matter. I left you and the family, not for lack of love but because the structure and privilege were stifling. There is a place downstream where the riverbanks close in and debris piles up, creating waters that stagnate and smell of rotting wood and leaves. Life in England was like that for me. The inertia was slowly killing my spirit.*

*I know Father never understood why I would give any of that up. He never understood why I would move an ocean away to live in makeshift structures in the woods when there were sweeping estates and land and wealth laid at my feet. They are all much better left in Daniel's care. He may be the younger of us, but he is better suited for it.*

*I know you always understood that. Perhaps that is why you gave me your inheritance. You told me at the time that it meant very little to you: the jewels, the things. You said you were partial to very little of it and that freedom, independence were far more precious a commodity. You told me to cherish the freedom and use it wisely. I have not forgotten.*

*Yet, wise or not, here I am, streamside, wishing I could linger. I am afraid if I leave on this journey, I will return to find her gone. Not drifting away like smoke on wind. She is far too real for that. She is like sunshine gleaming bright on a knife's edge; if she left while I was away, it would be on horseback with her long fall of black hair swinging in time with the galloping steed.*

*Still, I will go. I will keep my word because my business and some-times my life depends on it in this unruly land. I have used only two of the pieces of your inheritance for travel and to fund the supplies I have needed to start up this new business. The rest is untouched and will remain that way. My fortune lies in my own efforts. That, too, is part of my independence. I have been making deliveries, bringing post, trading, serving as a guide. Since my arrival, I have come to know the people up and down the river valley, their languages and customs. They begin to know me as well. I will travel now but hurry back to this woman. I do not know her well, but she calls to me, just as her name and its meaning call to me. Independence. I will keep the promise I made to you to cherish my independence and to use it wisely.*

> *Your loving son,*
> *Adam*

Jade made a copy before carefully placing the folder back in its place. Though her cabin was a mess, one place where Jade was meticulous was the office. She wrote a quick note to Matt, letting him know he could use her father's research, and placed it with the copied sheaf of papers into a manila envelope. She'd have Stu or Maddie drop it off later. It would be easier that way.

• • •

Matt was in his cabin when his cell phone rang. He checked the caller ID and sighed. "Hello, Mom."

"Oh, good. I'm so glad I got you instead of that infernal voice mail. How is your trip so far?"

"Great. It's nice up here. Very rustic."

"Ugh, sounds awful."

Matt laughed. "Yeah, it's not really your type of place."

"Indeed … which brings me to the point of this call. There is a fundraiser dinner at the Ritz-Carlton next week, and I'd like you to attend."

"With . . .?" This had all the earmarks of a setup.

"Amanda Carmichael."

"I wish I could, Mom, but I won't be back from this trip."

"I thought you were only staying a week."

"Change of plan."

"Samantha okayed it?"

"I'm a grown man. I pretty much get to dictate my own schedule now."

"Just how long are you planning on staying there?"

*As long as it takes, Mom. As long as it takes.* "I'm not really sure yet. It's very quiet up here. Perfect for writing. I'll just have to play it by ear."

"Well, that was non-committal."

"You know how I am."

Elizabeth McLaughlin sighed heavily. "Yes, unfortunately, Matthew, I do."

Matt smiled. "I love you, Mom."

"I love you too, Matthew."

"Bye, Mom."

"Call me next week."

Matt shook his head as he hung up the phone and settled down to write out what he knew about the Cartwright treasure.

• • •

Lakehaven was cloaked in the grey hush typical of fall mornings in the mountains. There was something caressing and intimate in the silence of nature that made Jade think of Matt with a delicious shiver. She shook off the thought and forced herself to think of something else.

The fog would burn off by noon, but at seven in the morning, Jade watched it curl around her feet as she made her way along the dirt path leading from her cabin to the main house. The tendrils of fog reminded her of a bracelet, and she filed the image away in her brain to sketch at her desk later. The lake stretched out to her left, completely still and pristine. She smiled at its graceful curve and wondered if she could work it into a necklace design.

Her pre-caffeinated brain jumped to thoughts of the day to come, the responsibilities that lay ahead and, of course, the first cup of morning coffee that waited for her in the kitchen. She had to make sure that the Kent sisters had enough blankets to keep them warm. The cabins had central heating and air-conditioning, but the sisters liked to keep the windows wide open while sleeping under piles of heavy blankets. Also, Mr. and Mrs. Bellamy had e-mailed last minute to see if they could reserve their favorite cabin for this weekend, and of course, it was already occupied. Jade would have to see if she could convince Mr. Boyle to move into another cabin and then arrange with Stu and Maddie to make it happen seamlessly while placating them for the inconvenience of extra work.

"Are you avoiding me?"

Jade jumped about a foot and let out a girlish yelp. Matt lounged against the frame of the door to his cabin with a coffee mug in one hand and the manila folder she had sent over the day before in the other. Steam swirled up from Matt's coffee. It smelled like something Jade would sell her soul for. His hair stuck up haphazardly, as if he had run his hand through it but stopped the gesture halfway. His Adidas track pants were slung low on his hips. A well-worn lacrosse t-shirt stretched across his chest and shoulders but hung loosely over his abs. Jade's eyes flicked back and forth between Matt and his coffee, sure that there was something she was supposed to say now, but she couldn't for the life of her think of what it was. Matt waited for her to respond.

*Crap on a stick!* Jade shifted her weight from her right foot to her left. She opened her mouth, closed it again, and shifted her weight back to her right. Matt lifted his eyebrows and sipped his coffee. Jade stared at his mouth. Sipping the coffee.

"Uh, what was the question?" Jade asked.

"Are you avoiding me?" Matt held up the manila folder for Jade to see.

Jade crossed her arms in front of her rib cage. "Not purposely. It's more of a convenient accident of timing. I just happen to be really busy this week."

"That doesn't seem convenient to me at all."

"Oh, I'm sure it's not convenient to *you*."

"Is this about our kiss? Because you seemed to enjoy it yesterday."

"Oh, I think we know whose enjoyment this is about."

Matt narrowed his eyes. "Excuse me?"

"Look, we both know where this is going."

"Do tell." Matt's eyes bored into her from over the rim of his coffee mug. He sipped at the heavenly brew with infuriating smugness.

"You'll have some fun then leave in a week and go back to your Manhattan lifestyle, where you are probably a member of the socialite-of-the month club, and you'll forget all about me. I'll be hurt and angry and eat too much, gain ten pounds, and eventually resume my solitary-but-completely-satisfying single lifestyle."

"Jeezus H. Christ, woman. You sure have managed to complicate this."

"Hey, I didn't *do* anything. It's already complicated."

Matt laughed. "Apparently so."

"Don't be condescending."

"Well then, don't be insulting."

"Bite me!"

"Uh, no thanks, I *kissed* you and look where that got me."

Jade threw her arms up in the air, professionalism long forgotten. "See, this is what I meant. It's complicated!" She was yelling by now.

"You keep saying that like it's a fact. It's not. But you insist on making it complicated. I bet you couldn't have a *simple* love affair if you tried." Matt began to raise his voice as well.

"I could, too! This is not about me. I'd *looooove* a simple love affair. I just don't think it's possible." Jade paced back and forth in front of Matt, but he just continued to lean against the door with complete insouciance. It was absolutely infuriating.

"I know it's possible. But I still bet you can't do it." Matt had a gleam in his eyes. He had dropped his volume, but his voice held a mocking tone that just pushed her every button.

"Can too." *Hah! So there.*

Matt tilted his head to one side. "Want to bet?"

"Oh yeah, you are going to lose this one, mister." Jade thrust out her hand and Matt shook it. Jade's eyes shone with anticipated triumph.

"Not a chance." Matt gave Jade his smug smirk again.

Jade had a feeling that between Matt and his biceps she had succumbed to a *Jedi* mind trick, but she ignored the niggling concern in the back of her brain and continued with her current bravado. "Oh, and what makes you so sure?"

"You know why I'm sure? Because I know that when you go out for coffee with a friend, you don't over think that. You don't go into a friendship wondering when, not if, but *when*, one of you is going to hurt the other. You don't wonder if you will disagree, or if one of you will move to another part of the country or when one of you will get angry and start a fight. You just connect with someone, relate to them."

"That is totally different."

"Maybe different, but no more complicated. You make relationships complicated. You have friends you love, right?"

Jade glared at Matt, almost unwilling to answer. Almost. Instead, she said, "Yes."

"So the only objection you have is the great sex."

Jade swallowed so loudly that she was sure Matt could hear her. "Great?"

Matt's eyes pinned Jade to the spot. He smiled and panned her body with his gaze, all the way down to her toes. He slowly took a sip of coffee. Jade felt the blood rush up her cheeks.

"Sex changes the relationship," she insisted.

Matt shook his head. "Jade, every relationship changes you, touches you, and if it's a good one, you evolve in it. It doesn't matter if it's a friend, a parent, or a lover. If you care about each other, then you make a difference for each other. You just *think* romantic relationships are different, somehow harder. But you're still *you* in each relationship. Sex or no sex, romance or no romance, a relationship will not make you perfect or complete. It can't because you already are."

Matt stared into Jade's eyes as she held her breath. A moment ticked by then another. Finally, Matt broke the silence. "By the way, check with Ben. I just extended my stay. I'm here for three months. The bet stands." Matt turned and went into his cabin, closing the door behind him with a quiet click, and leaving Jade staring at the blank door.

# Chapter 5

Jade stalked across the lawn of Lakehaven muttering to herself and gesturing wildly. It was a beautiful wide expanse of grass, perfect for Easter egg hunts in the spring and croquet games on warm summer evenings. The thick, lush plain stretched away from the house for a good sixty yards before gently sloping down to the lake. It was one of the highlights of Lakehaven's scenery and featured prominently in the brochure and pictures on the website. Adirondack chairs dotted the edge of the lawn facing the lake, providing a beautiful sitting spot to sip lemonade and gaze out at the water.

Jade's quick steps rapidly ate up the distance between her and her first cup of morning coffee. She was so intent on her destination and focused on her anger that she almost didn't notice the Kent sisters and Mr. Boyle standing in a circle staring at the ground. Well, technically it was a distinct absence of ground that they were staring at—a hole about three feet deep and four feet in diameter.

"It looks a bit large to be a gopher," Mr. Boyle said diplomatically.

"Quite right, Mr. Boyle." Beatrice batted her lashes at him and shot Adele a tight little smirk.

"I didn't say it was a gopher, specifically. I merely surmised that the hole may have been made by an animal of some sort *in the way* of a gopher," Adele clarified.

"What in the world is this?" Jade fumed. If she sounded a bit harsher than she had intended, it was only because a pompous guest had somehow goaded her into making a ridiculous bet.

"It seems to be a hole," Mr. Boyle clarified.

"A hole? A *hole*? No, that is a huge gaping maw of ignominy," Jade sputtered. This was not good. Jade had two responsibilities here at Lakehaven: keep the guests happy and keep Lakehaven running smoothly. The large ditch in the center of the gorgeous expanse of green lawn was not copacetic with fulfilling her duties. Come to think of it, yelling at Matt wasn't either. On the good side, the hole was occupying the Kent sisters. Maybe there was a logical explanation. Maybe Ben had some underground pipe maintenance scheduled, and he had forgotten to tell her about it. *Ugh.* It was just too much to digest before her first cup of coffee.

"Quite right, my dear. What do you suppose made it? We have a bet." Beatrice beamed.

"Of course you do," Jade snipped at Beatrice but then immediately felt contrite when she saw the woman's expression sag. Now she was being mean to a sweet seventy-year-old guest who used to give her candy when she was a girl. Jade took a deep breath. "I'm sorry, Ms. Kent. I'm having a difficult morning, and I seem to have lost all of my manners along with my sense. Please accept my apology for the sharp tone of my voice."

Beatrice nodded at Jade. "It's quite all right, dear. We thought we could hear you and Mr. Conner speaking loudly this morning. He must be quite confounding to get you so riled up." Bea's face lit up with a smile that twinkled all the way to her eyes. Jade frowned.

"Oh, now don't do that. You'll give yourself forehead wrinkles." Beatrice tsked.

Jade took a calming breath. "Okay, I'll go find Jeff and get him to fix this. Would you mind keeping an eye on things here until I get back? I don't want any of the Jordan kids to fall in."

"Oh sure, dear. Don't you worry, we'll keep an eye out. You don't think it was a large animal or anything, do you?" Adele glanced toward the surrounding woods and then back down toward the large pit.

Jade leaned closer to the edge of the hole for a better look. "Not unless the bears are carrying shovels. There are tool marks along the sides here that look to be the exact size of the shovel in the shed."

"Oh, very good, Jade! I hadn't noticed that before. Well, that settles the bet. So sorry Adele," Beatrice gloated.

Adele smiled back with a devious glimmer in her eye. "Not to worry. I'll win every penny back and then some."

"We'll just see about that … " Jade heard the sisters arguing as she walked toward the shed to see if Jeff was around and available to fill in the mysterious hole and maybe even provide some answers. She rounded the corner of the wood stack and stopped at the gaping shed door. Clanking and swearing came from inside.

"Jeff? Is that you?" Jade asked. More swearing from the shed. Jade peeked her head around the corner.

"Goddammit! I can't find anything in here!" Hedge clippers slid from where they leaned against the wall, smacking into the shoulder of the hunched figure. "Ouch, shit!"

Judging from the grey argyle sweater vest and the khaki pants, it was not Jeff. Jeff was more of the ratty t-shirt or flannel type.

"Uh, Ben?" Jade asked. Ben lifted his head and cracked it against a low shelf loaded with gardening tools. "*Oww.* Motherfucker, that hurt."

"Oh, I'm sorry. I'm looking for Ben Stuart. I had no idea they were holding a truck driver convention in the shed."

"Very funny. Why is this such a mess?" Ben carefully picked his way toward the open shed doors. He was cute in a geeky sort of way, with a medium build, reddish-brown hair, and wire-rimmed glasses that he was always pushing up his nose. He looked perfectly at home at the front desk but not so much in the shed.

"No one goes in here but Jeff."

"Ah, that explains a lot."

"Yeah, speaking of which, why are you in here? Have you seen him? And why is there a crater in the lawn?"

"Searching for a shovel, not this morning, and how the hell should I know?"

"Great." Jade chewed on her lower lip. "Well, this sucks."

"I cannot argue with you there. Any ideas?"

"Find the shovel? Fill the hole?"

"Easier said than done." Ben gestured to the tangle of tools surrounding him. "I'm amazed Jeff can find anything in here, and I'm starting to think the shovel is MIA."

Jade sighed. "All right. See if you can find rope and garden stakes to cordon off the area, then meet me in the kitchen when you're done. I'll go in search of Jeff."

"Aye, aye, Captain."

Jade rolled her eyes at Ben and headed back in the direction of the main house. After ten minutes of looking for Jeff with no success, she headed to the kitchen, hoping there was a cup of coffee there with her name on it.

Meg was already in. Jade poured herself a cup, tipped her nose toward the mug, and inhaled deeply. "You're here early."

Meg moved around the kitchen with an efficiency and ease that Jade admired. Meg could lose her vision tomorrow, and she would still be able to navigate around the room. "Yeah, Doug didn't have to go in to work until later today, so he drove the kids."

"Mmm." Jade nodded while she swallowed the first fragrant sips of fresh coffee. It was pure bliss. "Have you seen Jeff?" She closed her eyes as the warm brew slid down her throat.

"Coffee good?" Meg grinned.

Jade nodded enthusiastically then brought the mug to her mouth.

"Yeah, he was in here earlier, grabbed a muffin, and then left again."

"You don't happen to know anything about the hole in the lawn?"

"There's a hole in the lawn?"

"Yeah, it's huge."

Meg shook her head. "Some crazy gets it in their head to look for the treasure and next thing you know there's a huge hole in the lawn." A timer went off and Meg made her way to the oven.

Jade sighed. "I guess I was hoping it was some emergency plumbing issue rather than stupid treasure hunters."

Meg started to laugh. "One year Lester Manning got it in his head that the treasure had been buried at the edge of his property next to the outhouse. He dug too close and almost buried himself in poop."

Jade nodded. "I kind of remember that story. Jeez, this is such a pain in the ass. I'm supposed to be taking care of this place. I feel like I'm letting Aunt Bertie down."

Meg set a tray of cinnamon buns down on the counter to cool. "That's a bit harsh. I know Bert fairly well, and I'm pretty sure she would not hold you responsible for a mysterious hole in the lawn that I'm assuming you didn't dig and didn't hire someone to dig."

"Yeah. It just feels like I'm failing, you know? And who the hell digs a huge hole in a gorgeous, perfectly manicured, postcard-perfect lawn?"

"Well, if your intention is to control life's little road bumps, you are definitely failing. That's a game you can give up on right now. It's pointless. If your intention is to run Lakehaven smoothly, however, you're doing fine."

Jade straightened, pushing off from where she'd been leaning against the counter, and took one final sip of coffee before placing the mug in the sink. "I will be once I find Jeff. Thanks, Meggs."

•••

"Your mom is going to be very unhappy," Samantha complained over the phone. "What happened? Yesterday you were staying a week, and now it's three months. I don't get it."

"I just need more time than I thought." Matt swiveled in his chair away from the desk and his laptop. He picked up a pen from the desk and tapped it on his leg.

"Time for what? What in the hell is there to do there?" There was a pause on the line and a sharp inhale which sounded like Sam taking a drag on a cigarette.

"Nothing. That's the point. Are you smoking again?"

"Damn straight. Are you tapping a pen on your leg?"

Matt stilled the hand with the pen. "No."

Samantha laughed. "Liar. I promise I won't talk to your mother. What's going on?"

"Some intriguing developments." Matt started tapping his pen again. He swiveled his chair to face the window on the wall opposite his desk. Dappled sunlight filtered through the crosshatch of branches that arched over the cabin eaves, creating a mosaic of dark and light on the wood floor. He imagined Jade lying in that swath of light, the glow of it on her skin. Matt had a very good imagination. He smiled to himself.

Sam waited for a moment before prompting Matt. "I assume you don't mean with your story."

"Hmm?" Matt pulled his mind back to the phone call. "Oh, no, the story is fine. Writing is going well. Better than usual."

"A woman, then." It wasn't a question.

Matt laughed. "I'm that easy to figure, huh."

Sam sighed. "Maybe not for everyone. But I know you, Matt. Most people probably wouldn't figure you for a sentimental wuss. They see the successful writing career or the high-profile dating sprees and assume that your personality goes with the pictures in the paper. I know better, so spill! Don't leave me hanging."

Matt stood up and began to pace the cabin. "Okay, but if you talk to my mother about this I'll publish that picture of you with whiskey shooting out of your nose. She'd be up here in a heartbeat if she thought there was something to interfere in." He paced into the kitchen.

"Oooooh … It's that good?"

"No, it's nothing yet. It just has the potential to be something, which is why I want my mother as far away from here as possible. I want time to explore this, whatever it is." Matt leaned against the counter and looked out the window over the sink. The morning fog had already burned off. He turned back toward the living room.

Sam paused as if there was something important she wanted to say, but instead she just offered, "Okay, is there anything that needs taking care of here?"

"Just have Allison forward my mail. I'll take care of everything else." Matt flipped his cell phone shut and plugged it into the charger on his desk. He was surprised that he got service here in the woods, but the phone used up about twice the charge searching for a signal.

He wandered back to the kitchen and filled a teakettle with water. Each Lakehaven cabin came with a compact but tidy kitchen that was stocked with basic appliances and some simple pantry items. Now that he was staying for three months, he would probably make a trip into the town nearby to fill the tiny fridge with some of his favorite foods. He dumped the old grounds out of the French press sitting next to the sink, rinsed it, and filled it with fresh coffee. He leaned against the counter, arms crossed over his chest, and thought about the morning while he waited for the water to boil.

While diplomacy was not his strength, Matt didn't necessarily think of himself as a complete ass either, despite all evidence to the contrary. Part of what annoyed him was Jade's assumption that he was a shallow womanizer. As far as he knew, she wasn't even basing that opinion on the society pages in the *Times*, which did have a tendency to portray him in a somewhat salacious manner.

No, as far as he knew, she still didn't know his real name. She was either judging him based on the way he looked (which would be pretty shallow), or on some relationship in her past. That was the root cause of his foul mood. He was not about be punished for the crimes of some ghost from her past, and he was too damned attracted to her to let it slide. He was used to having a take-it or leave-it approach to relationships, even with women he had dated for months. He was always in control of his heart and his emotions. This was something else entirely, something a little wild. Being a bit out of control was new for Matt, and it had him off balance. But Matt was good at plotting, and tables were easy to turn … he hoped.

Matt poured boiling water into the French press and let it sit for a few minutes before depressing the plunger and pouring himself a fresh cup. He brought it to his desk and sat down to plot.

• • •

Two cups of coffee and a cinnamon roll later, Jade had her blood pressure back in the green zone. Amidst much grumbling, Stu, who had finally found a different shovel in the shed, was filling the hole in the lawn, and the local nursery and garden center was delivering some fresh sod later that afternoon. Now that Jade had dealt with that, she could focus on the other problem at hand. She had made a bet that almost *required* her to have an affair with Matt.

The kitchen was a large room with an open layout and a high ceiling with chocolate brown wood rafters. It had three doorways: one on the north wall that lead out to the hallway, one on the east wall that lead to the dining room, and one on the south wall that led outside. The south wall faced the lawn and, beyond that, the lake. A fireplace occupied the southwest corner, and next to that was an old wooden table where Jade sat cradling a mug in her palms and looking out the window at the lawn and the lake beyond.

Meg had finished cooking breakfast and began preparing lunch: cold pasta and chicken salad, Parmesan rolls, and a cold green bean salad. She sat with Jade while the pasta boiled. "So what are you going to do?"

Jade sighed. "I wish I knew. It's ridiculous, really. I should just apologize for losing my head and tell him respectfully that the bet is not really appropriate because he is a guest."

"Oh God, you're not going to be that big of a wuss, are you?" Meg got up and stirred the pot of pasta. She looked over her shoulder and raised her eyebrows.

Jade slumped down in her chair. "I don't know," she whined.

Meg rolled her eyes. "Wuss."

Jade stuck her tongue out at Meg. Meg just laughed.

"What if he's right? What if I really am incapable of having a simple affair?"

"Hey, that's a good point. What if you are? What happens if you lose?" Meg asked.

"Oh, that's a nice vote of confidence from my best friend," Jade said.

"No, I just mean, what are the terms of the bet?"

"We never came to terms. It all just happened so fast. I was so annoyed, and then the next thing I knew we were shaking hands, and … "

"Ooooh, this is great. He left himself wide open if you win. You'll just have to make sure you win."

"Do you think I can do it?" Jade asked.

Meg smiled devilishly. "You sure could have some fun finding out."

Jade just put her head down on the table and moaned.

# Chapter 6

Matt strolled into the main house at the tail end of the lunch hour. The Kent sisters were the only guests left in the dining room, and they sat at a table in the corner sipping tea. A haphazard pile of playing cards lay face-up on the table, and each woman had a neat stack of cards facedown in her hand. Matt watched them as Adele yelled out, "Two of clubs!" and then flipped a card from her hand onto the pile between them.

Beatrice replied, "Hah, not even close! Jack of hearts!" and flipped one card from her hand onto the growing mass of cards in front of her.

"Nice try, but no cigar!" Adele crowed. "Ace of spades!" Adele flung the card out, then both of them stared open-mouthed at the ace of spades staring up from the top of the pile. Adele was the first to recover. "Hah! I won! I won!" She jumped up from her seat and did a happy dance. Or at least Matt assumed that's what it was. He hoped she wasn't having a seizure of some sort. She giggled with glee and shouted, "*Booyah*! Take that, little sister! In your face!" She pumped a fist in the air and then turned toward Matt. "Did you see that? That was beautiful!" Adele sashayed over to Matt and took his hands and twirled him around in a circle. It was the first time Matt had ever been twirled by a woman, but he was so swept up in her enthusiasm that he just went with it, grinning from ear to ear.

Adele executed a final spin, ending up right in front of her chair and twirling Matt out in a move worthy of Fred Astaire and Ginger Rogers. Her cheeks were flushed, her eyes twinkled, and she was slightly out of breath. Matt stared at her, taking in the vitality and charm. She smiled at him, and he smiled back, giving her a courtly bow. He hoped that he had that kind of spunk when he got to be her age. That's what he was thinking when the swinging door smacked him in the back and knocked him forward.

He might have caught his balance and remained standing if Jade hadn't smacked into him next, at a full run no less. He did manage to turn himself over onto his back mid-fall to avoid an embarrassing face plant, but he couldn't do a thing to slow down the momentum. He landed hard, and Jade landed hard on top of him. She was small but still made an impact as she landed, forcing all of the air out of his lungs with a *whoosh*. They lay there for a moment, Matt trying to catch his breath and Jade with a stunned look on her face.

Then she started to squirm. "Let me up!" Jade wiggled against him.

Matt winced as he finally took in a breath. "Uh, you're on top."

"I know that! What kind of idiot stands right in front of a door?" Jade pushed her hands against Matt's chest and struggled to her knees.

Matt shifted suddenly when her right knee came dangerously close to making contact with his crotch. "I hope nothing's broken," he groaned.

"Of course not, I'm fine," Jade said as she crawled backwards on all fours down the length of Matt's body.

"I meant on me." Matt lifted his head to look down the length of his torso to where Jade hovered, her face directly over his crotch.

"Oh." Just then, Jade stopped what she was doing to look up Matt's body at his face. He dropped his head back onto the floor and draped his arm over his eyes, trying not to think about the proximity of her mouth to certain very interested body parts.

Jade glanced down directly into the fly of Matt's jeans. *Oh, dear God. Why does this happen to me?* Jade felt a flush run all the way down her body, heating her to her core. She scrambled the rest of the way down Matt's body and stood quickly.

*When embarrassed, bluff like crazy.* Jade planted her hands on her hips. "What the hell is going on in here? I heard Adele yelling!"

Matt just lay there, only moving his arm to look up at Jade. He didn't look inclined to give an answer. Or, maybe he was still out of breath from being crushed by her … awkward entrance. She glanced from one sister to the other. The sisters exchanged a look as Jade waited for an answer.

Beatrice was grinning. "Wow, I haven't seen anything like that since *I Love Lucy* was on the air."

"You know, you can still catch reruns of that on late night television," Adele piped in.

"Oh, yes, that was always one of my favorites. That and that *Gomer Pyle* thing."

Jade looked back and forth between the Kent sisters, bewildered. She was starting to feel like Alice down the rabbit hole. She shook her head. "I'm sorry, maybe I was mistaken."

"No, no. You heard correctly. Sorry if we disturbed you, dear. I won a bet and Matthew was kind enough to help me celebrate." There was warmth and pleasure in Adele's voice. "He's quite the dancer!" She looked fondly down at him and gave him a wink. Matt smiled up at Adele and winked back. Jade glared down at Matt, hands on her hips, stance wide, given that his feet were on the floor between hers. He looked fabulous stretched out before her, and she had to work hard to avert her gaze before her eyes met his.

"Are you sure you're okay?" Jade looked to Adele and Beatrice for confirmation. Both nodded in assent.

"I'm not," Matt complained. "Twisted my ankle a little in the fall."

The two sisters rushed over to him with sympathetic murmurings.

Beatrice jumped up with a spryness that belied her age. "Adele, could you come with me to the kitchen and help me get some ice?"

She stared pointedly at Jade. "You're much younger and stronger than us. Be a dear, will you, and help Matthew up and onto the couch in the great room. We'll bring the ice to you there."

Adele nodded enthusiastically in agreement and hustled out the door to the kitchen, leaving Jade alone with Matt.

Jade looked down at Matt and quirked an eyebrow at him. "A sprained ankle?"

Matt looked up at her. "Really. It's not too bad though."

Jade kept staring at him. She crossed her arms over her chest. "Hmm."

"Would I lie to you?" Matt kept eye contact, steady and open.

"Possibly. But if you are lying, you're very good at it."

Matt pushed himself to his elbows. "Hey, look, it's no big deal. I'm sure I can hobble to the couch on my own." Matt wiggled his foot a bit and winced.

Jade narrowed her eyes and pursed her lips. "I know what you're doing."

"Other than trying to walk, I have no idea what you're talking about." Matt pushed himself up onto his hands and looked up at Jade. He almost looked sweet and harmless. Almost.

Matt slid his right foot in toward his body and sat up a little higher, then paused. His brows knit together. Jade exhaled. "Oh, fine then." She stepped off to Matt's left side and extended her hand to him. He reached up for her and rolled up to a standing position, making sure to put his weight on his right foot. He did it with the fluid ease of an athlete. He took a quick step, favoring his left leg, and sucked in a breath of pain.

"Oh, for crying out loud. Here." Jade stepped under his left arm and let him take some of the body weight off his left foot. Matt's gratitude seemed genuine. Jade got him settled on the couch and waited in silence for the Kent sisters to return with the ice. Once they did, Jade figured she could leave them to coddle Matt while she made a hasty retreat.

Minutes ticked by. Matt lounged on the couch, looking comfortable and relaxed and like he was about to take a nap. The Kent sisters still hadn't returned. What the heck could be taking so long with a simple bag of ice?

"I'll be right back." Jade got up quickly, glad to have an excuse to get out of there. It was impossible not to be affected by him lying there. She found herself studying the planes of his face, the even rise and fall of his chest, the stubble on his jaw and thinking how he looked completely at home, like he owned the place—a place that had been her summer home for as long as she could remember. It was an uncomfortable thought.

When she got to the kitchen, she found a bag of ice sitting on the counter next to the freezer with a note lying beside it. It read: "Forgot that we promised Mr. Boyle we would meet him at three o'clock for bird watching. Take care of Matt's ankle for us. A & B."

Great. There went her escape. Even when she was young, Jade could count on the Kent sisters to be mischievous and a bit strange. That really hadn't changed in all the years she had known them. They were getting along in age and sometimes seemed scattered, but this sudden case of forgetfulness was suspicious. Jade had no doubt that they had left her alone with Matt on purpose. She shook her head; they were certainly sharp enough to exploit a matchmaking opportunity in two seconds flat. Jade was better off worrying about extricating herself from her current situation. She grabbed the ice pack from the counter with a frustrated sigh. Might as well get this over with.

Jade reached the arched doorway to the great room and pasted on a chipper smile. "Here's the ice. I guess Adele and Bea had to run ... " she trailed off as she rounded the arm of the sofa where Matt was stretched out. His face was turned to the side and his features were lax, making him seem boyish and innocent. Long lashes brushed the tops of his cheekbones, giving him the look of a fallen angel; one hand trailed off the side of the couch adding to the whole effect. Jade stopped in her tracks and just took him in. She smiled, imagining him dancing with Adele, remembering the glow of pleasure in Adele's voice. She tiptoed forward, slid a blanket off the arm of the couch, and spread it across Matt. Jade gently placed the ice pack on his ankle, resting it on the far arm of the couch and then turned back to the doorway and snuck out.

•••

Matt woke up and immediately wondered where he was. It was a couch but not the couch in his Manhattan apartment. That had white ceilings. Not wooden beams. Right, Lakehaven.

A blanket was draped across him and the hem of his jeans was … wet. Matt glanced down to the far end of the couch where a soggy plastic baggie lay on its side. He smiled. Someone had tucked him in and tended to his ankle. It might have been Adele, but he was betting on Jade. The thought made him grin.

He found her in her office huddled behind a large desk. It was a man's desk with heavy, dark wood—substantial, unadorned, practical. She looked like a kid playing at office. Matt was sure she wouldn't appreciate the comparison. Still, it made her seem cute and a bit vulnerable. Again, she probably wouldn't like those adjectives either. He leaned against the doorjamb and just watched her for a moment as she chewed on a pencil, wrote a note on a sticky pad with a purple-inked pen, and then swiveled in her chair to look at a computer screen. It was then that she noticed him and jumped. The pencil fell out of her mouth and onto the desk blotter with a plop.

"Crap, you scared the *bejeezus* out of me."

"Sorry."

She narrowed her eyes at him and tilted her head to one side. "How's your ankle?"

Matt pushed himself off the doorframe and shook out his left foot before standing with his weight on both legs. "Great. I'm a fast healer."

"Uh, okay." Jade looked up at him from under a thick fringe of lashes. "Is there something I can do for you?" The question sounded stiff and formal. Jade clasped her hands together and rested them on the desk blotter in front of her. It reminded Matt of Ms. Stockton, his high school librarian. The thought made him smile.

"Actually, I thought this would be a good time to discuss the terms of our bet."

"I'm not sure this bet is such a great idea." Jade worried her lower lip with her teeth, drawing Matt's attention to her mouth. Her lips were a deep cherry color even though she was completely without makeup. Either way, she was utterly kissable.

*Focus, Matt.* "Backing out?" he asked.

Jade crossed her arms in front of her chest. "I didn't say that. I just said it was a bad idea."

"But you'll do it anyway."

Jade sighed. "Yeah, it won't be the first bad idea I follow through on, and probably not the last."

"Great. When I win, you help me to search for the Cartwright treasure."

Jade rolled her eyes. "Please. Number one, you will not win, and number two, searching for the treasure is a huge waste of time."

"So what? It's my time to waste as I see fit."

"Okay, fine. And if I win . . ."

"Never happen."

"If I win," Jade spoke louder, "you . . . " she paused and looked thoughtful for a moment. Then, a look dawned on her face that ended with a bright gleam in her eye. "If I win, you have to escort me to my dad's retirement dinner."

"God, no! Not a room full of academicians!" Matt said with mock horror. "It's a deal. Especially since there's no way I can lose."

"How exactly are we going to determine the winner?"

"Easy. The second you make it complicated, you lose."

"And who exactly will judge this competition?"

"I'll be the judge," Matt volunteered.

"Oh, yeah, right. That's fair."

"I'm glad you agree."

"No, we'll have to come up with an impartial judge," Jade mused aloud.

"Who will be impartial? Everyone here seems to know you, and I'm a complete stranger. You have home court advantage, so to speak."

"Tough, you'll just have to deal. How about the Kent sisters?"

"No, they'll definitely vote for you. They've known you for over twenty-two years."

"How did you know that?"

"They're very talkative. They like to socialize." Matt gave one of his signature smiles, full of mischief and heat.

Jade glanced away. "Yes, they seem to have taken quite a liking to you. In fact, I'm not sure that they would be good judges after all. You might sway them with your manly wiles."

"I have manly wiles? I wish someone had told me sooner!" Matt quipped.

Jade crumpled a sheet of paper on the desk and threw it at him. It smacked Matt square in the chest. "Okay, smart ass. So who would you pick?"

Matt thought seriously for a moment. "Mr. Boyle."

Just as Matt's mouth formed the words, he realized Jade had said the very same thing.

Matt's gaze found Jade's, and they looked at each other for a beat. Matt smiled and, thank the Lord, Jade smiled back. It was like a beautiful light spreading across her face, and he felt simply stunned by it. Her smile was warm, and in it, Matt sensed a world of comfort and joy. The moment he thought it, he realized the implied danger, and yet he knew it was the truth with absolute certainty. *Crap, now who's going to make this complicated?* Matt winced at the thought.

Jade looked concerned. "Are you sure your ankle is okay?"

Matt was confused for a moment but covered quickly. "Yep, I'm fine. Okay. Mr. Boyle will be our judge. Now, when do we go out?"

"What do you mean, we?" Jade smirked at Matt.

"We, as in you and me."

"Why does it have to be me and you? The bet was whether I can or cannot have a simple affair. At no time did we specify who the other party would be."

Matt burst out laughing. "Oh, this is going to be *so* easy. You are complicating things already. You are attracted to me, and I am attracted to you, so the simplest thing would be that we start to explore that attraction. But you want to go out and find someone else to date?"

"Who says we're attracted to each other?"

Matt's laughter subsided and was replaced with an intensity that had Jade bolting up out of her seat and taking a step back from the desk.

Matt rounded the corner of the desk and Jade stepped back again. He came for her and she stumbled back until she was up against the filing cabinets. Matt stopped inches from her body; there was heat coming off her, filling the small space between them. It was such a slight gap that Jade's breathing almost had them touching. But not quite.

• • •

Jade could feel the heat coming off of Matt, smell his skin, spicy and warm, and if she tilted her chin up she could see the look in his eyes—a look that promised wanting and having. The combination had an answering heat flaring low in her body. Matt was still. God, why the hell was he standing still? He was just a hairsbreadth away. *Please.* She felt her body begging to touch him and almost swayed against him. She was breathing hard, their chests almost touching. Matt lifted one hand toward her waist, and she could almost feel how it would be to have him pull her hips into his body. She all but sighed in relief.

Matt lowered his head toward her and smiled, then dropped his hand to his side and stepped back. He was still only a few inches away, and he leaned over to whisper in her ear. "I say we're attracted to each other."

Jade swallowed then frowned. It was taking her mind a bit of time to catch up with her body. She felt Matt's warm breath on her ear and wanted to rub herself all over him, but she knew that his words should somehow piss her off. Matt took another step back and let out a slow breath. Jade felt the blood that had moved south rush up her body in a deep blush. Some weird adrenaline reaction had her shaking slightly, and she had to focus on staying steady. She pressed herself fully into the filing cabinets for support.

Matt had stopped smiling, but the molten look in his eyes held. Jade closed her eyes and just breathed. After a few minutes, she could feel her body's reaction settle and her breathing even out. She thought about not opening her eyes—just standing there with her eyes closed, head leaning back against the filing cabinets, ignoring Matt until he went away. Not a bad strategy if you wanted to take the wimpy way out.

Jade took a deep breath, opened her eyes, and met Matt's gaze. "Okay, one date."

# Chapter 7

The next few days passed in a blur. Jade kept busy, but it was always there in the back of her mind. She was going out on a date with Matt. She was excited about the idea of it, but given her history of scuttling even the most promising of dates, she was certain that keeping her distance from him in the days before the date was for the best. Still, that spectacular kiss kept creeping into the edges of her mind and she was worried. The more potential the date seemed to have, the bigger the disappointment when she messed it up. Not if, *when*. So she avoided Matt and tried to keep her mind on other things.

When she was anxious, she holed up in her cabin and occupied herself with some new jewelry designs for her fledgling business. She had some sketches for a line of bracelets called "Morning Mist" that she was still working out, and she had finished a series of pieces with a leaf design that she knew would be a success at some of the summer fairs. She wanted to mirror that design on her website, if she could only figure out how to do it.

The dreaded day got closer, and she thought about buying something new to wear. She dismissed the idea, deciding it would be taking things too seriously, something she definitely did not want to do. She filled Meg in on the bet, and they got down to strategizing.

"You know, this bet is really vague. Is Mr. Boyle going to accompany you on the date?" Meg asked while chopping carrots. Meggs still wasn't as fast as the tableside chef at their favorite Teppanyaki restaurant, but Jade could tell she'd been practicing.

"God, I hope not. That would be weird." Jade tried to imagine Mr. Boyle sitting at a table next to them on a date. She shuddered. "We haven't really asked him yet, but I was just thinking if we disagreed, we would plead our cases and he would make a decision. Like a judge in court."

"Either way, it's a little weird."

Jade lifted her eyebrows. "A little?"

"Yeah, you're right. A lot weird. But that's what I like about you. You don't let that stop you."

Jade laughed. "Thanks, I think."

"So, what are you going to wear?" Meg scraped the carrots into a large stockpot.

Jade picked at the paper label on her bottle of iced tea. "Nothing special. I don't want to encourage him."

Meg was over at the sink putting water in the stockpot, but she turned her head and shook it. "No, no, no. Make an impression. You want him to swallow his tongue."

"I'm not sure that's possible."

"It's a figure of speech, you dork." Meg rolled her eyes at Jade.

"No, really?! *Duh*!" She rolled her eyes right back. "I meant that I don't think Matt is that easy to impress. He seems like he dates high-maintenance." Jade began to tear the drink label into little pieces.

"One: You are a knockout. In the right dress, you could make a monk swallow his tongue. Two: I have seen Matt looking at you in denim and flannel, and you could definitely make that big of an impression. And Three: Did you just say 'duh'? What, are you ten?"

Jade stuck her tongue out at Meg. "Okay, a dress and heels."

"A dress and fuck-me heels," Meg insisted.

"Yeah, 'cause a twisted ankle is soooo sexy."

Meg set the stockpot on the stovetop and turned on the flame. "Don't be a wuss. You can take a little pain in order to make Matt squirm."

"Well, when you put it that way … " Jade's smile took on an evil gleam. Oh, yeah. This could be fun.

• • •

Matt didn't know enough about the area to pick a good first date spot, so he did what came naturally: research. Hopefully, Ben or Jeff would be around to give him some information. He found Jeff first just outside the porch area, trimming the edge of the lawn. Matt didn't intend to surprise Jeff, but between the earphones in Jeff's ears and the buzz of the weed-whacker, he jumped about a foot at Matt's approach.

"Geez, give a guy an embolism why don'cha?" Jeff said a little too loudly as he yanked the ear buds out of his ears.

Matt lifted his hands in surrender and stepped back quickly to avoid being whacked as Jeff spun around with his yard equipment. "Sorry."

"No sweat," Jeff shouted then turned off the weed-whacker. "Hey, you're the writer, right? I've got a great idea for your next book. We could make a fortune."

Matt smiled. "Thanks, but could we discuss that later? Right now, I was hoping to get some information about local date spots."

"Oh, right, for your current project." Jeff nodded slowly with an exaggerated up and down range of motion.

"Something like that." Matt found himself nodding back but stopped himself, mostly because he had no idea why they were nodding like idiots.

The two of them stood staring at each other for a moment, Matt waiting for Jeff to respond and Jeff waiting for god-knows-what. Finally, Matt raised his eyebrows, which seemed to rouse Jeff out of his reverie.

"Right, so you need to know … what exactly? Casual dining? Upscale restaurants? Forget that … Um … hot pick up spots?" Jeff squinted his eyes.

Matt thought about it for a moment. "I need a good first date place. Nice, but not too pretentious, with good food but not too loud."

"Wow, that's a lot of stuff. And we have a limited selection. Okay, here's what I'd do. Fitch's is low key and very local. The atmosphere is pub, the food is stellar, and the music is very low decibel, so you can talk. They have two pool tables if that's your thing. Tamblin's is more of a restaurant-with-a-view type place. Nice, but a little on the pricey side. If you take a date there, it's a *date*-date. Um, what else? The best dancing is at Wildflowers, and the best place to pick up hot chicks is the Grille. That just about covers it."

"Really, that's it?" Matt ran his hand through his hair and tried not to frown.

"Yep. Addie's is the best place for coffee and omelets, and then there's the deli for bagels and subs, but those are only open for breakfast and lunch." Jeff shrugged.

"Okay, thanks."

"Yeah, no problem. And don't forget my new idea for your next novel."

"Right." Matt waved as he made a hasty retreat.

After a day of book research at the library, he wanted to get a second opinion on the dating scene. Jeff seemed to know what he was talking about, but Jade had mentioned he was flaky. Matt decided to check in with Ben. At the same time, he needed to be careful not to embarrass Jade. It was inevitable that the staff eventually would know that he and Jade were going out—Lakehaven seemed too small and tight knit to avoid it entirely—but since Jeff had already jumped to the convenient assumption that this was research for his latest novel, Matt decided to go with that approach. He hoped the circumspection would earn him some extra points with Jade. She might be happier getting to choose how and when her staff found out they were dating.

Matt found Ben at the front desk behind a computer. When he saw Matt approaching, he quickly hit some keys on the keyboard and then stood at attention. Matt smiled. It looked like Ben hadn't wanted anyone to see what was on the computer screen.

Matt got right down to business and asked what he wanted to know. While Ben considered the question, he fiddled with a pen, lining it up precisely with the edge of the computer mouse pad. The pen was printed with the Lakehaven logo on the side, a leafy tree designed to form the "L" of "Lakehaven" with the tree's canopy providing shelter for the "a." It was a beautiful design that evoked the feel of the woods. The font used almost seemed to have a natural texture to it. Matt idly wondered about the design while he waited for Ben's answer.

"Yeah, I prefer going out for coffee. Less risk," Ben said.

Matt shook his head. "No, I'm talking about a real date. If you're going to ask someone out, you have to really ask. She'll say yes or no but at least everything is up front. I say make it crystal clear what you want."

Ben nodded. "Or you could just bet the woman to go out with you."

So much for circumspection. Matt nodded. "I guess that cat is out of the bag."

Ben gave a simple explanation. "The Kent sisters." He straightened some papers on the desk by his computer keyboard and then neatened the pamphlet display.

"Jeff thought the best bet would be Tamblin's."

"While I hate to actually agree with anything Jeff has to say, and particularly in the category of dating, he's pretty much right. Unless you want to drive an hour, maybe an hour-fifteen minutes away. Once you get closer to the college, you have a much better selection."

Matt saw an opportunity to win some points here. "Anything particular near the college that Jade might like?"

"Well, there's nothing really spectacular. Everyone at the university is more interested in the experience of exotic dining. It's like they want to be able to say, 'I had a great Nasi Goreng' or 'They have the best Doro Wat,' and then have everyone nod knowingly. Jade and I used to joke about it when we would meet up between classes. She'd probably rather just eat at Tamblin's." Ben pushed his glasses up the bridge of his nose.

Okay, that was interesting. It seemed that Ben and Jade were more than just co-workers. Matt saw an opportunity to pry. She was less than forthcoming about herself, other than the fact that she did not particularly want to date him. "You two went to school together?" Hopefully, that had come out sounding like a casual question. Although Lakehaven had a casual feel and the staff was very friendly, Matt wasn't sure how chatty Ben would be with a guest he barely knew.

"Sure, for a while." Ben nodded. "I've been going part-time for years. I commute during the day. It's taking a while, but I'll get it done eventually."

"And is Jade commuting too?"

Ben shook his head. "She was full-time and living on campus until she quit. We would get together for lunch sometimes because we knew each other. She spent every summer at Lakehaven when she was growing up, and I've had summer and part-time jobs here since I was seven. Mr. Sawyer used to hire me to collect kindling so I could earn money to buy my mom Christmas presents."

Okay then, no need to worry about Ben clamming up. He would be a font of information if Matt could get him to shift the conversation back to Jade. Matt debated how to ask a question that would steer Ben in the right direction, but Ben mistook the silence.

"Yeah, so … Tamblin's is your best bet nearby. Sorry about over sharing. If you need anything else, just let me know."

Matt decided he'd work Jade into a later conversation and let it drop for the time being. As he turned to leave, Ben turned his attention back to his computer screen. With a few deft keystrokes, he was surfing the Internet again.

• • •

"So, where is he taking you?" Meg pushed a pile of discarded clothing to one-half of Jade's bed and reclined on the other half.

Jade wore a black knee-length dress that was fitted through the torso. She pulled at her bra straps and adjusted herself in the dress. "I'm not sure." Jade shrugged and wandered over to her dresser, where various boxes and baskets overflowed with jewelry. She pawed through the piles, pulled out two different necklaces, and held both up for Meg to see. Meg pointed to the one in Jade's right hand. Jade smiled, nodded, and put the other one back in a box of carved wood.

The chosen necklace was one of Jade's designs and looked like lace and tree branches. The design was actually one that Jade had come up with while lying in the shade of a tree, looking up at the sky through the branches. It was a beautifully cast piece of gold with small stones incorporated in a rough, unpolished way. The design was both elegant and somehow raw at the same time. Jade loved the combination.

She handed the necklace to Meg and turned her back, sweeping her hair up and out of the way so Meg could lend a hand. "Well, my bet is on Tamblin's. Where else is there?"

"Thanks." Jade turned back around and presented herself with a goofy flourish. "Well? What do you think?"

Meg tilted her head in consideration then narrowed her eyes. The inspection made Jade shift from one foot to the other and roll her eyes.

Finally, Meg smiled. "Very nice, Sawyer. Lookin' good. How do you feel?"

"A little nervous. It's been a while."

Meg laughed. "Don't worry, I'm pretty sure it's like riding a bike. You don't forget how."

"What if you've always been terrible at bike riding?"

Meg looked confused. "You're not good at riding a bike?"

"No! I'm not good at dating. We were talking about the date, remember?"

"Oh, yeah. Really, you aren't good at dating? What, specifically, is the problem? Maybe I can help."

Jade threw her hands up in the air. "If I knew, I could fix it! It just seems, well … awkward and weird. Something always isn't right, but I never know what it is."

"That makes no sense," Meg mused, staring at the ceiling.

"I know it doesn't." Jade flopped down next to Meg, heedless of the pile of discarded clothes on the bed and heedless of her little black dress. She stared up at the ceiling and thought about the last date she had been on. It hadn't been pretty. They had talked, mostly small talk. Regular first date stuff. He was nice, but there had been no point to the conversation and no spark. He had put his hand over hers and rubbed his thumb across her knuckles, but there had been no excitement, no tingle. He was good looking, smart, and perfectly acceptable, but there was absolutely no connection. Jade sighed.

"Look," Meg said, "you claim you don't even want to date Matt, so that should take the pressure off. I mean, if it doesn't go well, he'll just lose interest that much sooner." Meg looked over at Jade. "Although in that dress, you could be a cardboard box and he might still be interested. Anyway, assuming he isn't too shallow or too horny and assuming you tank, he'll lose interest sooner and maybe even forfeit the bet. You should pray that you mess this up."

Jade cut a glance toward Meg. "It sounds good in theory, but I just know something will go wrong."

"Well, there's only one way to find out."

"Gee, thanks. That's comforting."

Meg smiled and stood up from the bed. "Hey! What are friends for?'

•••

Matt was nervous. It was weird. He had been on hundreds, maybe thousands of dates, and with women that were a lot higher maintenance than Jade. Technically, this wasn't even a real date. It was a *bet* date, whatever that was. He wiped his hands against his pants. Crap.

There had been a time when dates used to make him nervous, when he was in high school, before he had hit his stride. He had been gangly and awkward and had spent a lot of time in the library. He had had crushes and occasionally stumbled through a lame exchange of phone numbers, wiping his hands on his pants the whole time.

Then he went to college, put on a little muscle, and the girls suddenly viewed his hanging out by himself on the quad with a notebook as wildly mysterious and romantic. They would pursue him, give out clear signals, hand him a phone number, smile directly into his eyes, and ask him, oh so sweetly, to please call. The nerves had gradually disappeared. Matt had almost forgotten what it was like to be nervous around a girl … a woman. And, in a way, that was the whole point. Weren't you supposed to be a little nervous, a little excited, a little … alive?

Matt smiled. He headed out the door to pick up his date. *No guts, no glory.*

He took the brief walk to Jade's cabin, breathing in the crisp evening air, listening to crickets chirping in the underbrush, and wondering what Jade would be wearing. Ultimately, it wouldn't matter—she would be Jade no matter what. Prickly, sparkling, funny Jade. Nonetheless, Matt savored the anticipation of that moment when she would open the door and stand there, smiling or frowning or glaring. Again, it really didn't matter to him. He would breathe in the scent of her and sweep her face with his gaze, taking it all in. Taking her all in.

The walk from cabin seven to cabin nine was over quickly, and Matt was face to door. Music pounded from the cabin, and he could almost pick out Jade's voice belting lyrics inside. He knocked loudly and waited. Then he knocked again, harder this time. And waited.

# Chapter 8

Jade shimmied and strutted around her cabin singing loudly. She felt good. No, she felt really gooooood. Free. Meg's speech had sunk in and Jade had taken it to heart. She had given herself complete permission to fail. There was something wonderful in just accepting that this might go horribly wrong. It couldn't possibly be worse than her imagination, so there was nowhere to go but up. She smiled at her reflection in the mirror over her dresser as she danced past and waved. *Hi there, sexy!* The knock at the door hit off the beat of the music, or she wouldn't have heard it. She wiggled over to her stereo and turned down the volume, pulled at her dress, and then walked over to the door. *Okay, this is it. Deep breath.*

Jade opened the door and Matt stood there, a slightly goofy grin on his face. He was trying to keep his face straight, serious. He was going for the face he wore when he'd first arrived at Lakehaven, eyes hidden behind his aviators, where what you noticed first were cheekbones and a strong jaw. Yup, he was valiantly attempting his "shades face." Jade much preferred the goofy grin that was asserting itself. It was such a refreshing look that Jade felt laughter bubbling up from inside, and rather than stifle it, she just laughed. Yeah, she felt *that* good.

And why not? He was fun to look at: tall and lean, broad in the shoulders and so alive. So Jade just stared. It was a simple thing to stare and smile. So much easier than being careful. And that was her assignment, wasn't it? A simple date. Jade was good at assignments.

"I'll just grab my bag." Jade shot one more smile at Matt and turned to her cabin. She had picked up for a change and the cabin looked pretty decent. The tune of "Head over Heels" by the Go

Go's played in her head, and she walked in time to the beat as she crossed the room to pick up her purse.

...

Jade opened the door and all Matt's rational thought processes ceased. Holy mother lode. Her cheeks were flushed and her breathing was quick, which drew his attention to the neckline of her dress. Or maybe it was something else that drew his gaze downward. Like her exquisite … décolletage. Yeah, that could be it, too. Either way, he was *gobsmacked*, and it must've shown because, as he stood staring, she stared back and began to laugh. And he really couldn't blame her; the whole staring thing was pretty ridiculous. But he couldn't quite get himself to *stop*, so he slid his gaze down further. The dress was, *thank you God*, fitted, black, and just above the knee. And suddenly the patella seemed like a highly appealing erogenous zone, one worthy of worshipping with his tongue.

He was pretty much savoring that thought until she turned around to get her purse and then, *thank you, thank you God*, there were stocking seams and a rear view that included her sashaying across the room, causing her dress to shift back and forth across her butt. Her hair was a black curtain that swung from side to side across the satiny skin of her back, and the tiny portion of his brain that was still working could just imagine what all of that hair would feel like draped over his chest. Well, as to the question of what Jade would look like for their first date, there was his answer: *Stu-freakin'-pendous.*

Matt cleared his throat and smiled at Jade. "You look nice."

Jade smiled back. "Thanks."

...

Tamblin's was a perfect place for a first date. It was cozy without being too dark or intimate. There was a candle on each table, but the flicker was subtle rather than severe. You could hear your date across the table easily, but you were also afforded the privacy of knowing that the table next to you wasn't listening in on your date. It was Jade's favorite restaurant.

The best part about Tamblin's wasn't the atmosphere, it was the food. There was nothing pretentious or elaborate about the menu. Everything on it was easy to pronounce. It was also good. The chef had worked at a premiere steak house in Chicago and then moved back east about eight years ago to be closer to his aging parents. The end result was that this small town restaurant had pretty great food, and Jade would trade good food for atmosphere any day. It was a pet peeve of hers when some place became the hip new spot just because of its décor. If you really wanted décor, you could go to a Pottery Barn.

Most of the waiters at Tamblin's knew Jade, at least her face, and there were definitely some speculative stares as they took her in, her attire, and the hottie walking in behind her with his hand at the small of her back. Matt was behind her so she couldn't see him, but she would bet money that he had his "shades" face back on, even without the shades. If he did, he probably looked like a Michael Kors magazine ad come to life, like he owned any room he entered. It was both appealing and annoying at the same time.

They sat down and Matt helped to push her seat in. For the first time in Jade's life, the maneuver actually worked. Usually the timing would be off and the chair would hit her in the back of the knees or she would be forced to lower herself into the chair in slow, awkward degrees like some strange exercise program done in heels and a skirt. Mostly, she ended up looking silly and gritting her teeth until it was over. But, in either the most perfectly timed glide or by some alignment of the stars, the chair slid into place a hair's breadth behind her knees and at the precise moment that she was sitting. It was now wildly appealing and supremely annoying at the same time. Jade perused the menu and debated her choices. There were some really great dishes on the menu, but what she really wanted was the cheeseburger and fries. Granted, it was Gouda cheese and sweet potato fries. She should probably just order a salad. With dressing on the side.

"I assume you've been here before. What's good?" Matt asked.

"Yeah, I have. How can you tell?"

"You got a lot of looks on the way in."

Jade resisted preening. "You noticed that too?"

"Writer." Matt pointed to himself.

"Oh, yeah. Well," Jade said, scanning the menu, "do you prefer beef or seafood?"

"What are you ordering?" Matt asked.

"Um." Oh, what the hell. "Cheeseburger." Jade lifted her chin slightly and dared Matt to even look at her funny.

Matt smiled. "Great. We'll make it two."

"And a beer. They have my favorite microbrew on tap here."

"Two of those then." Matt snapped his menu shut and lifted his eyes to her and smiled. "What's your favorite animal?"

"What?" Jade was confused.

"Favorite animal?"

"I like the word platypus, but they're actually kind of creepy looking. I guess I like woodchucks because, well, they chuck wood, and what's not to like about that? Why do you ask?"

"This is the 'getting to know each other better' portion of the date. Aisle seat or window?"

"Are these questions from some male magazine article about dating?"

"No, but they should be. I'll write one."

Jade just rolled her eyes. "Yeah, that'll be a winner. Aisle. My turn. Favorite Hepburn: Audrey or Katherine?"

"Kate. I also like Kate Winslet and Catherine the Great, although I'm not a fan of Kate Spade purses."

"You know who Kate Spade is?"

"I dated this woman once who was obsessed."

Jade nodded sagely. "That can happen. I prefer Coach bags myself."

Matt shot Jade a worried look. "Please tell me we are not going to talk about purses."

"Okay, no purse talk, got it." Jade grinned at Matt. "May I assume that moratorium also applies to shoes?"

Matt grinned back. "You may."

The waiter arrived then to take their orders, and they quickly resumed talking. In some ways it was like any first date. They talked about themselves and asked questions. They smiled at each other and laughed at each other's jokes. But for the first time in a long while, Jade was actually interested in the answers. She thought she'd had this guy figured out. She had him fixed in her mind as a cocky New York writer with a social calendar and an entourage, but his answers just didn't fit. This person sitting across from her wasn't that at all. The cocky attitude was a façade to hide the normal, charming, funny person underneath. The question was, why hide that stuff?

Jade decided to find out. "Can I ask you a question?'

Matt laughed. "I thought that was what we were doing."

"This one's a bit more personal."

"More personal than sharing about your love of woodchucks? Uh oh."

Jade smiled. "Yeah, this is where I ruin things by getting serious." Jade made quote gestures in the air as she said, "serious."

Matt nodded. "Okay, I'm ready for it. Shoot."

Jade fidgeted with the silverware, flipping her fork tines down then back up again. She noticed herself playing with the silverware and could almost hear her dad say, "Jade, don't play with that." She stopped and looked at Matt. He was waiting patiently. "Okay, here's the thing. You have this persona, this slick thing you do where you ... I'm not even sure I know what you do, but I don't think it's you exactly. There's nothing wrong with it, it just seems so … not you."

Matt sat back in his seat and steepled his fingers. He nodded once. "My manager, Sam, hates it. I call it 'being Mr. Writer.' It started out as a kind of joke before I even sold my first novel. If I acted like this big hotshot writer, I'd be perceived as this big hotshot writer. Then later, I realized that it also kept fans from getting too friendly, which was convenient. Then I started to use it other times when it was convenient. Now, it's almost automatic, at least in public. Drives Sam crazy."

Jade smiled. "I bet. You guys have been friends a long time?"

"Forever." Matt smiled. He looked like he was remembering some past moment, some little piece of their history, one of the thousands of little moments that make up a friendship. It was a devilish smile, yet it somehow made Jade feel like she was in on the joke. Their eyes caught for a moment, and Jade felt a warmth spread through her.

"Meg—you met her in the kitchen—she and I have been friends for about fifteen years. I can't even remember what it was like before I met her."

"Mmm, I know what you mean. I don't have a huge circle of friends, but life would be weird without them." Matt leaned forward and rested his hands on the table.

The movement caught Jade's eye, and she just stared at his hands for a moment. They were lean and long-fingered. She could imagine them flying over the keyboard of his computer, and she could remember what they looked like wrapped around a coffee cup. They were tan and lightly dusted with blonde hair that you could just barely see when the low light of the restaurant hit them just right. They looked strong but not huge, and for some reason she had a sudden need to feel the texture of his skin. She reached out to touch them, and Matt sat there, stone still, and let her. He didn't move or turn his hands palm up to take her hand the way most men would do. She could feel him watching her as her fingers played, feather-light, across the backs of his hands. She started to pull back and he finally did roll his hands palm up, but still, he didn't grab her. He just cradled her hands in his, his fingertips warm against her wrists. She could feel his pulse at her fingertips, and it thudded there, tugging against things deeper in her body and making her catch her breath.

"Oh my God! Jade, is that you?" Just like that, the spell was broken. Jade broke contact as she swiveled toward the voice. A part of her brain, the part in denial, was confused and wondered who it was. Another part of her already knew, and stiffened up even as she turned to see the freight train of a blonde barreling down on their table with Jade's ex-fiancé, Nick, in tow.

*Well, this sucks.* Stacy-the-backstabber-Eames and Nick-the-cheater-Halloway were party crashing, and Stacy looked like she actually planned to stay a while. Never mind that Jade's posture had gone from relaxed to stiff and she was visibly scowling. That was just the kind of person Stacy was. Stacy would leave when she was good and ready and not before. She had always been pushy, even back when they were roommates. At the time, it was a quality Jade had admired. It made Stacy seem confident and bold. Now Jade saw it as insecure and rude. In another person, Jade might've chalked it up to stupidity, but she had learned the hard way not to underestimate Stacy. Stacy was anything but stupid. Even now, she wore a calculating expression, assessing the situation and checking Matt out from head to toe with interest.

Nick looked less than excited to be there, but Stacy had her hand wrapped around Nick's bicep and was pulling him closer to her and closer to the table. Knowing Stacy, Jade suspected that Nick got dragged around a lot. Not that she was particularly torn up about it. He got what he deserved.

"Hi Stacy, Nick." Jade stood up to discourage Nick and Stacy from staying too long. Matt stood at the same time and slipped closer to her side. Jade threw him a grateful look. She acknowledged her ex with a tilt of her head and Nick nodded back.

Nick was beautiful. There was no other way to say it. His features were absolutely perfect. Perfectly proportioned, perfectly hewn. His jaw-line was strong, his cheekbones high, and his nose aquiline. He had blonde hair, perfectly coiffed, if a little stiff. Even this late in the evening, his skin was perfectly smooth with not a hint of stubble in sight, as if his facial hair wouldn't have dared. He was tall and toned. He had always brought to her mind the image of Apollo here on Earth amongst the mortals. She hated him.

Jade squared her shoulders. "This is Matt." Jade gestured to Matt, and he shot the interloping couple a *GQ* smile that had Stacy blinking hard. "Matt, this is Stacy and Nick. They're … we went to school together."

Matt extended his hand to Stacy first. "Nice to meet you," she practically cooed at him. "A pleasure, I'm sure." *What the fuck?* Jade thought. Who the hell talks like that? Apparently, Stacy does when introduced to any attractive man whether he was available or not. Matt just lifted his eyebrows and glanced at Jade. She could practically read the thought bubble over his head: *Okay, interesting.*

Matt extended a hand to Nick and Jade watched nervously as they shook hands. Matt had a presence and confidence about him. He didn't get into a pissing contest or try to crush Nick's hand in his grip. It was like watching an alpha wolf approach a lesser pack member. There was no reason to assert himself. Matt's strength was just there, in every fiber of his being.

"It's been so long! What a year and a half, huh?" Stacy chatted on like they were old friends. They were anything but.

*Not long enough.* Eons, epochs, eras, and ages would not have been long enough. Until after Jade was dead and rotted to dust would not have been long enough. Eternity would not have. "Yeah, something like that," Jade agreed.

Stacy continued her friendly onslaught. "So, what are you up to these days?"

Jade debated being rude. She really didn't want to pretend that she was perfectly happy to chat away with a woman who had committed the ultimate roommate betrayal: sleeping with her fiancé. Jade took a deep breath. She was here with Matt, who really didn't deserve to be dragged into the drama and so, somehow, Jade found the fortitude to be gracious. "I'm managing Lakehaven for the winter and working on my jewelry business."

"That sounds so mellow! I'd kill to have such a relaxing schedule. Nick and I have just been so busy. We're finishing up our degrees, and Nick just got a fellowship, and of course there's the wedding to plan. It's a lot of work, but we're having so much fun!" Stacy clutched tighter at Nick's arm and pressed her Barbie Doll breasts against him. Stacy's breasts were pushed up and out of the neckline of her top, and she kind of leaned forward to wave them around in Matt's face. Or was it to rub Jade's nose in them? Nick was courteous enough to look embarrassed.

Jade gritted her teeth and glanced over at Matt. Matt looked amused. Jade looked back to Stacy, who practically oozed smugness. *Okay, you want to play? You got it.* "Yeah, I know exactly what you mean."

Stacy laughed. "Oh, God no. You have *no* idea how many little details there are until you actually have to deal with it all. You'll know what I mean … someday." Jade had seen cats lick cream from their whiskers with less smug satisfaction.

*Crap.* Jade just wasn't willing to give Stacy the satisfaction of gloating. She hoped Matt wouldn't be too pissed. "Well, that's why Matt's mother found us a great wedding planner. That way we can spend our time enjoying each other's company." Jade smiled brightly at Stacy, who stood there, stunned.

Jade held her breath for a moment, hoping that Matt would keep quiet. It was not to be. "Uh, Jade? That's not strictly true." Matt stepped up beside her. *Oh, crap on a stick.* He snaked his arm around her waist and she braced herself for the utter humiliation that loomed. "Remember, honey? We threatened to elope, and that's when my mother called Lady Carlyle to get her event planner." Matt then addressed Stacy. "Eve Stanford," he said, naming the premiere event coordinator in Manhattan. The one Jade had seen mentioned in magazines. Matt bent his head to kiss the top of Jade's, and she could feel him grinning into her hair, probably to keep from laughing.

Stacy looked ready to swallow her tongue as she glanced frantically at Matt and back to Jade. Matt was completely convincing, but Jade must've looked surprised because when Stacy caught Jade's eyes, Stacy's gaze narrowed. She looked pointedly at Jade's left ring finger, where there was a distinct lack of jewelry. And, of course, she couldn't let it go.

"Really? I guess you haven't had time to get a ring."

Matt chimed in again to save the day. "Oh, we've bought a stone, but with Jade's considerable talents, I didn't want to rule out the possibility of her designing the ring herself. She's such an amazing artist." Damn, he was good at this.

Jade tilted her face up to Matt and gave him a beaming smile. It was only pretend, but Matt was giving an Oscar-worthy performance. She snuggled closer to him as his hand at her waist opened and flared down across her hip. His touch sent little licks of heat lower, and her breath hitched. She could feel Matt's thigh pressed against her, warm and firm. All she could do was stand there feeling all of it as sensation and lust coiled through her. It hung in the air between them until Matt spoke.

"Well, it was nice meeting you both. I don't want to keep you from your dinner, and Jade and I are eager to get back to our meal as well." Matt spoke with an authority and finality that had Stacy and Nick docilely drifting away.

Jade stood there pressed against Matt for a moment, enjoying the feel of body-to-body contact. Finally, he cleared his throat and stepped away from her. He grinned down at her, sending another flutter of butterflies through her stomach. Then he spoke: "Really? That's your idea of uncomplicated?"

# Chapter 9

Jade and Matt sat at the table as the waiter brought them each another beer. Jade had a sudden moment of shy apprehension as the waiter left them, so she grabbed the burger in front of her and took a healthy bite. Matt watched with amusement as she attacked her food with gusto. She kept chewing. She wasn't one to hold back or eat daintily. She saw him watching her and raised an eyebrow at him until she was done with the bite and could talk again. "Are you going to eat that?" Jade gestured at Matt's untouched plate.

"Why? Do you want mine too?"

"You're watching me eat. It's weird."

"It is weird. Sorry." Matt shook his head at himself and reached for his burger. They both took a bite and ate for a bit in silence. The burger was good, as usual, but Jade was having trouble enjoying it. She stopped eating and looked at Matt. He was dipping his fries, three at a time, into the plum sauce that came with them and then eating them. He didn't hold back either. She waited until he was done with his bite.

"So, you aren't even going to ask about it?"

Matt shook his head no and took another bite of burger, followed by a sip of beer.

"You aren't just a tad curious?"

Matt shrugged. "Some of it I can guess. The rest I'll make up, and you'll correct me when you're ready."

Jade tried for a pout, but she wasn't very good at it. "This is much more fun if you have to drag it out of me, huh?"

Jade sighed, which she was good at. She waited a beat, but Matt was deliberately silent. "Okay, you've talked me into telling you the whole sordid story."

"Ah! Sordid?" Matt fought back a grin. "You didn't mention that earlier or I would've tried harder to drag it out of you."

Jade shot him a look that was part *very funny* with overtones of *okay, smartass.* Matt just tried to look innocent.

"We were engaged."

"Really? Stacy just doesn't seem your type."

Jade smiled weakly at the joke. "She was my roommate at the time."

Matt nodded. "She seems the type."

"To be a roommate?"

"To create soap opera level drama around her."

"I thought I liked her at the time; I thought I loved him. It seemed a huge betrayal, and yes, very dramatic. There was much wailing and gnashing of teeth." Jade stopped for a moment, tracing a finger down the side of her glass, creating a trail through the condensation.

She tried to put herself back there, back three years. It really had been painful and crazy and dramatic. She tried to recall the exact feelings, the despair, the hurt. They were so diluted now that she could barely remember them. It was like some ball of black emotion buried deep in her belly had suddenly just disappeared. It was such a surprise to her that she jerked her head up and started to laugh. Her eyes met Matt's. He didn't seem confused or worried by her laughter. He just waited and listened. "It's so weird. Seeing them tonight. If you had asked me how I thought I would feel, seeing them together, I would've said devastated. Crushed. But it's not like that. I don't love him, I don't miss her, and I don't even wish a house would fall on them. I can remember that time, how hard it was, but it's like it happened to someone else."

Matt smiled at her. "Maybe you were someone else then."

Jade nodded. "I was. I tried really hard then. To fit in, to belong. I never really wanted college. It was expected of me. My *dad* wanted it. And Nick, he was a graduate student—really bright and totally hot." That got an eyebrow raise and a smirk from Matt, but Jade just continued. "We fit together in a convenient way. It was something I thought I wanted for myself, but now, looking back … " Jade shook her head. "Maybe it was what I thought my parents would want for me. I caught Nick and Stacy leaving a restaurant together, but I told myself that it was just friendly, that he was probably just giving her some advice or tutoring. I was going to head on over to them, say hi. Then he leaned down and kissed her. I mean *really* kissed her, full on the mouth. Maybe they did me a favor. It shook me out of my … complacency, I guess. It was a perfect excuse to quit school, which I hated anyway. I had been making jewelry between classes instead of studying. After I quit school, I took some courses: metalworking, casting, gemology . . ."

• • •

Matt had been listening intently to her the whole time. He was gazing at her, his eyes fixed on her face, watching the play of emotions there. She was so vital, glowing and alive. When she started to speak about making jewelry, his gaze shifted downward—down her throat, across her collarbone, and lower. Her skin had a slight sheen and glowed softly in the low candlelight of Tamblin's. It was a perfect backdrop for the pendant she wore.

The piece was a rough-edged weave of gold with delicate little stones embedded in the junctures. The stones were pale blue, green, and brown. It hung from a black silk cord around her neck. He reached out to feel its texture. The gold was warmer than he expected. It had absorbed her body heat and was the same temperature as the skin beneath it. Her skin was silky-smooth and the pendant was slightly rougher. He rested his hand there for a moment, thinking if they were someplace else … he would keep going.

He could feel her eyes on him, and he slowly looked up at her. Her lips were slightly parted; her eyes looked dark and dreamy. He could feel her heartbeat under his hand, which rested lightly on the pendant, which rested low on her chest. He could almost imagine what it would feel like to have all that warm skin underneath him. And that was a bad direction for his thoughts to take if he wanted to stand up from the table any time soon. Which he did—as in immediately—want to get up from the table, leave the restaurant, and drive like a bat out of hell back to his cabin. Her breath came faster now, and he could feel it in the rise and fall of her chest. He wasn't sure what she was breathing since it felt like all of the oxygen had been sucked out of room. He knew that she had been saying something. He just couldn't remember what they had been talking about. He looked at his own hand, dark against her pale skin and at the gold glinting out from behind his fingertips. *Bingo!* He gently lifted the pendant from her skin.

"You made this." It was a statement, not a question. Jade nodded. Matt rotated the piece in the half-light of the darkened room. The small nuggets of color winked, reflecting the glow of the candle flame. "It's beautiful."

Jade smiled in a flush of genuine pleasure. "Thank you."

"You're a talented artist."

"Don't stop." Jade's grin widened. "No, really, don't stop!" she insisted.

Matt leaned toward her and spoke in a low tone. "I can think of a couple of situations where I would love to hear you say that." He sat back and continued. "None of them in public."

Jade took a long slow sip of beer. "No, really." She ran her tongue suggestively across her top lip. "Don't stop."

Matt held up two fingers and flagged down the waiter. "We'll have the check now."

• • •

The drive home went quickly. They talked music as Jade set Matt's radio to stations that she thought he would like. Their conversation was peppered with silence as they listened to the music. There was a sexual tension in the vehicle that wrapped around both of them, while they both pretended they were not about to have mind-blowing sex. Jade even sang aloud with some of her favorite songs, something she usually reserved for later in a relationship. Matt drummed to the beat with his fingers against the steering wheel. They reached Lakehaven, and Matt pulled his SUV to an easy stop. He walked around to the passenger side to let Jade out. She felt stupid waiting when she was perfectly capable of letting herself out, but she didn't know Matt well enough to gauge whether he would be insulted or appreciate not having to walk around the car.

"It must be great living in the city," Jade commented. They made their way up the trail toward their cabins. It was dark, but Jade moved confidently along the path, even in the fuck-me heels.

"It has its moments. But I'm sure you could say the same of living in the mountains."

"Mmm," Jade agreed. They strolled along, taking their time, Jade's face tilted upward as she watched the pattern of moonlight filtered through the branches. "Do you miss the action? I mean, it's pretty quiet out here. You'd eventually get bored."

Matt didn't answer right away. He took his time thinking about it. "Yeah, I guess sometimes you want that energy, but then you start to feel crowded in and want some space."

They got to Matt's cabin, and she slowed as they got near his door.

"No, I'll walk you back to your door," he said.

"You don't have to. It's okay." She tried to wave him off.

"It's the least I can do … now that we're engaged." He wiggled his eyebrows at her and continued on up the trail past his cabin.

"Oh God, I almost forgot that!" Jade put a hand to her forehead. She sighed, and her next words were meek. "I guess, technically, I lost the bet."

Matt laughed softly. "Yeah, technically."

"I don't suppose you could be persuaded . . ." Jade trailed off as they reached her cabin door. She turned to face him.

"Try me." The walk back had seemed casual and relaxed, but his next move was anything but. He stepped into her, crowding her. She took a step back until she felt her door at her back. He looked down at her and, despite the teasing tone of his words, there was no ambiguity in his eyes. His intentions were clearly written there, and they were anything but pure.

He moved closer still, and she tilted her head back to look up at him. The planes of his face stood out, heightened by the play of moonlight there. She let herself take him in. Earlier, he had been gorgeous in the candlelight as they ate dinner. Now, his features had shifted, made fierce by the night shadows wrapped around them. There was not a soft line on him, except maybe his lower lip, which Jade could imagine nibbling at and then licking. That thought had her knees turn to liquid, along with other things as she leaned into the door for support.

• • •

Matt watched her eyes go molten, black pools surrounded by a rim of green. Her lips parted slightly, which was really working for him. But he still couldn't get past the amazing column of her throat, alabaster in the moonlight. It had to be one of the seven natural wonders of the world. He reached out. His fingers traced feather-light touches there, the pad of his thumb circling the hollow at the base of her throat. She jumped and gasped. Her quick intake of breath turned him on a little more, if that were possible. He moved in closer to touch more of her with more of him. His knees mingled with hers. His thighs pressed into hers. Her soft breasts pillowed against his ribcage, and his erection pressed into her belly. She was definitely going to notice that. Not that she was complaining at this point.

He slid his hand around to cradle the back of her neck and leaned in to kiss her. He moved slowly, giving her plenty of time to make up her mind. He wanted her full participation, and if the look in her eyes was any indication, he'd get that and a whole lot more.

As his lips touched hers, she responded. She pushed her hips into him and met his mouth with hers. Her arms came up around his shoulders. She clung to him as they kissed and it was a done deal. She went off like a Fourth of July three-stage firework. Kissing, nipping, gently flicking her tongue at the corner of his mouth. His hand slid down her back so he could mold her more closely to him. He heard a soft whimper and was pretty sure that it was her. It was not helping his self-control at all. They had been kissing for maybe only a minute, and he already wanted to break her door down and tumble her onto the floor of the cabin. Right now.

Her hands had slid to his waist and below, and he had certainly missed something, because his shirt was already untucked and her small fingers were sliding up and down his torso. He was pretty sure she could have asked him for a secret code to detonate a nuke right now, and he would have given it to her. She kept exploring, found his waistband, and slid her hand down the front of his slacks. Her fingers found him and, *holy heaven*, she stroked them along his shaft. He groaned into her mouth and thought he felt the corners of her mouth tip up in a smile. It was hard to be sure with his attention divided between what her mouth was doing to him and what her hands were doing to him. *Holy heaven, indeed.* He managed to speak, his voice rough, "Inside." He hoped it hadn't sounded like begging.

• • •

Jade had him exactly where she wanted him. Well, not exactly. Laid out on a bed would be nice, or the floor, or the kitchen table.

Or buried deep inside her, like five minutes ago. She heard him growl, "Inside," and was trying to process how to make that happen with the half of a brain cell she had left functioning. What *was* functioning was her body. On all cylinders. And her imagination; that was on overdrive and already had him naked with his legs between hers and his fine backside in her hands so she could pull him in closer, deeper. She eased her hands around to the back of his body to test what that would be like to have her hands pull him closer, and it was stupendous. Except for the clothing. There was still *waaay* too much of that.

"Please ... " She didn't finish the sentence, but there were about eighteen different ways she wanted to. Please get naked, please faster, please kiss me here, please take me, and just please, please, please. At this point, begging seemed like a very good plan, if it would get her what she wanted.

• • •

He heard them first, and for a moment just thought, *fuck it.* I don't care what anyone thinks. Then he heard the kids' laughter and scuffling footfall. He had kissed his way to her temple and was working his way toward her ear. His plan was to whisper in her ear, get her to open her door, and move inside faster. She would have to take her hands off his butt to do that but it was a small sacrifice. One he was willing to make if it meant getting her inside. Her dress was hiked up her thighs and Matt's number one goal in that moment was to get her out of the dress entirely. Or at least that was the plan, until the crazed raccoon came on the scene.

The noise of the approaching family had probably frightened it out of the brush, and unfortunately, the damn thing ran directly toward Jade and him. It ran across their feet, and Matt could feel its claws scramble for purchase against the leather of his shoes. Jade's feet weren't nearly as well protected and the moment the panicked raccoon came between them, she shrieked and jumped away. He pulled his head back, but wasn't quite quick enough to avoid getting clipped in the chin. In a matter of seconds, they had gone from a total wet-dream lip lock to a scene out of *The Three Stooges*. Jade was hopping from foot to foot, making little yelping noises. Matt rubbed at his chin and ran his tongue across his teeth, checking for any chipped edges. He had to take another step away from her to avoid getting bumped again. This never happened in Manhattan. He looked down at her feet to check for blood, but it was dark, and she was moving too much.

"Are you okay?" he asked.

"Aaaahhh!"

"Hold still for a sec."

"Omigod … Omigod!"

"Jade. Hold still."

"Was that a raccoon?"

"Yep. Hold still. Let me look at your feet."

She stopped hopping but stepped away from Matt. "They're fine."

"Let me just see."

"No, there's nothing wrong with them," she said.

"Then why can't I see them?"

"I don't want you looking at my feet."

Matt stared at her. He felt like he had missed something here. They had been kissing and maybe moments away from doing way more, and now she didn't want to show him her feet? "Really? Jade, what's wrong?"

"Nothing. I just … " She blew out a hard breath. "Look, this is going to sound stupid, but maybe this is a sign."

"A sign?"

She nodded. "Yeah, like from the universe. Maybe we should hold off on this for now." She waved her hand back and forth between them as she said *this*.

Matt wanted to roll his eyes at her but didn't think that would win him any points. He thought about it from her point of view. They hadn't known each other for very long, and she was definitely gun shy around romantic relationships. Physically she was ready but maybe not mentally. At least she had said *for now.* That was a good sign. Matt called on every reserve of self-restraint, gently kissed her forehead, and said goodnight before he stepped away and turned toward his cabin.

"Good night." Her soft voice floated toward him as he walked away. He thought about their vicious wildlife encounter and chuckled to himself. It was either laugh or howl in frustration.

# Chapter 10

"How could you lose the bet on the very first date?!" Meg asked. She bustled around the kitchen, peeking in the oven at some pastries and putting a kettle on the stove.

Jade responded with a shrug and a one-word answer, "Stacy," as she sipped her morning coffee.

Meg just shook her head.

Jade threw her hands up in the air. "What? I was just supposed to let her walk all over me? I have my dignity! I have my self-respect!" She clunked her head down on the table in defeat. "I have no self-control."

Meg laughed. "Well, on the plus side, you don't have to date Matt anymore." She was washing a platter at the sink and facing away from Jade, but Jade could hear the smirk in her voice.

"Yeah," Jade said with a sigh.

"I hear a big *but* coming … "

"I could make a joke here, but I'm too depressed for witty repartee."

"Now you *want* to date him?"

"It was good." Jade thunked her head on the counter a few more times for good measure. "Oh, who am I kidding? It was great, fabulous, stupendous. *Ahhrgh*."

"Talking about me again?" Matt poked his head in the doorway. His right hand held the coffee carafe from the dining room. He thrust it forward and wiggled it around. He smiled charmingly at Meg. "Needs a refill, when you get a chance."

Jade hid her face in her arms, which were crossed on the countertop.

"Please?" Matt said.

"Sure, I can refill that," Meg said. "For a price." She waited a moment. "You have to take Jade out on a few more dates."

Jade lifted her head long enough to mumble, "Oh, that's just great. Now men have to be bribed with caffeinated beverages in order to go out with me."

Matt rubbed his chin where Jade's head had smacked into his. There was a purplish bruise there, and Jade felt her cheeks heat with embarrassment. She buried her face again. He was already too good-looking, too urbane for her. Last night's incident was just more evidence that she was not in his league.

"I don't know. Given the rodent attack … she is kind of dangerous."

"It was not a rodent! It was a raccoon."

He paused a moment longer. "Throw in a cheese danish and you've got a deal."

"Sold!" Jade heard Meg grab a plate and walk over to Matt.

"Oh God, is this still warm? You're the best!"

Great. Now she felt like cattle at the county fair in addition to feeling like a goofy klutz. Jade grunted into her forearms then mumbled, "Could this be any more humiliating?" Meg and Matt ignored her.

Matt groaned in pleasure. "Mmm." Then he called out to Jade, "I'll pick you up at seven!"

Jade thunked her head on the counter top one more time.

• • •

Jade spent the early part of her day catching up on paperwork, bills, supply orders, and payroll. She couldn't be sure, but it felt like the paperwork had been shuffled around a little, like someone had been in the office poking around. She figured it was just Ben looking for a reservation confirmation or some other paperwork and shrugged it off. At lunch she socialized with guests then worked through her hospitality to do list, making sure everyone was well taken care of.

Next, she made a stop to check on Jeff. She had Jeff cutting back some of the brush down by the lakeside that was beginning to encroach on the lake view from the lawn and porch. The bushes and trees that ringed the lake separated Lakehaven from structures on the opposite side, creating a magical world cloistered from the rest of civilization. There were private residences and the country club with a lakeside restaurant over there, and it was important to maintain the intimacy of her resort (*When had she started thinking of it as hers?*) without blocking the view. It was a tricky balance, and though Jeff knew what he was doing, he did sometimes have his moments of unreliability. She was too humble to stand there and order Jeff around without also lending a hand, so she spent the next hour dragging branches onto a tarp and then dragging the tarp across the grounds to dump the branches onto a pile for clearing. At least she wouldn't need a workout.

On her way back up to the lawn, she checked to make sure that the Jordan family in cabin four had their parcel of towels and finally went back to her own cabin for a shower. Then hopefully, she could finish some work on her jewelry website. At least, that was the plan. She completed only an hour of frustrating work before losing consciousness. She drifted up from sleep to the sound of someone knocking on her cabin door. The blankets were shoved down to the foot of the bed, and her laptop lay on the mattress next to her, its screen saver cycling through various images. The windows were dark. A quick glance at the alarm clock on the bedside table showed a glowing 7:00 P.M. *Crap!*

"Just a sec!" she called out.

She rushed to the door and threw it open without really thinking it through. She had thrown on an old pair of boxer shorts and a tank top after her shower. Without underwear. Or a bra. And her hair had dried while she slept on it. She reached up to feel the back of her head and … yup, it felt rough. She hoped it looked tousled, but she was guessing it was more … matted.

And there he was, over six feet of muscle in a worn pair of jeans, fitted black t-shirt, and leather jacket. His hair was mussed, but almost artfully so, and it curled just the slightest bit at the nape of his neck. She wanted to run her fingers through it and— Okay, now she was in a tank with no bra and *hellooo, nipples.*

"Okay, I admit, when I mentioned casual I had something else in mind." Matt's eyes zeroed in on her top. "Although, I could be talked into this. This is a *very* good look."

Jade crossed her arms over her chest and mustered a weak smile. "Okay, yeah, I fell asleep and—Can you give me just a moment to get myself together?"

Matt's grin widened, and he shrugged. "I kind of like you falling apart." He hooked a finger under the strap of her tank top, which she promptly batted away. Jade stepped back quickly and ushered Matt into her living room.

"Make yourself at home. There's beer in the fridge." She gestured toward the kitchen then ducked into her bathroom.

Matt grabbed a beer and sat. He was accustomed to waiting for women to get ready. Though usually, he was wearing at least a suit and tie. Sometimes a tux. The women he dated always wanted to go out on the town and mostly made their preferences known. He'd take jeans and a t-shirt any day. The beer was also a nice change from the glass of Pinot he usually was offered. He leaned back into the cushions of the couch and took a pull from the bottle of beer. He was surprised when Jade came out of the bathroom five minutes later. He was expecting twenty. She wore a pair of jeans that she filled out nicely and a top that clung in all the right places. It was a t-shirt material but somehow didn't fit the category of t-shirt. He found himself leaning forward in his seat and setting his beer down without taking his eyes off her. She looked fresh and glowing, all of that black hair swinging around her shoulders, and more alluring than any socialite in a little black dress. Just looking at her spiked his heart rate. She wasn't tall, but in those jeans her legs looked long, lean, and toned. She wasn't full-breasted either, but her breasts were high and lush and palmable. His hands wanted to reach out and touch. He stood and put his hands in his pockets to keep them out of trouble.

"I'm ready. I hope jeans are okay." She opened her arms out to her sides, palms up, framing her figure.

Okay? That didn't begin to cover it. He just smiled and nodded. Very much okay. Eye-crossingly okay, *okay*? "So, where are we going tonight?"

Matt finally found his voice. "Fitch's."

She smiled broadly and practically bounced over to a low table by the front door where her purse sat. "Great! That'll be fun."

Hmm, fun. Yeah, at the very least they would have fun.

# Chapter 11

Jade and Matt pulled up to Fitch's. Much like their entrance at Tamblin's, they drew stares. Most of the stares were from women. If it made Matt uncomfortable, he certainly didn't show it. He was either used to the attention or unaware of it. She guessed as a writer, he was very aware. He reached over to her, slipping his arm around her waist. She paused for a moment and then decided it would be easier, and nicer, to slide close to him. She was right. On both counts.

Jade didn't draw too many second glances, but it wasn't because she was plain. She was, however, a familiar face, and when people reacted to her here, it was with warmth. She truly belonged here and felt it down to her core. Like most people, Jade hoped to travel someday and see the world. When she did, Lakehaven would be the place she'd come home to.

She smiled with the confidence of that thought. Matt looked down at her that very moment, and he almost stopped walking. Jade turned to see what had stopped him. He was smiling down at her, and she would've stood staring at him all evening if Fitch himself hadn't waved them over to the bar with a jovial greeting.

"Jade, m'love! Where've you been? This place is just pining for your pretty face to liven it up!"

Fitch was a big bear of a man in late fifties, with a shaved head. He was vital, and despite his age, still in his prime. He was handsome, had the charm of the Irish, and even though he wasn't for Jade, she'd always thought of him as a sexy guy who could make some woman very happy. Jade was still trying to work out which woman.

She glanced around the bar, packed with familiar faces. Many of them pretty women. Jade just shook her head. "I don't know. It looks pretty lively to me, Fitch."

"Ah, true enough, but none of them are you." Fitch leaned over the bar and slid a glass across to her before dropping his voice in a conspiratorial tone. "And none quite so pretty."

Jade rolled her eyes at Fitch and then took her glass. "Fitch, you charmer." Fitch bussed her cheek from across the bar and then pulled back to eye Matt.

"It's true that I'm charming, but perhaps not so much as the gentleman who got you out here tonight."

Jade shifted to her left to make room for Matt beside her at the bar. "Fitch, meet Mr. Connor."

"Oh, Mr. Connor is it?" Fitch took Matt in with an assessing gaze.

Matt stepped up beside Jade and offered his hand. "Just call me Matt."

"Well then, Matt, what can I get you?"

A slight smile played at the corners of Matt's mouth, as if what he was about to say wasn't necessarily what he was thinking. "I'll have what the lady's having." He gestured toward Jade's glass.

"Good choice, lad." Fitch winked before he turned away to grab a glass for Matt, filled it, and then slid it over to him. Matt thanked Fitch and tipped his glass in salute before he and Jade moved toward the back of the bar. There were other shouted greetings as they crossed the room from people who knew Jade or her parents or her aunt and uncle.

It was pretty crowded already and the tables were all taken, so they ended up standing at the back of the room near the hallway that led to the restrooms. There was a narrow shelf that ran the entire perimeter of the bar to rest your drinks on. Here and there, were stools to pull up to the ledge, but it was Saturday and those were taken, too.

They stood close and leaned in to one another to talk and be heard above the general din of the bar. Matt spoke first.

"I want you to know … "

"What?" Jade asked, leaning in.

Matt bent down and put his mouth next to her ear. She could feel his breath warm on her face. "You don't have to help me search for the treasure."

Jade lifted her face to bring her mouth closer to his ear. She resisted the urge to run her tongue along the curve of his jaw. For now. "You think I'm going to renege on my end of the bargain? No way!"

"Okay, I just want you to know I won't hold you to it. It was really just a ploy to get you to date me." Matt's breath on her ear sent shivers down Jade's spine. The thought of having to be coerced into dating this man was laughable. The bet seemed like eons ago, and the issue of not wanting to date him seemed like it had occurred in another lifetime. Sort of like saying, I'll give you a million dollars if you eat this piece of cheesecake. It was a no-brainer.

The gentle scent of him, his soap or cologne or maybe it was just his skin, enveloped her. Her body practically wanted to meld with his.

She laughed softly. "Mission accomplished."

Matt leaned in closer, his lips touching her ear, the soft fabric of his shirt and the hard chest underneath brushing her cheek. "Yep." Jade could feel his words vibrate through his chest and tickle her earlobe.

This time her body pressed in to his. She wanted him to kiss her, right here in Fitch's with everyone watching. She stood still against Matt's chest and fought it. It wasn't desire. That was too nice a word for what was coursing through her. It was lust, plain and simple. Raw lust ran through her, and she flushed hot with it.

She closed her eyes and stepped back, reaching for her beer. She took a sip and looked back at Matt. He stared at her, a smile playing about his mouth. "Wow, this is a great beer." Jade said taking another sip.

Matt grinned wider. "Mmm, great." He paused to take a drink of the topic of discussion. "You're sure you don't mind going on a wild goose chase with me?"

Jade considered for a moment then shrugged. "What the heck. I always wanted to be a part of a Scooby-Doo caper."

"Daphne?"

Jade snorted with derision. "Uh, no. Velma."

Matt nodded slowly over the rim of his beer. "Hot."

Jade managed a smile and waggled her eyebrows at Matt. "Hmm, you have untold depths."

"Oh, you have no idea." He gave her a look that melted everything south of her waistband, and she was pretty sure the temperature in the bar spiked about a billion degrees. Plus, her mouth was suddenly very dry. She took a big sip of her beer, which went down the wrong way, leaving her coughing and sputtering. *Suave.* Matt patted her on the back until her coughing subsided.

The two women standing behind Matt turned to watch Jade's choking fit, pausing long enough to eye Matt with interest before turning back to their conversation. This somehow left Jade feeling like she didn't measure up. She could see the scene through their eyes, and all of her insecurities flared to life. She could easily imagine Matt in a James Bond tuxedo with a cool blonde on his arm, sipping champagne that cost hundreds of dollars a bottle. What was she doing here? More to the point, what was he doing here? With her? All of the reasons why this was a bad idea flooded her mind, and she stepped back out of Matt's reach. He dropped his arm, slid his hand in his pocket, and leaned against the drink ledge.

Jade pulled it together enough to actually look Matt in the eyes. He was watching her carefully.

"Where did you just go?' He reached over and tucked a piece of her hair behind her ear.

She shook her head. "On a little head trip."

He smiled down at her. "Have fun?"

"God, no. Don't go there—it's a bad neighborhood."

Matt took another drink of his beer. "I don't know. I might like the neighborhood."

Jade laughed. "Nah, it's pure anarchy and chaos with some tap dancing lemurs thrown in."

"Okaaay, so we'll leave your internal monologue alone for now."

"Yeah … so, what's our plan? Split up to look for clues? Participate in a musical chase montage and then unmask Mr. Withers?"

"Actually, I do have an angle."

Jade smirked. "Why am I not surprised?"

"Because you're aware of my innately clever nature?"

Jade rolled her eyes.

Matt barreled on. "Your dad's notes seem to be mostly from travel diaries and business ledgers, plus some letters between other guides from the area written after Cartwright's death. In fact, most of the research I've come across so far has been from these types of sources. But all of these sources only speculate as to the fate of the treasure. They cite evidence of its existence, and they speculate that it was buried. The problem, as I see it, is that the only people who know for sure where the treasure was put to rest are the Native American tribal members who buried it. Most of their history is oral, and what was recorded was by white settlers who were basically playing a huge game of telephone. By the time the facts were actually written down, they were distorted."

"Yeah, I'm with you so far, Sherlock."

"I thought we were the Scooby gang."

"Yeah, I was going to go with that … but I realized after the speech you just gave that *you* are Velma, and I would have to be Scooby or something. Not interested."

Matt just stared at her for a beat before continuing. "I started to think that we need a new approach, something outside the box a little." He waited for her response, which in this case was a raised brow and a head tilt. He took that as a go-ahead. "There are two angles that haven't been explored. I had a research assistant out of London, someone I've worked with before, track down both provenance papers for most of the pieces in the treasure and letters from Adam Cartwright to his mother. Either one may provide us clues as to where the treasure was buried."

The blonde behind Matt bumped her hip into him, and when he turned to look, she smiled and purred an effusive apology. It was pretty crowded in there, so Jade did her best to ignore the incident.

She shook her head. "I don't see how. Neither of those sources would be likely to have information about how an unrelated Native American tribe would think or behave."

Matt lifted his eyebrows.

"What? I went to college. I've done research before."

"So has everyone else who searched for the treasure … but with no results."

"Okay, so we work outside the box. What are we looking for?"

"I don't know." Matt shrugged. "But we'll know it when we see it."

The two were standing close again, speaking in low tones. Jade noticed some of the bar patrons glancing their way. She couldn't tell whether they were just curious about a new face at Fitch's, or whether they were curious about their conversation. Maybe it was her imagination, but for some reason she felt like carrion circled by vultures.

Some of the glances were from men. Those looked less than friendly. The women, on the other hand, were more than friendly, with toothy smiles and pronounced eye contact. The blonde behind Matt eyed him and whispered something to her friend.

The friend giggled. Matt was ignoring it all, but it was starting to piss Jade off. *What? Am I invisible?*

Jade mumbled to herself, "Okay, enough is enough." She smiled brightly at Matt. "Come on."

Matt gave her a confused look. She grabbed his hand and began to pull him to the pool table at the other end of the room. It was crowded, and she had to weave her way through the shoulder-to-shoulder people, glancing back at Matt as they went along. He was smiling slightly, but the look in his eyes was wary. They got to the table at the exact moment that the Wilson brothers were leaving. Jade waved to the twins who were younger than her but had gone to the same school. Surprisingly, there was no one queued up, and she and Matt got the table immediately.

"Do you play?" Jade grabbed a rack and began to gather the balls in it.

"No. This really isn't my game." Matt threw Jade an apologetic look. "Did I miss something?"

Jade kept her voice low enough so only Matt could hear her. "Probably. You're just going to have to go along with me here." She finished racking the balls, and hung the triangle back on the wall where a row of pool cues was hanging. She grabbed one and handed it to Matt.

Matt took it but was shaking his head. "No, you don't understand. I really don't play."

Jade stepped in very close to Matt, pressed up against him and whispered, "Don't worry. I don't need you to play pool, and you'll do fine at what I do need you to do." She smiled her best flirty smile at him and hoped she didn't look maniacal.

Matt's eyes grew speculative. "Mmm hmm. And what might that be?"

"Chalk your stick."

"Uh, is that code for something?"

Jade spoke loudly so that the women nearby could hear. "Is this what you want, *honey*?" Jade reached behind Matt to the wall rack where the cues and small cubes of chalk were lined up. She had to rub up against him to reach the chalk, but that was better for the show. She slowly slid the chalk around the tip of the cue Matt was holding and then rubbed herself against him again to return the chalk to the shelf. Matt, trooper that he was, didn't complain once.

Jade sauntered up to him. "Tell me to turn around and bend over."

Matt stared at her, speechless.

She hissed at him. "Come on, Connor. Snap to. And make it look believable."

Matt blinked, but the command in Jade's voice had him moving. He slid his free hand to her hip and turned her body away from him and toward the pool table. In one smooth move he crowded her to the rail of the table and stepped up tight behind her.

She turned over her shoulder and beamed a smile up at Matt. "Okay, good." She caught a glimpse of Fitch, who might've been smirking behind the bar. Anyone else who was watching seemed to be buying the show.

Matt took advantage of his position and pushed in closer, if that was possible. He leaned down over her, tucked her hair behind her ear, and whispered, "Anything else I can do for you?" His breath tickled against her ear.

For some reason, her voice came back breathy as she gave him his next order. "We need to break."

"Uh, *honey*," he leaned in to whisper again, but punched up the volume on the endearment so that those around them could hear it. Jade smiled. He had caught on to the game quickly and it pleased her that he played along without needing an explanation. He trusted her. Completely. The last time she had trusted anyone that way, she had been falling in love. The thought had her reeling, and she swayed back into Matt. He slid his arm around her torso to steady her.

"Are you okay?"

Jade took a deep breath and nodded. It scared her, but she couldn't expect trust from him and not give trust in return. She kept her smile firmly pasted on her face and stared at the table in front of her. *Focus.* "We need to break."

Matt whispered, "Yeah, about that. I *really* don't play pool." Matt's hand rested lightly on her ribcage, and she imagined all sorts of places it could explore from there.

"It's okay, just put the cue ball—that's the white one … "

His jaw was against her temple, and she could feel him smile. "I know what a cue ball is." Matt stepped up, bracketed her feet with his, and pressed her forward until her hips were up against the table. She put her right hand out on the rail to keep from being laid out flat on the felt. Taking his time, Matt reached around her for the cue ball. His chest curved around her back. In front of her, the pool table was solid and cold; behind her, Matt was solid and warm.

"Great, it goes behind the … "

"Head string. I know the rules. I just can't play." Matt leaned down to put the cue ball behind the head spot.

"Okay, I'll do the aiming. You just put some, uh, thrust into it."

Matt chuckled. "With pleasure."

Jade smiled to herself. She loved Matt's quick mind, his charm, his easy and playful nature. And, let's face it, the man was easy on the eyes. She could feel him behind her and … *Okay, Sawyer, keep your mind on the game.*

Jade took the cue stick from Matt with her left hand and then shifted it to her right. She knew she handled it with an ease that spoke to her skill as a player. She debated whether to risk a glance to the other side of the room to see if she had an audience, mostly to check and see if some of the other women were finally getting the hint. It would've given her a great deal of satisfaction to see a look of jealousy on the women's faces, but she decided that it was enough to impress Matt with her ability as a pool player.

Jade raised the cue and dropped her eye level down toward the table to make the break. This forced her hips back and into Matt. Specifically, into his arousal. Matt quickly shifted his body to the side, which had the unfortunate effect of bumping his hand into the butt of the cue. Jade smiled in anticipation as she drove the cue stick back to take her shot. What she didn't anticipate was Matt knocking the back of the stick right up toward his own face, and though the force was not that great, the angle and aim were perfect.

The thwack would've been satisfying if Jade had been *trying* to injure Matt. It was followed by a grunt and a spurt of warm blood that landed in flecks on Jade's forearm. She was confused for a moment and began to turn toward Matt, bringing the pool stick down suddenly as she pivoted. She nearly smacked Matt again, this time in the crotch. Luckily, his fast reflexes saved him further bodily harm as he deflected the shaft of the pool cue to the side.

While his right hand was busy saving his nether parts, his left was cupping his nose, attempting to staunch the flow of blood. Jade gasped at the sight that met her as she turned, blood dripping down between Matt's fingers onto his gorgeously chiseled chin. It seemed an awful large amount of blood, and some of it was flowing from the bottom of his hand down his wrist. The room flashed hot, and Jade felt suddenly nauseous. She swallowed hard and heard Matt speaking, but it sounded far away.

"Are you okay?"

Jade nodded weakly and wondered why he was asking her that. Shouldn't it be the other way around? She did feel a bit dizzy though, and using the pool stick for balance, slid herself down to the ground. It struck her as funny that she was still holding on to the cue, and she started to giggle, which almost caused her to smack Matt with it again. Matt caught the stick and laid it on the ground next to her hip. Some of the noise in the bar had died off, and Jade could feel the other people in the bar looking at her. She was still feeling woozy and only vaguely heard her name being called as people asked if she was okay. Matt was the one with the bloody face, and they kept asking about her. She giggled harder.

She heard Matt call for a wet cloth. She laughed until he bent over her to press her head down between her knees. A drop of blood landed with a splat on the floor between her feet and suddenly breathing seemed to take all of her focus. Fitch came over with the cloth but rather than place it over his nose, Matt used his free hand to scoop Jade's hair up and over her shoulder and then took the cloth and draped it across the back of her neck. It felt cool on her hot skin. She noticed a scuff mark on her shoe that looked like a profile of Elvis. She giggled again. Matt gently caressed the back of her neck, and something in her chest loosened so that she could take deeper breaths.

• • •

Fitch came back with a dry cloth for Matt. He took it and absently mopped the blood from his face. His focus was on Jade, who seemed to be alternately hyperventilating and giggling at her shoes. He had hoped to charm her on this date to make up for the previous one. He grinned at his absolute failure. He was usually better at this.

God, he wanted her to like him. He sure as hell liked her. Matt thought about the way she had grabbed his hand and pulled him across the bar to play pool. He thought about the confident way she had bluffed Stacy the other night. He remembered the way she had run to make sure Adele and Beatrice were okay when she heard Adele's shouting. He thought about her chopping firewood on the lawn. Yeah, he really wanted her to like him.

He hadn't been this concerned with impressing a woman since college … God, back then he had thought he was so in love. It was nothing compared to what he was feeling now. Matt froze. *Where the hell had that thought come from?* This was supposed to be fun and sexy. Instead, he was nursing a bloody nose, and she was practically passing out. His worry for her had his stomach twisted in knots, and on top of that, he thought he might be falling in love with Jade on their second date? *Very suave, McLaughlin.* He shook his head and chuckled. Jade's head came up quickly to look at him.

"What are you laughing at? I broke your nose."

Matt shook his head at her. "It's not broken."

"Are you sure? That's a lot of blood." Jade dropped her head back between her knees. "How do you know?" she continued weakly.

"I've broken it before. It's not broken. What were you laughing at?"

"I have Elvis on my shoe."

"Really? Where?" Matt tried to get her attention off of his bloody nose. The more focused she was on other things, the easier she seemed to breathe. He could feel the tension in her, and more than anything he wanted it gone. He wanted to be the one to do that for her.

"Here. In profile." She gestured to the toe of her right shoe. She licked her thumb and reached down to try to rub the scuff mark.

Matt reached for her wrist to stop her. "Don't lick off Elvis! That's a special scuff mark."

She was still talking to the floor. "Well, it's not Jesus or anything. If it were Jesus, or Mary, I wouldn't lick it off."

"Still … it is Elvis."

Jade stopped rubbing at her shoe. "Yeah. How did you break your nose?"

Matt sighed. "I'd rather not say." He pulled the cloth away from his face and touched the back of his hand to his nose. There was only a little bit of blood and Matt could tell the flow had slowed. *Good.*

"Was it traumatic?" Jade blurted. "I'm sorry, it's none of my business. I don't mean to be nosy." She looked up at Matt's swollen nose, realized what she had said, and clapped her hand over her mouth. "I didn't mean that."

Matt laughed and pulled her hand back down. "It's okay. You can ask. It was more embarrassing than traumatic." His hand stayed on hers, and he could feel her small fingers, cool against the inside of his palm. He had the overwhelming urge to kiss them, but didn't. He dropped her hand and brought the cloth back up to his nose.

Jade smiled. "Now I really want to know the story."

Matt thought he detected a distinct glint in Jade's eyes and the color looked like it was starting to come back into her cheeks. He smiled at her. "How are you feeling? Can you stand?"

Jade took a deep breath. "Yeah, I think so."

Matt stood up and gently pulled her up with him. He slid his hand up to her shoulder to steady her as she stood.

"Thanks."

"You're welcome." Matt grinned and slid a sidelong glance toward the pool table. "Do you mind if I take a rain check on that game of pool?"

Jade laughed, and it was a full, vibrant sound with none of the breathiness of before. Matt laughed with her, relieved.

She grabbed his free hand and pulled him toward the door. "Let's get out of here." She pulled the damp bar towel from her neck and dropped it at the bar.

She leaned over the bar to kiss Fitch on the cheek and say good-bye.

Fitch grinned down at her. "See, m'love! I told you you'd liven the place up."

# Chapter 12

Matt was quiet on the ride home, leaving Jade to her own thoughts, which were pretty grim. She had now managed to mangle two dates and embarrass herself in front of a bar full of people, including the man she was trying to impress. If she was out of her league before, she had cemented that status by beaning Matt in the head with a pool cue. She was starting to feel like she was living a Lucille Ball comedy routine. *I suck, I suck, I suck.* The refrain echoed in her head. Meg would hate that kind of thinking.

"You are thinking way too hard over there."

Jade looked up from her lap and over at Matt. "It's that obvious?"

"Yeah, I'm a little worried about it." Matt slid his glance toward her, then back to the road.

"About my thinking?" Jade narrowed her eyes at Matt, prepared to get defensive.

"Yeah." Matt smiled a little.

"Why?"

"Well, what are you thinking?"

"That I suck."

Matt laughed. "That's why."

Jade shrugged and felt hot tears pushing at the back of her throat. Oh, no. No crying. That would not be cool on a second date. And of course, right at that moment Matt chose to glance over at her again. He pulled the car over to the side of the road. They were only about halfway back to Lakehaven, and he just pulled over to the side of the little two-lane road like he had arrived at his destination, and pulled her into his arms.

She really couldn't stop the tears then. "Oh God, I am so sorry."

Matt just gathered her closer and stroked his hand up and down her back. "You don't suck, Jade. You don't," Matt whispered. "You are the most … incredible woman."

Jade nodded in agreement, channeling her best friend. "I am!"

Matt laughed and gathered her closer.

Jade lifted her head and wiped at the wet spot she had left on Matt's shoulder. "I got snot on you."

"I like snot."

Jade shook her head. "I don't get it. You are a sophisticated, creative, super-hot guy with a great sense of humor who could date anyone. This doesn't make any sense. You going out with me. I mean, yes, I am awesome, when I'm not clumsily smacking guys in the face with a pool cue. But there is absolutely no reason for you to like me."

"I'm super-hot?"

"That's not the point. Focus here, Connor."

"No, that kind of is the point, Jade. You think I'm super-hot. That means something. Not everything, but something."

Jade rolled her eyes.

"Why do you like me?" Matt pulled back to look down at her.

"What?"

"I'm serious. Why?"

Jade smirked. "You're super-hot."

Matt grinned down at her. "Yeah. And?"

There was a long silence as Jade pretended to think.

Matt looked like he was starting to get worried. "Uh, can you come up with anything?"

Jade laughed. "Yeah, I just wanted to make you squirm a little."

"Oh, I haven't taken enough abuse tonight?" Matt gestured toward his nose, which looked slightly swollen and a little red.

Jade smiled weakly. "God, I really am sorry about that."

Matt waved off her apology. "Nah, it was my fault anyway."

"See, that's why I like you. You'll take a perfectly disastrous date and turn it into fun. You'll take the blame for something that I did, just to make me feel better. You're creative and intelligent. You're funny, charming, witty, and a good kisser."

At Jade's last words, Matt's gaze heated and drifted to her mouth. She could see his intent before he even moved. She knew he was going to kiss her, and she almost sighed with pleasure when his mouth met hers. His lips were firm but still soft, and his kiss was impossibly gentle. His hands slid up her back to her neck and then cradled the back of her head, his fingers working into her hair and massaging her scalp. Her breath caught as he took the kiss deeper, pulling her into him with the slightest pressure of his fingers. She flattened her palms across his abdomen and felt the tightening of the muscles there as she ran her hands across his stomach and out to the sides of his waist. *Heaven.* Having his hands on her, her face bracketed by his forearms, his scent wrapped around her in the close confines of the car *was* heaven. She wanted to lick him there, on the inside of his wrist, to taste his skin, but that would've meant breaking off the spectacular kiss. She wanted more, but she also didn't want him to stop kissing her, *ever.* The sensation was so full, so rich, she felt suffused, drunk with the kiss.

Jade was a short heartbeat away from crawling onto Matt's lap when he pulled out of the kiss with a groan. She could hear his ragged breath and feel his abs rise and fall with it.

"Why did you stop?"

"We're still in the car." Matt dropped his head forward and raked his hand through his hair, leaving it sticking up at odd angles.

Jade nodded. "Right."

Once his breathing started to slow, Matt turned to look at her. "Look, you want to know why you? That kiss says it all. When I'm with you, I can't get enough, Jade. I can't know enough about you. I'm fascinated, intrigued, impassioned, and flattened by you. I can't hear enough, I can't look enough, and I can't touch enough of you to stop wanting to know you, hear you, look at you, be with you. I don't know how to explain it any better than that. It doesn't have to make sense to me. It just is what it is."

Jade looked Matt in the eyes, searching there for something, some way of knowing if it was the right thing to do, the right choice to make. Then, in a moment, she chose. She chose him; she chose the situation; she chose her feelings. She felt the resistance in her slide away, and every cell of her being acquiesced. The air in the car went from charged to crackling, and Jade nodded at Matt. "Let's go home."

• • •

They slipped into Jade's cabin, already wrapped around each other but, surprisingly, only slightly disheveled. They had strolled the path to her door with false patience. They had touched and kissed leisurely along the way, each time holding something back.

Jade locked the cabin door behind her and leaned against it. Matt reached over her shoulder slowly and turned the light on. It was a soft light, playing across Jade's features, her small nose, the wide, sensuous mouth, big green eyes. He took his time looking at her, drinking her in. *Beautiful.* Matt smiled at the inadequacy of language to really express it. *Exquisite.* Yeah, maybe that was closer.

He reached out to touch the bridge of her nose, the seam of her mouth. Her breath caught, and he stepped in to her. She pushed in to meet him. Goddamn, he wanted her. Badly. He took a deep breath to steady himself as she wrapped her arms around his neck. Big mistake. He breathed in her scent—mint, pine, and something richer beneath that—a smell that was simply her skin, and he felt the heat coil tightly in his belly and shoot straight to his groin. If it weren't their first time, he might just bury himself in her right now. He tried to concentrate, but he could feel her fingers playing lightly across the nape of his neck, and all of her pressed against him. His control was slipping.

He stepped away, and she made a little noise of dismay. She took a step to him, and he stepped back again. She glared at him and followed, reaching out to grab his t-shirt. "Where are you going?!"

Matt looked down at her small hand, fisted in the material of his shirt, and smiled.

Jade shook her head. "There's nothing funny here, mister."

"No, ma'am." Matt nodded at her but the corners of his mouth gave him away.

She shook her hand, which was still twisted up in his shirt. "Take this off."

Matt raised his eyebrows.

"Now." She started to pull the hem of his shirt up his torso, and her hands brushed against his skin. He stilled under her touch and let her struggle to pull it over his head. It was sweet torture, and when she was done he was breathing hard, and she had a look of triumph on her face.

Matt's control slipped another notch. He needed to do something now to slow this down. "You don't want to talk?"

Jade stared, dumbfounded, at his bare chest and licked her lips. "Uh, no." She reached for him, but he intercepted her hands and held them in his.

"I never told you how I broke my nose. Don't you want to know?"

She wiggled her hands to try to free them, but his grip held firm. "Tempting, but later." She pulled at her hands again. "Come on, let me touch you." It came out like a little growl, and he could feel himself get harder with the demand in her voice.

He seriously thought about giving up then and there and just letting her do whatever the hell she wanted to do to him, but there was his pride. Or what little of it he had left. "I was with my best friend, Sam, and we were playing *He-Man* and *Skeletor*."

That got her attention, and she stopped struggling against him. She looked up at him and smiled a devilish smile. "We could play *She-Ra* and *Sea Hawk*."

Matt sucked in a deep breath at the thought, but he continued with his story as if he were unaffected. "We were wrestling."

"I'll wrestle with you." Jade's hands were still shackled by Matt's, but rather than try to pull them out of his grip, she changed tactics. She was leaning forward, pressing her breasts into the back of his hands and rubbing them against him. When he felt her nipples pebble under his knuckles, he had to stifle a groan. The stalling tactics were backfiring big time.

His voice came out strained, but he was determined to continue with the story. "We were rough housing and got a little out of control."

Jade purred. "Out of control? I know the feeling." She stepped back and bent her head over his hands, flicking her tongue over his knuckles. Her tongue was warm and pink, and she slid it up the length of his finger to the tip and swirled it there.

Matt dropped her hands like he had been burnt. He was pretty much done for and couldn't even finish his thought. There was very little blood flow reaching his brain at this point, and he let instinct take over. He reached for her, sliding his hands up her sides, over her ribs and up under her breasts. He filled his hands with her and stepped closer.

Now that her hands were free, they worked the button-fly on his jeans while her mouth and tongue explored his chest. She made a little noise in the back of her throat and that was it. He was done playing. He needed her now. He picked her up and strode back to the bed. He dropped her there on her back and watched her wiggle her way back up. *Nice.* As she slid her body further onto the bed, her breasts shifted and her hips lifted in a symphony of movement.

•••

Jade watched him watch her. His eyes darkened and passion played across his face as he stood at the foot of the bed. His shoulders were steeled with tension, and she could see the play of muscles across his arms, chest, abdomen. She had managed to unbutton his jeans, and they must've slid down his hips when he carried her to the bed because they hung low on his hipbones. She could see the shadow of hair that started below his belly button, where it trailed down his stomach and disappeared under the waistband of his underwear. Her mouth felt dry, and she had to lick her lips for about the hundredth time tonight. The movement caught his attention, and he smiled a wolfish grin. "Do that again."

Jade complied. He slid his thumbs into the sides of his waistband and Jade sat up suddenly to get a better look. Matt lifted an eyebrow but didn't move.

Jade begged. "Please." Her voice was husky, which wiped the smile off Matt's face. He slid the waist of the jeans down an inch then paused. His eyebrows pulled together. "You still have all your clothes on."

She slid her shirt up over her head and lay there in jeans and a black lace bra so filmy that her nipples were clearly visible through the thin fabric. She leaned back on her elbows then glanced at his waistband and stared back up into his eyes. "Now you."

Matt eased his jeans the rest of the way off and climbed up on the bed with her. He was big everywhere, and his weight pressed her into the mattress. Jade gave into a sigh at the feel him on her. He leaned his head down to her breasts and licked a nipple through the lace of the bra. The fabric seemed to melt under the moist touch of his tongue, and she savored each sensation. He sucked harder and snaked his hand around her back to undo the clasp. His mouth stayed where it was, even as he gently slipped the straps down her shoulders and peeled the fabric away from the tops of her breasts. He moved up to her mouth as he pulled the bra the rest of the way off, and she pushed back onto the sheets. He slid further up her body. He inched up her torso until he was over her completely, his arousal hard up against the seam of her jeans. She slipped her hands around to the base of his spine then slid them lower, tracing the contour of his lower back as it arched into his fabulous butt. She could feel the muscled planes of him flex as his hips pushed forward, and she felt herself go wet with need.

Her jeans had to go, but Matt was too busy taking small nips at her shoulder. She gasped and shuddered with the feel of his teeth gently gliding on her skin. Her body involuntarily arched up into him. He moved to the base of her throat and licked there. It was slow torture, and she was panting with the strain. Matt seemed leisurely, but she could feel a sheen of sweat between them as their bodies slid together. "Help me get these off!" she moaned as she tried to work her hands between them to get to the button of her jeans.

Matt lifted his hips and jerked at her button, popping her waistband open with one pull. He circled his tongue around her nipple as he slid his hands down her hips, pushing her jeans and underwear down her legs. His mouth moved lower as he worked the jeans down her calves and she felt his breath hot on her belly. He tried to slip her jeans over her ankles and feet then paused. They were stuck. He tugged at them a little harder.

He had managed to twist the fabric around her ankles but not quite pull the jeans off. They had bunched around her feet and pooled there. She wiggled her feet to try to free them, but it didn't help.

Jade pointed her toes hard to make it easier. "Try now."

Matt pulled harder but the jeans stayed put. He grunted as he pulled. "Almost."

Jade pointed her toes harder to try to help him. "How about now?"

Matt tugged one last time and the jeans suddenly came free, and he sat back hard on his heels.

"Oww, oww, cramp!" Jade was twitching her foot crazily.

"What's wrong?"

"My foot, it's cramped. Help." Jade was laughing but wincing at the same time. "Oww, oww, oww."

Matt grabbed her foot and started rubbing. "Here?"

Jade dropped her head back on the bed. "Almost … lower."

Matt lowered his voice an octave. He sounded like a James Earl Jones impersonator. "Better?"

Jade laughed again. "No, toward my heel, you idiot."

"That's no way to talk to the man who is about to rock your world!" Matt boasted.

Jade rolled her eyes. "Yeah, all talk and no action."

"Oh, you want action?" Matt swiveled his hips, which made his penis bob up and down. Jade laughed again. Here was a Greek god come to life: sculpted shoulders, chest tapering down to a trim six-pack, and all of it glistening in the low light of her cabin, but he was making her laugh in the midst of what promised to be the hottest sex of her life. Was it possible he didn't take himself too seriously?

He bent over her and kissed her forehead gently. She reached for his face but her thumb caught him in his red and swollen nose.

"Oww!" Matt pulled back suddenly.

"Oh God, I'm sorry!" Jade pulled her hands away as Matt jerked his head back. "Are you okay?"

Matt rubbed his nose. "Do you have a nasal fetish? It's okay if you do. I'm just curious."

Jade sighed. "I'm not very good at this."

"What?" Matt looked flummoxed.

"This sexy, seduction stuff. It's not in my skill set."

Matt shook his head disbelievingly. "Are you kidding?"

"Uh, *hello*. I just picked your nose in the middle of sex after accidentally bashing it in with a pool cue. I'm not even mentioning the foot cramp. Not sexy."

Matt wiggled his eyebrows. "Are you kidding? I'm incredibly turned on."

Jade narrowed her eyes. "Are you into S&M?"

Matt smiled a naughty smile but didn't answer her question. "We were not quite in the middle of sex, anyway. Not yet."

Jade frowned. "Whatever. I'm not good at this."

Now Matt frowned. "Whatever gave you that idea?"

Jade shrugged. "I don't know. It's supposed to go more smoothly than this."

Matt caressed her cheek. "Says who?"

Jade didn't say anything.

Matt leaned down to kiss her. It was a tender kiss, sweet and gentle. Jade relaxed back into the pillows. Her eyelids drifted shut.

Matt kissed her along the jawline. "What if it this is exactly how it's supposed to go?" He flicked his tongue along her neck and collarbone.

"Mmmmm." Jade stretched like a cat.

"See? You're very good at this." Matt worked his way lower, nuzzling her cleavage. Jade arched her back and moaned. Matt grinned and slid lower. "Really good." His voice sounded like velvet and gravel.

He worked his way down her body with his tongue. His mouth played along her skin. It was warmer than the cabin air, and she shivered at the contrasting sensations. He explored her curves reverently—where her rib gently jutted out below her breast, where her waist curved out to hip and then back down to her thighs. His every movement aroused her. She shivered when his hair gently brushed across her sensitized skin as he made his way back to her center.

His head rested at the V between her legs, and he looked up at her to make sure she was with him. "Open up for me." Jade hesitated but then gave in to him. He bent her knees and slid her feet over his shoulders, caressing the arch of her foot and the curve of her calf as he did. He slid his hands up to her hips to tilt them upward. She fought to keep her head up to watch what he was doing, but finally just dropped back to enjoy his touch on her body.

His hands played along the inside of her thighs and then she felt his finger slip inside her. Her hips jumped with the pleasure of it, and she felt him exhale against her sensitive flesh. He bent his head to taste her then, and the intensity of his touch, his mouth, had her hips bucking off the bed again. She moved against him but he tightened his grip on her to hold her where he wanted. She struggled to push up toward him but he moved slightly out of range, teasing her with his hot breath. He slid his finger out and in again, and she twisted to try to get closer. "Please … "

His response was to flick his tongue out and lick her. She was slick with desire, and his quick movement pushed her a little closer to the edge. She shivered against him, and he bent down to suck at her. She made a little noise at the back of her throat, and Matt had to stop what he was doing to catch his breath. She could feel the roughness of his stubble on her tender inner thigh. She could feel the warmth of him, but was losing track of where he was and where she was and who was who. Time stretched. She floated between reality and pure sensation. It was a lovely place to be, but she wanted more.

"Don't stop!" she begged. Even as she said it, she reached for him, pulling him up to her. She wanted him with her this first time, face to face.

"I just need to … " Matt paused to kiss her ribcage, caress her waist.

She pulled at his shoulders again. She felt the tension in his muscled back as he moved up along her body. Felt him grasping for control but, in her mind, control was way overrated.

"I'm apologizing now, in case this is over before you … "

Jade made a sound. It was like a switch was flipped and Matt on top of her, raining kisses on her, and she felt him against her, thick and heavy. Ready.

"Condom." She reached for the little bedside table and opened the drawer.

But he was one step ahead of her. "It's on." His voice sounded tight.

He pressed into her, shifting his hips and sliding into her slowly. Jade gasped. "Oh God … "

Matt paused for a moment, attempting to slow things down, but Jade would have none of it. She reached around him, her hands on his behind, and pulled him closer, lifting her hips at the same time to force him deeper. She sighed. He pulled back and then pushed forward again. She moved with him, and they found a rhythm that was working. "Jade … " he whispered.

She felt the change in him and saw the moment his expression changed. There was some gentle emotion in that look. Her heart stuttered for a moment, and she forgot to breathe. He pushed into her one last time. She flew apart and he followed.

They were wrapped around one another. Jade's face pressed into Matt's side, and the rhythm of his breathing was putting her to sleep. She was halfway there when she heard Matt say, "I told you I would rock your world."

Jade punched him in the arm, rolled over, and fell asleep.

# Chapter 13

Jade woke in the morning to the sound of rain patter on the roof and the feel of hands running up and down her sides. She lay there for a moment trying to get her bearings. They were male hands, large and a little rough. She could feel soft hair brushing across her abdomen and warm lips pressing kisses in a circle around her belly button. Then he moved lower and she jumped.

She flipped the comforter off and the cool cabin air was a shock to her heated skin. Matt lay sprawled across her legs and lower torso, pinning her to the mattress. He looked up from his task, his hair standing up crazily in some spots and flat and matted in others. He still took Jade's breath away, which only made her grumpy.

"What are you doing!" Jade wiggled underneath Matt, trying to get some space.

"Uhm, pretty much what you think I'm doing." He raked his hands through his hair and glanced up at her for a moment, before leaning down to swirl his tongue around her hipbone. His hand found its way to her breast.

"Now? This early?!"

Matt moved to her other hipbone and swirled his tongue around that one. He looked up at her and shot her a sinful smile. "Breakfast of champions." He inched lower and gave her a good lick. The sensation shot through her like electricity. She bucked underneath him and pulled her knee up simultaneously. He was thrown to her right at the same time as he jerked away from her oncoming knee, and pitched over the edge of the bed. He landed with a thud. A muffled, "I'm okay" came from the floor below.

Jade sat up and leaned over the side of the bed. "What are you doing down there?"

"Recovering."

"Oh. Did I do that?" She gestured to him where he was spread out on the rag rug beside her bed. She looked concerned.

"You just surprised me. I lost my balance."

Jade smiled sweetly. "You're awfully clumsy, aren't you?"

Matt smiled back. "I guess so." He reached his hand up to her. "Help me up."

She reached her hand out to pull Matt up, but he yanked. She landed hard on him, but he was braced for it and she was naked, so she guessed he really didn't mind.

Jade lifted her head from his chest and gave him a glare. "You did that on purpose!"

Matt raised his eyebrows innocently. "Gee, I'm sorry. That was an accident. I'm just so clumsy."

Jade bent down and nipped at Matt's lower lip. Matt growled, "You'll pay for that." He flipped her on her back underneath him and slid down her body. "Where were we?" Then Matt got back to business.

Matt slipped his hands down to her thighs and moved them apart, then played his thumbs over the tight springy curls between her legs. He eased her open and licked her.

Jade gasped and fought to regain sane thought. "Uhm," was all she managed to say.

His tongue played over her folds, and she could feel her body coiling under his care. His tongue found the sweet spot and just barely skimmed it. *Again*, she thought, but her mouth couldn't form the words and all she managed was a sharp intake of breath.

He pressed harder with his tongue, taking his time with it. He was achingly patient and thorough. The slow pressure built up in her, and she shook with the pleasure of it. It was like a warm bath, filling her up, the pleasure level rising, closer and closer toward the edge until it spilled over, unable to be contained.

...

When Jade had finished, Matt inched up and rested his cheek on her belly. He could feel her heartbeat, fast and furious at first, then gradually slowing. She sighed, and he smiled in triumph.

He was still hard as a rock and ready to go, but it also felt nice to lie here listening to the rain on the roof and the beat of Jade's heart. Her skin was warm and smelled like a combination of her and some lingering scent of vanilla. The air of the cabin was cool and smelled like rain and pine. It was a moment of beauty, filling his senses in a way that left him feeling powerful and alive. There was nothing missing in that moment. It was pure contentment, and just like that, a piece of the puzzle clunked into place. He *knew*. The feeling that had been dogging him, that vague feeling that there was something missing in his life became clear. What had been missing was her: the intimacy, the laughter, the loving—a life. His career, his success, none of it mattered without someone who mattered.

Matt lifted his head up to look at her. She was glorious with her jet hair draped out over the honeyed tones of the rug and oak plank floor. Her eyes were closed, lashes fanned over her flushed cheeks. Her skin was pale and creamy with the exception of her nipples, which were a dusty rose. He could see a future with her, and it scared him to think about it.

She reached a hand down, and without opening her eyes, found the top of his head and wove her fingers into the tousled mess of it. He felt her fingers exploring his scalp and the softness of his hair. Here was something worth having, if only he could figure out how to make it work. Matt took a shaky breath and blew it out. If he managed to make a life with her, it would be perfect. Already, he could see how many ways he could fuck it up. And suddenly he recognized one way he already had.

Matt sat up abruptly, yanking his head away from Jade's hands.

Jade's eyes flew open. "What's wrong?"

Matt froze. What was he going to tell her? How was he going to tell her? Up until now, he had brushed the whole name thing under the rug, writing it off as not that big of a deal. He was betting good money that she wouldn't see it that way. *Fuck!*

He accused her of complicating relationships, but this one was plenty complicated and he had no one to blame but himself. *Double fuck!*

"Matt! What's going on?" Jade was sitting up now. She had pulled a pillow off the bed and held it clutched to her chest, a worried look on her face.

Matt dragged his hands through his hair and then dropped them helplessly to his side. There was really no way out of it. "Okay, honey, I have something to tell you, uh, something you are not going to like … "

Jade paled a bit but didn't interrupt him.

"I was going to tell you before … before last night, before we … " Matt cleared his throat.

"You're married," she whispered, her top lip trembling.

Matt looked confused. "What? No! No, that's not it."

"You have a girlfriend!"

"Uh, no, I'm completely available. I just haven't been completely honest … "

Jade glared at him. "You better not tell me you have some . . ." She waved her hand in the general direction of his penis.

"No! Definitely not that." Up until that point, he had forgotten that he was naked. He glanced around until he found his underwear on the floor.

"Well what, then?"

"I'm not who you think I am." He put the underwear on and started to pace the room.

"You're a secret agent?"

"No, I'm a writer."

"You're not published?"

"No, I'm published. And successful."

"Well then, what is it?" Jade threw her hands in the air.

Matt bit the bullet. "My last name is not Connor."

Jade jumped up and put her hands on her hips. She glared at Matt. "What?! You lied about your name?"

Matt nodded. "My name is Matthew Riley McLaughlin."

"You lied about your name?"

Matt nodded again. He looked worried. "I'm so sorry. I meant to tell you about a hundred times, and there just never seemed to be … " He trailed off, the excuse sounding lame even to his own ears.

"Wait a second." Matt could see the moment Jade put it all together. Her eyes widened. "Matthew *Riley* McLaughlin? As in *the* Riley McLaughlin?"

Matt nodded unhappily.

"International bestselling author Riley McLaughlin? *That* McLaughlin?" Jade laughed raggedly. It was not a happy sound.

Matt held out his hands, palms up. "Jade … " He was afraid to say anything more than that. There was nothing he could think of to say that would make the lie better, and he certainly didn't want to make it worse.

Jade was pacing the floor now, gesturing wildly and ranting. "Oh, the joke's on Jade … Too stupid to know. You lying son-of-a … " Jade paused and gasped. *And* I've seen all of your movies … with Ben!" Jade gasped again. "With *Nick*! *Three* of them!"

Matt mumbled another apology, but Jade wasn't really listening to him now. She was on a roll. "I slept with you!" Jade turned to face him and jab her finger at him. "You … you … poop! Get. Out."

Matt should have expected it. What he had done was shitty, and most of what she was saying he deserved. But, more than anything, he wanted a chance to talk, to try to say whatever it was that would convince her that they could get past this and make a future together.

Jade picked up a Chia Head plant sitting on her bedside table and threw it at him.

It exploded in a fantastic burst of pottery and dirt at Matt's feet. *Or maybe they could talk later.*

# Chapter 14

*Hudson River Valley Outpost 54*
*September 12, 1616*

*Dear Mother,*

*I am sorry it has been so long since my last letter. The summer was full and quite productive. Pierre and I collaborated again on business ventures. Together, we were able to map out much of the valley as well as establish alliances with other trappers and guides from the area. Neither Pierre nor I wish to form a permanent business arrangement, but we do work well together and will most likely do so in the future. Our success has sustained us financially, and I have had no need to spend anymore of your generous gift to me. With luck, those pieces will be passed down to your progeny.*

*What may be of more interest to you, dear mother, is the news of another alliance that I have formed since I last wrote, this alliance being one of the heart. I wrote to you about meeting Alsoomse before and since then we have had opportunity to spend more time together. As you can no doubt guess by her name, she is native to this land. We met when I consulted with her tribe about known travel routes through the mountains, and her father agreed to allow her to guide us. She is a magnificent tracker with far greater skills than my own and a wonderful horsewoman. If she ever crosses the ocean, you will finally have some female company on the hunt. Mother, you would find her a kindred spirit and a true friend.*

*In fact, much of her reminds me of you; her intelligence, strength of character, fierce loyalty, and pride are all qualities you and she share. Perhaps that is why I find myself so taken with her. I have endeavored to remain careful in this matter, but unfortunately my heart rushes forth heedlessly.*

*I intend to ask for her hand by the end of fall. I do not yet know whether her traditions demand a long engagement, but I am hoping for a wedding after the spring thaw.*

*When possible, I will keep this outpost informed of my location and situation. If you were to write to me here, the letter would work its way to me. I may not make it back this way until spring, but I promise to write you before then. Send my love to all.*

*Affectionately yours,*

*Adam*

•••

"You did *what*?!"

Matt pulled his cell phone away from his ear to keep Samantha's voice from blistering his eardrum. "I told her who I was *after* I slept with her."

"I hope she threw something at you."

"A Chia Head."

Samantha laughed. Hard. Three minutes later she was just starting to catch her breath. "I like her."

"Yeah, the truth is, you would if you met her." Matt tried to sound annoyed, but there was a tinge of desperation to his voice. "So, are you going to help me or not?"

"That depends."

"On what?" Matthew heard the click of a lighter through the phone and waited for Samantha to inhale.

"Is being an asshole a genetic thing, or can you control it?"

"I know. I know. I'm an idiot. But I've never really been in love before. I'm new to all of this. You have to account for the learning curve. Please, I need you."

Samantha laughed again. "Oh, this is great. The great Riley McLaughlin, international man of intrigue, lady-killer, in love and begging for help!"

Matthew dropped his head into his left hand and tried not to damage his cell phone in the crushing grip of his right. "Just … please."

Samantha stopped laughing. "Oh, sweetie, of course I'll help you. You're like a brother to me. Which is why I can't resist torturing you just a little. Look, this is completely fixable. Just leave it to me. But I warn you, it's going to take some finesse. Meaning no rushing in. You'll have to hang back and be Mr. Sensitive for a change."

Matt heard the confidence in Samantha's voice and for the first time since that morning, he was able to breathe. "Yes. I can do that."

•••

Jade made her way to the main house. *Please let Meg be there.* Unfortunately, she had to make her way past every other cabin to get there. She picked up her pace as she passed cabin eight and didn't slow down until she reached the kitchen. Luckily, she managed to avoid any tall, good-looking, internationally famous writers along the way.

Meg was rolling dough out on the butcher block and Jade was so relieved that she could feel the knot in her stomach release.

Meg looked up as Jade entered the room. "Uh oh, what's wrong honey?" Meg stopped what she was doing and immediately went to the coffee maker to pour Jade a cup.

"He's Riley McLaughlin."

"What?" Meg brought the cup over to Jade.

"Matt. Mr. Connor. He's actually Matthew *Riley* McLaughlin."

"Holy crap! You're kidding." Meg looked speculative. "Okay, so he's not only drop-dead gorgeous but talented and successful too. And this is bad because . . .?"

"He told me *after* he slept with me."

Meg gasped. "You slept with Riley McLaughlin … *the* Riley McLaughlin!"

Jade rolled her eyes. "Uh, *hello*. You are missing the point here."

Meg started dancing around the kitchen. "I can't believe Matt is Riley McLaughlin. How did we not know?"

Jade waved her hands in the air. "I don't know. It's like Robert Ludlum; how many people know what he looks like? I just didn't think that Matt … We didn't Google him. He doesn't have a photo at the back of his books. We're idiots?" Jade thunked her head on the counter.

Meg stopped abruptly. "Okay, spill! How was he?"

Jade's head shot up. She gasped. "Meg Hammond!" She shot Meg a glare.

"What? You slept with Riley McLaughlin, and I am your best friend. I am bound by duty to ask."

"Well, I'm not saying a thing." Jade crossed her arms under her chest until she realized she couldn't drink her coffee that way. Coffee was way more important than indignation.

"Oh, no … that bad?"

Jade spewed coffee all over the counter. "*No!* I didn't say that!" For some reason Jade felt compelled to defend Matt's sexual prowess.

"Ooooh, he was great, wasn't he?" Meg grabbed a paper towel and handed it to Jade with a smile and an eyebrow waggle.

"Meg! Focus here. Matt is a jerk! He lied to me! You're supposed to be supportive and sympathetic." Jade waved the paper towel around in between mopping up her mess.

Meg sighed. "Oh, okay. Do you want feminist outrage or just maternal compassion?"

Jade narrowed her eyes and pursed her lips. "Hmm, let me think … How about outright pity?" Jade dropped the act, waving Meg off instead. "Forget it. You're just no fun to whine to."

Meg smiled. "Ah, now we are getting somewhere. Jade, why do you think Matt chose to tell you who he was now?" Meg walked back to the butcher block to work the dough.

Jade thought about it for a moment. "Overwhelming guilt?"

Meg smiled. "Okay, maybe. Maybe he is basically a decent guy with a conscience who didn't want to keep lying to you … "

"Or … ?"

"Or he actually likes you and wants your trust."

Jade frowned. "That's a stupid way to get my trust. How does lying to me earn my trust?"

"Think about it. He's Riley McLaughlin working on a new project in a place where he can have relative anonymity. He books under a fake last name. He doesn't know us, doesn't know if he can trust us. Probably has people bugging him all the time in New York. Not because they like or even want to know him, but just because they want to get close to Riley McLaughlin, the celebrity. Meanwhile, he just wants to write and live like Matt. Can you imagine trying to get to know people and never really knowing if they're for real or just putting on an act?"

Jade stared up at the ceiling, avoiding Meg's gaze. "I hate you."

Meg smiled and cocked her head to one side. "Do I have to buy you another Chia Head?"

Jade thunked her head down on the counter and groaned.

• • •

Matt spent the rest of the day writing and nervously running Sam's words through his head. He had enough provisions in his little kitchen to avoid going to the main house, but by the next day, he was tired of peanut butter and jelly sandwiches and oatmeal. He went out in search of food and perhaps a little advice from Meg. She seemed to know Jade better than anyone else, and Matt figured he could get some information and maybe even plead his case to Meg. If he could convince her of his honorable intentions, maybe he would have an ally in his court. At this point, it couldn't hurt.

When Matt got to the kitchen, Meg was nowhere around. He was just about to leave when the Kent sisters came bursting on the scene.

Adele was shaking a long bony finger in the direction of Bea's face. "No, you can't."

"Why not?" Bea came gliding in, wearing a diaphanous dress and looking like she would slide into an arabesque at any moment.

"Because they have feathers, you dolt. Hello, Matt!" Adele smiled coyly at Matt.

"So what? Hello, Matthew." Bea floated over to Matt and bussed his cheek.

Then Adele asked: "Matt, can you shave a penguin?" She thrust her angular hip to the side and placed her hand there, jutting her elbow out. She looked like a tall glass pitcher of mint julep.

"Umm, is this a trick question?"

"No, no. No trick, dear."

Matt mused for a moment. "I'm going to go with plucking, but it's just a guess."

Bea sighed. "Oh, well. You can't win them all." She paused a moment and looked closely at Matt. "You don't look well."

Adele paused in her gloating and leaned toward Matt. "Oooh. You're right, Bea. He looks … strained."

*Oh, great. Just the look I was going for*, Matt thought.

Bea looked a bit closer and *tsked* at him. Then she spoke to Adele as if he wasn't even there. "He hasn't been sleeping."

Adele's head bobbed on her narrow neck. "Mmmm. Must be a woman."

*How could they know that?* Bea clucked and ushered him to a seat. "Come here, dear. We'll work this all out."

Adele had already worked her way over to the stove, snatched the teakettle off the burner, and brought it over to the sink where she was filling it with water.

"So, what did you do?" Adele winked at Bea.

Bea snapped back at Adele. "Oh, stop. Can't you see he's suffering?" She turned back to Matt. "Now, how did she find out?"

Matt's gaze shot to Bea and then to Adele. "Find out . . .?"

Adele nodded. "Mmm hmm. You went on a date last night."

"It seemed to be going well. We were just returning to our cabin after a lovely game of Canasta with the Bellamys."

"They're a lovely couple," Adele smiled.

"Yes, quite. And we happened to overhear you." Bea nodded.

"You were walking through the parking lot."

Bea practically sighed then. "You seemed so … "

Adele got a faraway look on her face. "Yes."

"But this morning, not so … and so naturally we assumed she found out."

Adele nodded furiously. "Your secret."

Matt looked from one sister to another. "But how did you … ?"

Bea and Adele exchanged a grave look. Adele moved over to the stove and turned the burner on under the kettle. She nodded at Bea to go ahead. Bea patted Matt gently on the shoulder. "Oh, we have *The New York Times* delivered here. Special delivery."

Then Adele piped in, "We just love the society pages. You photograph very well."

Matt shook his head. "You never said a thing."

Bea smiled. "Certainly not. You were entitled to your privacy."

"Even if it meant hurting Jade?" Matt would give anything for it not to have happened the way it had. Anything to go back in time so that Jade wouldn't get hurt. Now it was too late and his privacy or any other reason he may have had for lying seemed insufficient.

Bea smiled down at Matt where he was sitting. "We knew you'd eventually put things right."

Matt wasn't one to dwell on past mistakes. He was more of a man of action. "Yeah, about that … I don't suppose you have any ideas."

Bea gasped softly and placed an open palm on her chest. "We wouldn't dream of interfering in Jade's," she cleared her throat daintily, "affairs."

Adele had moved over to the cabinets to pull down some mugs and a box of tea. She turned away from Matt and coughed. Bea shot her a dirty look and then smiled down at Matt. "Jade was always such a competitive young girl, wasn't she, Del?" Adele nodded as she put tea bags into the mugs and poured water over them. Bea continued, "Very territorial."

Adele carried two of the mugs over and set them on the counter in front of Matt and Bea. She picked up the thread of the conversation. "Oh, yes. I remember this one time she had a GI Joc doll and her sister Libby wanted to play with it."

Matt mumbled something. Adele stopped and asked him, "What was that dear?"

"It's an action figure. Not a doll. GI Joe is not a doll."

Adele's left eyebrow shot up. "Riiiight. Okay then, she had this GI Joe … action figure … and Libby wanted to play with it. Well, would Jade loan it to her? Goodness, no. You would've thought it was the key to the kingdom the way she went on about it." Adele went back to the opposite counter for the honey and some spoons.

Bea was nodding and smiling. She jumped in. "Oh yes, I remember that. The funny thing about it was that Jade wasn't even playing with the doll … er … action figure … when Libby asked to borrow it. Jade wasn't all that interested in him until someone else wanted to play with him."

"Yes, she's always competitive that way, and very possessive." Adele set the honey and a spoon down in front of Matt. "There you are, dear boy. Drink your tea."

Bea was dunking her tea bag in and out of her mug and nodding in time. "Indeed, you'll feel better after some tea." Bea sighed. "I just wish we could have been more helpful to you, Matt. But, you're a clever man. I'm sure you'll figure it all out." She took a sip of tea and smiled at him over the rim of her mug.

# Chapter 15

Jade and Matt skillfully avoided one another for the next five days. Jade knew she owed Matt an apology for trying to pummel him with vegetation and was slowly working herself up to the task. She worked tirelessly the entire week and when she wasn't taking care of Lakehaven, she was holed up in her cabin designing jewelry and working on her website.

She avoided thinking about Matt during the day, but nighttime was a different matter. She had strange dreams where he was standing outside her door, knocking incessantly in the cold with no shirt and bare feet. It took her three nights to realize there was a low-hanging tree branch knocking against her bedroom window. She cut it down on Thursday. Thursday night, she dreamt they were swimming in the lake together at night. The images were vivid: moonlight glinting off of his wet shoulders as his strong, sure strokes broke the silvered surface of the lake. But no matter how long he swam, he didn't ever get any closer. In the dream, Jade could tread water easily but couldn't remember how to swim. She could see Matt swim, but her brain couldn't tell her muscles how to do it. They were stuck, separated by the expanse of dark water. Though the air was cold in the dream, the lake temperature was a balmy 98.6 degrees Fahrenheit.

By the time Friday afternoon came around, Jade was ready to talk to Matt again. She still didn't trust him and hadn't forgiven him, but she was at least ready to act like a civilized adult and say she was sorry for throwing the Chia Head at him. She showered and spent the extra time needed to do her makeup and hair. She put on her best fitting jeans, the ones that hugged her hips and ass, and she picked out her favorite push-up bra and a tightly fitted Henley shirt. Unbuttoning an extra button on her top, she smiled at her reflection in the mirror. She looked great, but he probably wouldn't even notice. She stuck her tongue out at herself and headed out the door to do battle.

Jade walked to his front door, took a deep breath, and then knocked. She waited, but there was no answer and she wondered if she had knocked too softly. She knocked harder this time and waited again. She could feel her heart-rate speeding up and tried to give herself a pep talk. *You can do this. It'll be fine.* She waited another minute, but there was still no response. She blew a breath out. *Okay, no problem. I can apologize later. He's probably just out on a hike.*

•••

"I'm just pulling down the driveway now."

"Watch out for potholes."

Sam laughed. "Is that what you call these craters of suffering?"

Matt smiled to no one in particular since he was in his cabin alone. He grabbed his jacket off of the back of his chair. "I'll meet you in the lot."

"Are you nervous?" Sam sounded surprised.

"Yes. I hope you've come up with something."

"Will she be around?" Matt could practically hear the gears turning in Sam's head as she thought through the situation.

"Somewhere, but I think we can avoid running into her long enough to strategize. I'm pretty sure she's been avoiding me."

"Okay, that's good. Don't worry. We can turn this around. See you in a sec." Sam hung up.

Five minutes later, Samantha Parker pulled into the lot behind the wheel of her silver Aston Martin. She currently embodied what Matt thought of as her "Hot Secretary" persona. Her hair was twisted artfully at the back of her head, and she wore a tight business suit skirt and a precisely fitted white button down shirt with one button undone. She slid out of the front seat of the car, and when she spotted Matt her face broke into a wide grin. "Matty!" She started to run toward him, but her heels were not made for running on gravel, and she pitched forward as one heel got stuck in the rocks and she struggled to keep the shoe on. Matt was quick and closed the gap between them with one long-legged stride. He caught her by the waist to keep her from face planting in the driveway. Sam was pure elegance to look at, but to Matt she would always be a scruffy eleven-year-old klutz. He looked down at her face, all smooshed up into his shoulder, and started to laugh. It was the first time he had laughed this week. "Nice one, Parker."

Sam's hands went to Matt's shoulders so she could leverage herself into a less awkward position. "Yeah, yeah. Yuck it up now, Mr. Smooth. Just remember, I came all the way out here to the other side of this god-forsaken mountain to help you win back your ladylove. So quit being an asshole."

Matt chuckled. Seeing Sam was like sunshine (maybe acerbic sunshine, but sunshine, nonetheless), and he instantly felt the tension he had been holding onto all week seep away.

She smiled back up at him and brought her hand up to his face. "You look like shit on a stick, buddy."

Matt grinned down at her. "Not sleeping much."

Sam sighed. "Oh man, this is worse than I thought."

Matt nodded. "I'm afraid so. The situation is dire."

"I was thinking catastrophic, or maybe even cataclysmic. Speaking of which, your mother asked about you again. She wants to know when you'll be back. Mostly to set you up with Amanda Carmichael."

Matt was about to respond when Samantha's cell phone went off. It played the first two bars of "Live and Let Die." Samantha pulled out of Matt's arms. "Shit, sorry, it's the office. Gotta take this one." She flipped the phone open with one hand and handed

Matt her keys with the other. "Hi, Camille, what's up?" She dismissed him with a wave toward her car and an upper crust eyebrow raise. He swatted her tush but headed for the trunk of her car to grab her luggage. She flipped him the bird as he walked past.

Matt just laughed. He pulled her weekender out of the trunk and turned to head back to the cabin, gesturing for Sam to follow. She took a careful step on the gravel, and Matt offered her his arm for balance. She spoke into the cell phone, "Right, well, they can play it that way, but in the long run it'll cost them, and then we'll step in to snatch him up." She smiled up at Matt, nodded, and rolled her eyes all at the same time. Sam was a one-woman army in Jimmy Choos. Matt smiled at her and felt lighter than he had in days. Until he glanced up to see Jade stepping out of the woods ahead. *Shit.*

• • •

Jade made her way down the path toward the main house. She was still in the woods when a sleek silver sports car pulled down the drive. She watched as it glided to a stop in the graveled clearing that served as a parking lot. There were already eight vehicles parked there, ranging from Jeff's POS truck to a minivan to Jade's serviceable Honda Civic. None of them were particularly sleek. Perhaps that's why the driver of the sports car parked slightly off to the side of the lot. There were no scheduled check-ins for today. In fact, all of the cabins were occupied, so if the owner of the sports car was a drop-in, they were out of luck.

Jade moved forward to get a better look, but her view of the car and driver was partially blocked by the trees to her left. It was then that she noticed Matt approaching the car, his long legs eating up the distance. Jade froze. She stared as a tall, blonde Bond girl emerged from the driver's side, squealed at Matt, and threw herself at him. Matt caught her in an embrace. Jade could hear his rich, warm laugh as he smiled down at her.

Jade sucked in a breath and narrowed her eyes. Everything about the blonde was perfect and polished. She looked like her car: sleek, refined, and fast. Matt and the woman were at ease with one another. Matt's hands rested comfortably on Miss Sports Car's waist, and her hands were on his shoulders. The blonde was a tall woman, and since she wore heels, was only a few inches shorter than Matt. They fit together in a glossy magazine way. They were smiling and talking with one another and though they weren't exactly hugging anymore, they were still holding onto each other. Jade felt pure jealousy heating her cheeks. The blonde paused to take a phone call and handed her keys over to Matt. Matt smacked the *valkyrie* on the butt. Jade shoved her hands into her pockets to keep them from tightening into fists. She continued to watch as Matt pulled a weekend-sized bag out of the trunk of the sports car and turned back toward the path where Jade was standing.

Jade stood rooted to the spot while she debated the pros and cons of stepping out into the clearing to face Matt or running back to her cabin to avoid them. She barely noticed as Matt approached his guest and offered her his arm. They started toward her and Jade was just about to run when Matt looked up and caught her eye. *Crap!*

•••

Jade looked amazing in a pair of jeans that was more fitted than what she usually worked in. Her tight shirt was unbuttoned at the top, and Matt instantly wanted her. He wanted to undress her right there, to have the taste of her on his tongue, to feel her hairbrush against his skin and her body surrounding his. He stopped short, and Samantha stumbled against him. He looked down in surprise. For the space of a second, he had forgotten she was there.

She looked up at him and mumbled something into her phone before snapping it shut. Matt watched as Sam turned to look at Jade. Sam tilted her head and gave Jade an assessing gaze. Then she smiled and elbowed Matt hard in the ribs.

He couldn't think of a single thing to do or say. He turned back to Jade and looked. It had been almost a week since she had kicked him out of her cabin and he had spent the time thinking, writing, calling Sam, and thinking some more. Plus doing his best to follow Sam's instructions to give Jade some time and space. But here she was right in front of him and she was so heart-stoppingly beautiful that he couldn't breathe. How had he forgotten? Her eyes glittered large in her face. Her black hair moved in the air, brushing against pale pink cheeks. Her shoulders were squared, and her hands were shoved deep into her pockets. She looked fierce and proud. He wanted to cup the back of her head in his hand and drag her into a deep kiss.

Sam moved forward with bright smile and a hand extended. "Hi, I'm Samantha Parker."

Jade took the hand and shook it. Hard. "Jade Sawyer." Jade shot a look at Matt. "I'm so sorry. No one told me you were coming or I would've arranged for … " Jade trailed off.

Sam shrugged it off. "No problem. I don't need anything special. I'm just going to crash with Matt for the weekend."

Jade stiffened and smiled weakly. "Well, I certainly hope you have a pleasant stay. Let me know if there is anything I or my staff can do for you, Miss Parker." She took a deep breath and looked at Matt. "Bye." His heart was in his throat as he reached his hand out to her. She turned back to the main house and walked away.

• • •

Samantha was grinning as she stepped into Matt's cabin. "This place is cuter than I thought it would be."

Matt dropped her bag on the floor and threw himself down on the couch. "That sucked." He pressed his palms into his eyes and rubbed.

"I thought she'd be taller."

Matt shook his head, which was still in his hands.

Sam put a hand on his shoulder. "Don't worry, I'll figure something out. We'll win you back your lady. You just need to have a little patience."

"I don't want to do it this way anymore. It's too hard. I just want to crawl across broken glass on my knees and grovel. It'll be less painful."

Sam rolled her eyes. Then she suddenly turned away from Matt. "Ooooh, hey, I have a present for you." Sam crossed to the door where Matt left her bag.

"Cyanide tablet?"

Sam rolled her eyes. "Drama queen." She rifled through her bag and pulled out a large envelope. "I checked in with Allison before I left. She said some extra letters were sent in from London. She was going to forward them, but I told her I'd deliver them in person." Sam handed the envelope to Matt. He waved it off. Sam dropped the envelope on the coffee table in front of Matt and sat on the couch beside him. She draped her arm around his shoulders and bumped against him playfully.

"She's great, Matt. Short, but great," Sam said softly.

Matt smiled sadly. "How can you tell? You barely met her."

"I negotiate for a living. All I do is read people. She was pissed, but she cares deeply. She's passionate and feisty. I'm surprised I don't have blisters after the look she gave me. And she loves you." Matt's head jerked up. He looked at Sam. She patted him on the knee. "Come on, buddy. It'll all work out. Trust me."

• • •

Jade stalked into the kitchen for a cup of coffee. She took her anger out on the cabinets and drawers, banging them as she got out the necessary items. It hadn't taken long for Matt to call in his socialite-of-the-month. *Slam.* Of course, she was as mad at herself as anyone else. *Bang.* If she had gone to Matt and apologized for overreacting, he might not have invited Miss Hottie-Mc-Sports-Car. *Whap.* But honestly, it had only been a week and if Matthew Riley Mc-Any-Warm-Body-Will-Do was that fickle, it was better to know now and shut the whole thing down. *Bam.* "Asshole." Jade muttered under her breath as she flounced out of the kitchen and into her office.

The office was cluttered, and it took her twenty minutes of tidying, filing invoices, and entering notes into her calendar before the desk was clear enough to work. She cleaned with a vengeance until the surface was clear, then she stared at her desktop and tried not to think about Samantha Parker. In Matt's cabin. With Matt. It was interesting that she had called him Matt and not Riley. They must be close. Her jaw was beginning to hurt from grinding her teeth. If she kept this up she wouldn't have teeth left, just nubs and some white dust. The thought made her smile, sort of. The phone rang and jolted her out of her reverie. Jade just stared at it for a moment. *Now what?*

"Lakehaven Resort. Jade speaking." Her greeting was terse.

"Uh, Jade? It's Dad."

Jade sighed. That answered that question. "Hi, Dad."

"You okay?"

Jade forced a chipper tone. "Yeah, fine! What's up?"

Jade's father paused for a moment but seemed to accept her answer and then went on. "Well, I don't know if it'll be useful to your writer friend, but I'm cleaning out my filing cabinets at work and I came across some additional Cartwright papers that I had completely forgotten about. Would you like me to drop them in the mail?"

Jade's laugh was dry. "Sure, that'd be great."

"Are you sure you're okay, Pumpkin?"

"Absolutely." She started doodling on the blotting pad on the desk.

"Okay then. Uhm. I'm sure you don't need the reminder, but your mother wanted me to mention the retirement dinner next week. She said, in case you needed to shop."

"Right, Dad, I'm on top of it." *Not.* She had completely forgotten.

"It's cocktails at seven and dinner at eight."

"I know." Her doodle started to take the shape of a sports car. There was a freakishly tall woman crushed under the front tires. With x's for eyes. Jade wrote, *7:00 P.M.—retirement*, next to the drawing. Then she added a road with two high heel shoes strewn across it.

"Your mom RSVP'd for two, just in case."

"Ok, thanks." Jade wrote "two" next to the time. *Crap.* Maybe Ben could take her. She hoped he didn't need to wear a tux. "It's black tie optional, right?" Jade started to draw a broad shouldered figure in a tuxedo next to the car. She drew an anvil over his head.

"Yes. Your mother is making me wear a tuxedo though. She says I'll look dashing. Like James Bond."

Jade paused for a moment and thought about clunking her head against the desk. At this rate, she would soon have a large bruise on her forehead. She decided against it. "She's right, Dad. You should go with the tux."

Jade heard her Dad chuckle on the other end of the line. "As if I have a choice? This is your mother we're talking about." Jade's mother was a soft-spoken bohemian poet with a stubborn streak a mile long.

Jade smiled as she thought about how that conversation had probably gone. She had never seen two people who were so in love but could disagree so often. "Yeah, but this time she's right. Wear the tux." Dr. Sawyer was a lean, small-boned man who looked lanky in his usual wardrobe of baggy khakis and sports coats but managed to look dashing in a well-fitted tux.

"So … How's the jewelry coming?"

Jade sighed again. "Good. It's … almost ready." Jade felt like she had been putting the final touches on the line for months now, getting it ready. It was never quite perfect.

"Oh, good. I can't wait to see it." There was a brief pause on the line, and she could hear the sound of shuffling papers. "Well, take care of yourself."

"I will."

"I love you."

"Love you too, Dad. See you next week."

They hung up and Jade laid her head down on her arms and cried.

# Chapter 16

*Hudson River Valley Outpost 54*
*March 13, 1616*

*Dear Mother,*

*We have made it back to our valley and to what I am coming to think of as home, my true home. This is genuinely a beautiful land. A silvery lake nestles among the mountains and hills with hundreds of thousands of trees shading and sheltering us. I am aware that some of our European friends would call this land barely civilized, yet there is nowhere else I feel as comfortable. We have none of your conveniences, but still I am at ease and free. This is Alsoomse's land and her home as well, and perhaps that is also why I have taken it as my own.*

*Alsoomse and I are well matched, though I am unaccustomed to her strong will. You would laugh at how many arguments she wins. Before meeting her, I would have said it was not possible for a woman to be so certain minded and stubborn. I had no idea that it would be so easy and yet so difficult to be in love. I am happy.*

*She makes me take notice of small things like sunlight on the floor of the forest, morning mists that swirl around our ankles, and the exquisite design of an owl's nest. She is so aware and takes such pleasure in the form and intricacies of nature.*

*We had a difficult winter with little food, unfriendly terrain, and bitter cold. She stood it all without complaint. When we were ready to quit or too tired to go on, she would tease and cajole Pierre and me into continuing on our way. She was highly competitive and would stir the same spirit in us. We found it in ourselves to explore farther, more treacherous routes than ever before. Pierre and I would then end the day enlivened and proud, feeling more like men than when we set out that morning. She brings out the best in those around her.*

*When she and Pierre speak in French, heads close together, she can see my envy and lightens it with a caress and a tender word. She does not fault me my immaturities. She is brave and bold but innocent, too. I would worry and fret over her, but she just laughs. I have never had a more tumultuous time or a more exhilarating time in my entire life.*

*She has agreed to marry me, and I hope to gain your blessing. We will marry in the fall with the leaves blazing around us in a multitude of colors, for this is Alsoomse's favorite time. For myself, I do not care how or when it happens. I just await our joining with great impatience.*

*With your permission, Mother, I hope to give her the ring with the brown diamond and emerald leaves. Its woven metals and natural hewn beauty seem made just for her. She does not seem to be particularly enamoured of baubles and trinkets, but she does love nature. I hope she will find some pleasure in its artful design.*

*I do miss you dearly, but know that I am truly as happy as a man can be in life.*

*Your loving son,*
*Adam*

• • •

Matt finished reading the letter and smiled. At least he wasn't the only guy to have a rough time of it. If things had worked out for Adam and Alsoomse, maybe there was hope for him.

• • •

After dinner, Jade went out in search of Ben. Most of the guests were already back at their cabins, although a few stayed behind to play cards in the game room. Thankfully, Jade had managed to miss dinner and avoid seeing Matt and Miss Sports-Car. She had grabbed her own dinner from the kitchen and then gone directly back to the office to finish up paperwork and some simple tasks on the computer.

It was difficult to focus, and she ended up doodling some new designs on scraps of paper. The drawings all resembled the woven branches of trees and bushes in the area, similar to the ones she and Jeff had cleared out of the paths around Lakehaven. Jade was sure that the renderings would make beautiful jewelry, but she was starting to think that some of the designs would also make wonderful stationary and note cards. Jade distracted herself with daydreams of a whole "woven branches" line of accessories.

By the time she had finished drawing and stuffed the sketches into a folder, it was after eight and, she figured, safe enough to leave the office.

Jade found Ben manning the front desk, or at least sitting at the front desk and surfing the Internet on his computer. He saw Jade approaching and quickly tapped a few keys.

Jade smiled. "I know what you're doing."

Ben looked confused. "What?"

Jade shrugged. "You always close down your internet window right before I get here. Don't bother, I know what you're doing."

"I'm not doing anything."

"Uh-huh."

Ben crossed his arms in front of his chest. "I'm not."

Jade made it to the front desk and leaned against it. The desk was a beautiful expanse of rough-hewn wood cut from a single log. It was rustic and natural; the light stain highlighted the whorls, knots, and wood grain. Its glossy surface glowed in the soft light of the foyer. Jade ran her hands lovingly over the wood. "You do know that anyone can check the history of the websites you've visited?"

Ben's face flushed pink, and he glanced down at the computer screen. He straightened the pad and pen on the desk next to the computer. "I don't have anything to hide."

Jade laughed. "Okay. Whatever you say. How was the evening?"

Ben smiled. "Do you want the good news or the bad?"

Jade frowned. "There's bad news?" She could feel the knot forming in her stomach.

Ben shrugged. "It's all relative. Nobody died or anything."

"Well, that's something then." Jade let out a slow breath. Ben seemed relaxed about the whole thing, so Jade tried to stay calm while she waited for him to continue.

"Yeah. Everyone loved dinner. I think the catering is going to work for Sundays or anytime Meg can't be here."

"I thought we were doing bad news." She was getting a bit impatient. She really needed to know how bad it was.

"Oh, right. Well, uh, the Kent sisters created a bit of a … disturbance." Ben pushed his glasses up the bridge of his nose.

*Gee, that was nothing new.* Jade raised an eyebrow and waited for the rest of it.

Ben nodded. "They were trying to decide who was hotter: MacGyver or Michael Knight. You know from that show in the '80s?"

"That's completely subjective. How can they decide who's right?"

"That's where the disturbance part comes in. They decided to poll the other guests. Mr. Boyle refused to answer, which upset Beatrice. Adele asked Mrs. Anderson, who voted for MacGyver, but Mr. Anderson disagreed. Then, Mrs. Anderson said it was just because Mr. Anderson liked the black car and not because he liked Michael Knight, and Mr. Anderson said he was pretty sure he knew who he liked, thank you very much. Miss Parker didn't like either of them, but said she always loved the physicist from *Quantum Leap.* "

"Dr. Sam Beckett."

Ben gave Jade a funny look. "It's sad that you know that. Well, that started a whole new argument between the sisters. The new couple in cabin two left dinner early. I think they expected a quieter evening."

Jade sighed. "Okay, I'll talk to the Kents. You send an apology note and a bottle of wine to cabin two."

Ben nodded. "Already done."

Jade paused before she asked the next question. "Who did Mr. … Connor vote for?" By now most of Lakehaven's staff had been informed that Matt was Riley McLaughlin, but everyone had decided to maintain his cover and allow him his privacy.

"Matt? He couldn't. After Sam, that is Miss Parker, put a vote in for the *Quantum Leap* guy and the Kent sisters started yelling, he was laughing too hard to speak. Miss Parker threw her napkin at him, which just made him laugh harder. Then she started to laugh. That got the Davis family from cabin five laughing so hard that Nick Davis, he's the ten-year-old, shot milk out of his nose. That's actually when the Martins got up to leave."

As usual, Lakehaven was a well-oiled machine. Jade looked longingly at the surface of the front desk. This was a head-thunking occasion if ever there was one. Unfortunately, she had given that up. To avoid bruising.

"Well, at least they liked the food," Jade finally said. Ben nodded. Jade picked up the pen and Lakehaven pad in front of her and started to doodle woven branches. "Ben, I actually need to ask you a favor."

Ben pushed his glasses up the bridge of his nose. "You can't borrow my Radiohead CD. It's signed and I don't sleep well when it's not in its special place."

Jade blinked at him. "No, it's not that. I need a date."

Ben laughed. "Don't we all! I personally am working my way up to asking out Samantha. That woman is so … well, you know."

Jade rolled her eyes at Ben. "You don't think Matt might object to that?"

Ben shrugged. "I don't see why. She's his manager and some kind of an old family friend, but they aren't hooked up or anything."

"How do you know that?" Jade asked. And why had no one bothered to tell her? Though now that she thought about it Matt had mentioned a manager, someone named Sam.

"She called before she drove up. Man, she has a great phone voice. She was going to get her own cabin, but we were booked. She asked if it would work just to stay in the cabin with Matt, if there was enough room for two people who weren't, you know, hooked up."

Jade smiled. "So she's not here to … "

Ben shook his head. "Nope. She said she had some project that she and Matt needed to work on, and she couldn't lure him back to the city so … " He thought for a moment. "You know, you are very interested in their personal relationship or lack thereof. Why don't you just ask Matt out on this date?"

Jade wondered what their project was even as she answered Ben. "Look, it's complicated. What I really want is an escort. To my dad's retirement dinner. This is his special night and I'd like it to be free of drama. You already know all of these professors and you can talk to them. You only have to wear a suit, the food will be good, and it'll take about four hours. I will cover two of your shifts if you do this for me. Please?"

Ben smiled and pushed his glasses up his nose. "Any two shifts of my choosing?"

Jade nodded. "With twenty-four hour notice."

Ben's smile turned mischievous. "So, for example, if Samantha agreed to go out with me, you'd cover my shift?"

Jade laughed. "You think you have a chance with her?"

Ben pushed his glasses up the bridge of his nose. "Are you kidding? She likes the physicist from *Quantum Leap*. I am *so* her type!"

Jade smiled at his optimism. "We have a deal then?"

Ben nodded. "You, m'lady, have an escort."

•••

Matt glanced at Sam. She looked completely different from the woman who had arrived the day before. Her hair was sticking out in a scary way, and she was dressed in sweat pants and a t-shirt. The tee was printed with a picture of Shakespeare and said, *"Prose before hos."* She sat on the couch with her laptop open to an Excel worksheet. Her cell was next to her on top of a stack of pillows and blankets that Matt had used the night before. She wore a pair of Ralph Lauren eyeglasses and mumbled under her breath. If Matt didn't know her, he would've thought her imbalanced. He knew her well enough to know that she was just Sam.

He loved Sam, loved having her company. Dinner the night before had been fun. Sam was boisterous and sharp and funny. The problem was, she wasn't Jade. Jade was grounded and peaceful; she exuded comfort and whispers of home. Jade had something indefinable too, whether it was her scent, or an expression or the way she walked. There was just something about her that twisted him up inside.

Matt turned back to his desk and stared at his laptop. The cursor blinked ominously on the blank document as he tapped a pen on his leg. It was the end of a long day of writing in fits and bursts. He was not at his most productive. He wasn't even sure that what he had written was usable. He glanced back at Sam tapping on her keyboard with lightning speed.

They had eaten a quick lunch at the main house while Sam filled him in on the latest gossip, some of it was from the city, but some was from Lakehaven. She hadn't even been here a full day and already she was collecting intel. He had listened with half an ear while scanning the doors for any sign of Jade. She hadn't made an appearance. Sam had been great, ignoring the fact that Matt wasn't really listening.

They had gone for a swim in the lake and Sam wore the tiniest bikini Matt had ever seen. Unfortunately, that just made him imagine what Jade would look like in equally small scraps of fabric. That, at least, had made him smile.

Jeff had been mowing the lawn at the time, and he seemed to appreciate Sam's suit. He mowed over the same area for twenty minutes before Sam got out and wrapped herself in a towel. He had even taken off his flannel shirt and conspicuously mopped sweat off his chest for Sam's benefit. Sam had pretended not to notice, much to Jeff's dismay.

After the swim, Matt and Sam had gone back to the cabin where Sam was hard at work and Matt was still staring at his laptop screen. Blink, blink. The cursor was starting to annoy him. He tapped his pen against his leg. He glanced back at Sam again. He was trying to be patient with her method of problem solving. She had come to help him win back Jade, but he knew how she operated. She first would gently fish for information, get the lay of the land, get to know the situation and the players, and then she would let various scenarios roll around in her brain until the perfect solution clicked into place. To an outside observer, it looked like she wasn't doing anything but Matt knew better. She had been his manager since the very start and she was a genius at managing anything. Sometimes it took weeks for her to steer a situation in the direction she wanted it to go, but she always got the job done. Always. He just wished it would take less time. He wasn't great at waiting.

Without looking up she spoke. "What's wrong?"

"Nothing."

Sam typed out a few keystrokes. "Bullshit."

"What the fuck does that mean?" Matt slammed his laptop closed and turned to face Sam. He knew he was being a baby, but he just couldn't help himself.

"You're tapping your leg."

Matt stopped tapping his pen. "Okay look, I've got to do something. This is driving me crazy."

"Okay. Go for a walk. What time is it?"

"Around five."

"Where will she be?"

"I don't know, somewhere in the main house. It's near dinner so … kitchen or dining room … maybe her office, if she's hiding from me."

"Okay, run into her accidentally and then be casual. See what happens."

"Really?"

Samantha nodded. "Yes, but don't spook her. Be casual. I mean it."

Matt grabbed his jacket off the back of his chair and bounded toward the door like a puppy. He was out of the cabin in a matter of seconds. Matt looked in all the places he thought Jade might be, with no luck. He checked the game room and the porch that looked out over the lawn toward the lake. He glanced out at the lawn through the screened-in area. Off to the left, in the direction of cabin four, he could see Jeff working in the brush around the path. Matt strode over to ask about Jade's whereabouts. Jeff pulled his headphones off long enough to tell Matt that he wasn't sure, but she might have gone up the path.

In the time that Matt had been at Lakehaven, he had only been hiking that second day, the morning Jade had taken him. The morning they first kissed. The path had been a gradual slope uphill, but followed the shore of the lake. This path led in the opposite direction. From the maps Matt had seen, it looked like this was just the other end of a large loop around the lake. There were various trails that branched off the main loop, but if he stayed on this path it would eventually circle all the way back to his own cabin.

The path in this direction wove its way past cabins three, two, and then one, before starting to slant uphill. Here the path was wide and edged on the left with low bushes that left the lake view unobstructed. To the right, the only thing visible was a forest of trees.

Matt looked to his left. At this time of day, the late afternoon sun was throwing stardust trails of gold across the darkening water. It had been a sunny day and there was still warmth in the air, but Matt could feel it fading and knew in an hour it would be chilly. He made his way up the hill, and after a five-minute walk, the path began to narrow. The bushes got taller and were gradually replaced by trees that blocked the view of the lake. There were openings in the tree line to his right leading off to other trails, but a solid wall of greenery to his left. The lake mostly curved to the left, but here it bent right for a way before curving back in the other direction. Much of the lake line was like that, creating small coves and shallows perfect for fishing or swimming. He walked farther, listening to the breeze running through the branches and the cadence of his own footfalls.

Suddenly, he was aware of a third sound up ahead—a splashing below him and to the left. It was a rhythmic sound but not the same as the lapping of lake water on its own. It was closer to the sound of an animal drinking or wading in the water. He walked twenty yards until the sound was directly below him and looked around. The path was dark here, and in the waning light, it was getting darker by the minute. Matt looked closely at the trees bordering the lake side of the path. There were bushes filling in between the trees, and after a careful inspection, Matt noticed a small opening between the greenery. He gently drew the branches aside and sure enough, there was a narrow path angling downward, presumably toward the lake's edge.

He moved slowly and silently, hoping to see a deer drinking from the water and not wanting to startle it. The thin trail made a series of switchbacks, zigzagging across the steep slope and winding its way down to the lake. As he approached the bottom, he could see the darkness of tree-cover give way to light. He slowed his pace even more as he approached the shore, hoping not to disturb whatever was ahead.

The sun had dropped to the horizon line and glowed orange on the water. The same warm glow glinted off the midnight blue silhouette of a naked woman, outlining her against the gold-flecked water. Her body stood in profile, and her head was turned toward the center of the lake. Even so, Matt could tell it was Jade. He froze at the edge of the tree line, deciding what to do. Or not deciding.

She had waded in to mid-thigh and bent over to trail her hand lovingly through the water. The waning light glinted off her hip, the curve of her lower, lower back and everything in between. *Holy God.* Matt sucked in a breath. She waded in deeper and the water lapped at the apex of her thighs. *Lucky water.*

He stood frozen as she slipped lower into the water, dunked herself completely under, and then came back up, facing the other direction. She wasn't quite facing him, but from this angle, he could see more of her. She was sliding her hand over her hair, water sluicing off her body and pouring down in rivulets between her breasts. He could tell the water was cold.

She dove back under and disappeared for a bit. She rose up out of the lake a few yards from where she had gone under. She reminded Matt of a water nymph.

Without turning, she spoke. "Are you coming in or are you just going to gawk?"

Matt found his voice on the third try. "Can I just gawk?"

She shrugged. "Suit yourself." Then she disappeared beneath the lake's surface.

He waited for her to rise again, holding his breath and scanning for her figure. She came out of the water facing him, and he could feel desire pour through him. He loved the tease of it, could almost see it in slow motion. Each part of her was gradually revealed from her lovely shoulders, her high, round breasts, the slope of her ribcage down to her abdomen. His whole body tightened for her. He almost groaned aloud.

She smiled at him where he was, still standing at the edge of the trees watching. "I'm glad you're here, actually. I wanted to talk to you."

Matt just nodded. I mean, what could he say to her right now? Certainly nothing coherent.

Jade continued on as if she were standing in her office fully clothed. "I wanted to apologize for … overreacting last week. I guess it can't be easy, the fame and the lack of privacy. I shouldn't have thrown plant life at you." She turned away from Matt and looked out at the water for a moment. Matt stared at her backside and marveled at the glory of nature. He was starting to rethink the decision to just watch. Part of him wanted to shuck his clothes, rush in, and lick lake water off her, then drag her back to shore and slide inside of her. He was hard just thinking about it.

She dove under and this time came out of the water several yards closer to Matt. This time she actually was slowly, purposefully gliding up out of the water. When she was standing fully, she tilted her head back and lifted her arms to squeeze the water out of her hair. It was timed just right so that her breasts tilted up and her back arched just so. Her lips parted slightly and she paused there for the slightest moment. Okay, now he was really hard.

She smiled slightly and slid her gaze over to Matt. "Oh, I have a surprise for you."

Matt thought about pinching himself to see if he was dreaming, but that would look embarrassing if he wasn't and would wake him up if he was. There was absolutely no reason to wake up from this kind of a dream.

Jade turned toward him. The golden sunlight was gone, replaced by silvery moon glow. The water glistened off her body, highlighting each and every one of her perfect curves. She started out of the water toward the shore, toward him. She shivered a little as the cold air hit more and more of her skin. Matt shivered for another reason altogether.

Jade smiled. "I'm sure you'll like it." She walked closer.

Matt pulled his gaze away from her body and forced himself to make eye contact. He smiled. His voice was deep and husky. "I'm sure I will."

Jade nodded. "My dad found some more Cartwright papers in his office." She veered toward a rock and leaned over to pick up a towel. Somehow, Matt had failed to notice it sitting there in the fading light. Jade continued speaking. "He was cleaning out his filing cabinets and found them." Jade wrapped the towel around herself and picked up the pile of clothing that was on the rock next to it. Somehow, Matt had missed that, too. "He's mailing them, so they should be here in a couple of days. Isn't that a great surprise?" She secured the ends of the towel under its edge and tucked her clothes under her right arm.

Matt nodded, stupefied. "Uh, great." He was supposed to be good with words but that was the response he came up with? It seemed that most of his brain was stuck thinking about Jade—naked.

He was sure he was awake now because this was not how he would have scripted the dream. Jade sauntered past him and up the trail. Her shoes were in her left hand, but even in bare feet in the dark, she was sure footed. She had obviously been here many times.

She took a few steps up the hill and turned. "I'm glad we had this talk. I hope you can forgive me."

Matt waved his hand in the air, but kept his back to her, his gaze on the lake. He cleared his throat. "Nothing to forgive. Apology accepted."

She paused and said, "Thanks," then turned and continued up the hill.

He knew he would come up with the perfect words to woo her about an hour from now. For now, the only word that came to mind was *pathetic*. Matt took the few strides to the rock where Jade's towel and clothes had been. He sat down hard. The rock was still warm. He rested his elbows on his knees and stared out at the water. He nodded to no one in particular. *That went well.*

# Chapter 17

Two days later, Jade received her father's newly discovered papers and decided to deliver them to Matt's cabin in person. Matt's friend Samantha had gone back to the city. She must have liked Lakehaven, at least enough to book a cabin for the following weekend.

Ben insisted that there was nothing going on between Sam and Matt. He pointed out that Sam had called to ask him to bring an additional set of blankets to the cabin. Stu and Maddie had mentioned seeing the same blankets on the couch. Jade was still suspicious. She knew what she would be doing if she were locked in a cabin with Matt all weekend. She could feel her body tighten at the thought.

Jade sighed at her traitorous body and tried to pull herself together. If she arrived at Matt's cabin like this, she was likely to jump him. She was pretty sure after the skinny dipping episode that he wouldn't protest. That had been fun, to have the upper hand for a change, but for now, she was trying to keep a little distance, sort of. She really wanted to stay mad at him; it was safer for her heart if she did. When her relationship with Nick fell apart, she had made a promise to herself: never again. She could feel herself relenting bit by bit, and it wasn't the most comfortable feeling. She was freaked out by how quickly she had fallen for Matt. When he'd confessed his real identity, it had pulled the rug out from under her, and now she was just trying to keep her equilibrium. She didn't want to really care about Matt, and she still wasn't sure if she was anything more than a vacation fling for him. Not that he didn't genuinely like her; he probably did, but beyond that she couldn't tell. It felt like he always had an edge over her, somehow, that left her scrambling to come out on top. The moment the phrase *out on top* popped into her head, her mind turned wicked. She had an instant image of Matt flat on his back underneath her, her thighs straddling his waist and her hair draped over his naked chest. Jade frowned and tried to think about something else.

She got to his cabin and knocked, then glanced at the large envelope in her hand. She was still looking at her father's scrawl when the door swung open, and just like that, he was there in front of her. Suddenly, all of her concerns seemed to fly out of her head. She had avoided seeing too much of him lately. Down at the lake's shore the other day it had been dark, and he had been hard to see. He wasn't hard to see now. The over six feet of potent male standing in front of her rendered her speechless. He wore faded jeans, slung low on his lean hips, and a grey t-shirt stretched taut across his beautiful broad chest. Her breath caught in her throat. All she could manage was to raise the envelope and wave it about in front of him.

For a moment, Matt's face was completely expressionless. Jade was betting he was a really good poker player. Then he broke into a casual smile and stepped aside to usher her in. She paused before entering. It hadn't occurred to her that he would invite her in. She was pretty curious to find out what was in the envelope and maybe a little curious to find out where they stood with each other. The truth was she flat out missed him, his warmth, his humor, his scent. She walked in.

The cabin was tidy. The pile of bedding provided by Ben sat neatly folded on one end of the couch. Other than that, the place was spotless. Matt had a lot of papers on the desk, but even they seemed to be well organized.

Matt shot her a thousand watt smile that made her stomach jump. "Let's see what we've got here." He opened the envelope and slid a sheaf of papers out. Some of them were old and yellowed, while others looked more recent. Matt spread them out on the coffee table and invited Jade to sit. He sat next to her, not so close as to crowd her, but close enough. She could smell his soap and that other warm scent that seemed to be just him. He picked up one of the more yellowed papers and slid in toward her. "What do you think?" It was an old map.

"Well, it's not original. If this were four hundred years old, it'd be crumbling under our touch. It could be this lake, though."

Matt shrugged. "It's not proof of much of anything."

Jade nodded her agreement. They started to sift through the rest of the papers on the table. His hand brushed hers as they both reached for a paper that looked like another map. Her stomach jumped again, and she quickly pulled her hand away.

He stopped what he was doing and looked at her. "This is ridiculous. We're lovers, for crying out loud! We should be able to touch each other without being awkward."

Jade sighed. "Are we?"

"Are we what?"

"Are we still lovers?"

Matt ran his hand through his hair and looked into her eyes. His eyes were a stormy grey with a dark black ring around the iris. He had small lines at the corners of his eyes that crinkled with concern. He laughed, but it came out choked. "Just say the word and … " He opened his arms. It was both an invitation and a surrender.

There was a moment when she almost did it. It would be so easy to take off her clothes, take off his, and lose herself in pleasure. That thought stopped her—*losing herself*, all of herself—the fear of losing her heart and her soul to him. It would be so easy to give them away, but could he hold them dear and keep them safe? Was she brave enough to take that risk?

She pulled back from him and gave him a wistful smile. "I don't know how to … "

His smile turned teasing. "As I recall, you know how to ... really well."

Jade grabbed the pillow off the stack behind her and smacked Matt in the face with it. "That's not what I meant." His teasing had helped though, and now her smile was relaxed.

"Okay, look. Whatever it is you think you don't know, we'll figure it out. Together."

She nodded and took the pillow and put it back on the stack. "I'll definitely consider it." She turned back to the papers on the coffee table and picked up a map.

Matt exhaled and gave her a small smile. He must have been satisfied or at least had decided not to press his luck because he, too, turned back to the coffee table. He picked up a paper covered in small, precise lettering—a woman's handwriting. He read the first line and smiled.

"Jade, listen to this!" Matt began to read the letter aloud:

*London, England*
*October 28, 1616*

*Dearest Adam,*

*I have just received your most recent correspondence regarding your nuptials. Your description of the occasion was wrought with such loving detail and depth of feeling that I have taken the earliest opportunity to write these few lines hoping they find you in good health. I must admit your letter moved me to tears. It is no doubt feminine folly to be so emotional over a letter, but I blame the romantic sensibilities of a loving and devoted mother. I can imagine you there, looking out at the lake as you took your vows. You are a special son, and if I am a bit overcome with happiness at your joyful union, it is, I imagine, quite forgivable. I am only sorry to not have been there in person.*

*If your father were well, you can be certain I would have made the ocean journey. As it is, I worry for him. He is not as hearty as you would remember. This bout of illness has aged him much. It has slowed him and eased his temperament as well. He is changed. It is possible you would even enjoy his company now . . .*

• • •

Matt trailed off, reading the rest of the letter to himself.

Jade was outraged. "Don't stop now!"

Matt glanced up at her. "I thought you weren't interested in this stuff!"

Jade scooted herself closer to Matt. She bumped him with her hip and he held the letter closer to her, pointing out where he had left off so she could read for herself.

They finished the letter, but there was no other mention of the wedding ceremony of Adam Cartwright. Adam's mother went on to write about Adam's brother, sister, and a parade of other names. She detailed the events surrounding those lives, filling him in with news of family and friends and the life he had left behind.

For some reason, the details of the wedding ceremony seemed important, like a clue to the whereabouts of the treasure might be found there. It was a total hunch, but Matt was a good judge of human character. It was what made him a good writer, getting into the minds of people. He had spent a lot of time with the Cartwright story and Adam's life. It seemed like a long shot, and yet his gut was telling him to follow this clue. The location of the wedding was somehow significant.

Somewhere out there was a letter from Adam to his mother, if it hadn't been destroyed or lost.

Matt went to his desk and shuffled through the folders until he found what he was looking for. He handed the folder to Jade.

"These are copies of the letters my assistant found in London. They are copies of Adam's letters to his mother."

Jade opened the file and began to sift through. These were typed, probably transcribed from the originals, and much easier to read. She glanced up at Matt and her eyes were sparkling with excitement. "Is the wedding letter here?" She didn't even wait for him to answer before turning back to the folder. She was already reading some of the earliest letters.

Matt had his own hunches, but he was curious as to why Jade had singled out the wedding as well. "Do you think it's important?"

Jade shot him a look. "The wedding? It was to them."

Matt nodded and declared again, "I thought you weren't interested."

Jade smiled. "I said I wasn't interested in the treasure."

Matt persisted. "You called me a romantic. And not in a nice way."

Jade shrugged and ignored the accusation. She went back to reading the letters. "The wedding is important."

Matt gestured to the folder she was holding. "It's not there. I've read all of these, and none of them describe the wedding."

Jade ran her hands through her bangs. "These are good." She pointed to one of the letters. "Here. This sounds like the north side of the lake. There's a clearing like the one he describes here. The light filters through the trees and in the spring, the pollen is so thick it's like fairy dust in the light shafts. Here, read."

Matt read the paragraph she pointed to. It was good writing, vivid and emotional. "He loved this land."

Jade nodded. "If we can find that letter, and he describes the wedding site in this kind of detail, I think I can find it." She was excited about finding the treasure; Matt could hear it in her voice. Her enthusiasm made him smile. Somehow, Ms. Cynical had turned into a five-year-old on Christmas morning and Matt had a ringside seat. If he weren't enjoying her so much, he might have made fun of it. Instead, he just grinned.

"Okay," he said, "I think I have some connections that might help. I'll make some phone calls and see if we can find that letter. No guarantees though."

Jade smiled up at Matt. "There's no guarantee that when we find the wedding site there will be anything there, either. That's not the point. It'll be fun to look and see, find out what's there. It's all about the journey."

Matt thought about the two of them, Jade and him, about their relationship. He nodded at her. "I couldn't agree more."

...

A frustrating five days later, the Aston Martin was back. Jade gave a heavy sigh. The exhale was forceful enough that Meg turned around and slammed her hands down on her hips. "That's it! You are done with being pathetic and mournful. Get your ass off of that stool and go have sex with that man now, or I am revoking our friendship."

Jade raised both eyebrows high enough to get them lost in her bangs. "Should we do that here, on the countertop, or do you recommend the parking lot? Maybe on the hood of Ms. Parker's car?"

Meg fought a smile by glaring at Jade instead. "I don't give a good goddamn where you do it. You can do it in the middle of the lawn with Jeff watching for all I care—"

"Eww!"

"—but just stop sighing!"

"Ooooh, are we talking about what I think we're talking about?" Beatrice Kent swept into the kitchen with an empty platter in her hands and set it down on the counter. "I once did it on stage. Of course, not with an audience present, but *oh my!*" She gave a little shiver and sat down on a stool next to Jade.

Adele stalked in three steps behind Bea, rolling her eyes heavenward. "Oh Lord, not this story again."

Bea turned to Adele and stuck her tongue out. "You're just jealous."

Adele barked out a laugh and shook her head. "What on earth of? I've done it in much more exotic places than on a stupid stage."

Jade shot Meg a pleading look, but Meg pretended not to notice. She was not going to help.

Bea narrowed her eyes. "Oh, really? Like where?"

Jade was thinking about putting her fingers in her ears and chanting, "La, la, la, la, I'm not listening." She might have done it, too, but just then Samantha Parker strolled in from the hallway, looking like a million dollars.

Her hair fell in a golden curtain around her shoulders and swung when she walked, almost in perfect time with her trim hips and skyscraper legs. Her eyes glittered, and her golden skin glowed. She wore another slim pencil skirt, this time with a snugly fitted v-neck sweater made of tissue thin cashmere. The outfit hugged every important curve, which for Samantha meant all of them. She was in three-inch heels that looked like they cost more than Jade's entire wardrobe. Everything was black except the gold and stainless steel Tag Heuer watch at her wrist. If she had earrings on, Jade couldn't see them. Samantha's hair was that thick. Jade tried not to glance down at her own cotton t-shirt and khaki pants. She hoped they weren't covered in coffee stains.

Samantha paused for a moment at the door and looked around. Adele was still talking. "It just so happens that I can name about a half-dozen interesting places I've had sex!"

Sam's mouth had opened to say something, but at hearing Adele's declaration, she quickly shut it. She leaned casually against the doorframe with her arms folded across her ribcage. She was settled in for the duration. Meg feigned disinterest as she walked to the fridge and took out a new tray laden with small crust less sandwiches.

Bea challenged Adele. Apparently, the presence of a newcomer was not going to dissuade her in any way. "*Harrumph*. This I'd like to hear! Name them."

Adele thrust her hand out at Bea and counted each one off on her fingers. "Well, there was the bearded ladies tent, a dental chair, in front of the wax figure of Clark Gable at Madame Tussaud's, the bullpen at Yankee Stadium, the bathroom of a 747 … "

Jade shot a pleading look at Meg, who finally took pity on her. She thrust the tray of sandwiches into Adele's hands and gently led the sisters toward the door to the dining room. "Would you ladies mind setting this out on the side board? Thanks so much." Meg nudged them out the door with a pat on the back. They were still arguing as they left. "The airplane doesn't count; it's too mundane."

"It does too count!"

Samantha quirked an eyebrow at the retreating pair. "Are they always like that?"

Meg and Jade answered simultaneously, "Always."

Sam shook her head and laughed. "How did they even end up on that topic?"

Meg shrugged. "Who knows with those two? They do end up on some pretty strange tangents."

Sam smiled. "I guess at their age you've covered all of the boring stuff. I hope I'm still having those … *interesting* conversations when I'm that old."

Meg nodded. "It sure beats talking about the weather!"

Samantha laughed. "I was thinking the exact same thing!"

There was a moment where no one said anything, but before it could turn to awkward silence, Samantha continued. "So, I just dropped in to find out what there is to do around here."

Meg made her way toward the counter to continue stirring the dough for breakfast scones. "You mean, other than hiking, swimming, sailing, canoeing, fishing, horseshoes on the front lawn, or general lazing about? Oh, and don't forget canasta with Mr. Boyle. He's a real card shark. Plays every Sunday after brunch without fail."

Sam laughed and jerked her head toward the dining room door. "With those two ladies?" Meg just nodded in response. "No thanks. I'd lose my shirt!"

Meg smiled slyly back at Sam. "No, their strip poker game is Saturday night."

Sam cringed. "That's a … vivid image."

Meg had bent down to pull a baking sheet out from the cupboard. She popped back up to answer with a shiver, "Yeah, a little too vivid."

Meg wiped her hands on a rag on the countertop and walked toward Samantha, hand extended. "Meg Hammond."

"Hi, I'm Sam Parker."

"Yeah, so I hear." The two women shook hands and smiled at one another.

Jade sat and watched in horror as her best friend and Matt's friend made nice. Then something occurred to her. "You go by Sam mostly, right?"

Sam nodded. "Unless I'm trying to be snotty or pretentious."

Jade tilted her head. "Did you … " She thought about how to phrase it delicately, without offending, then gave up. "Are you the one who broke Matt's nose?"

Sam laughed. "Yep, that was me." She lifted her right arm, put her right hand on her own shoulder, and presented her elbow. "I was a bony kid. Smacked him with this. Hit him just right, too. There was this great spurt of blood. It was everywhere. All over the rug, the couch, on the silk throw pillows. It cost a fortune to clean them. Aunt Elizabeth was so furious." Sam paused in the story and looked carefully at Jade. "I'm surprised he told you about it."

Meg asked, "Why?"

Sam lifted a shoulder. "He probably wouldn't like me saying this, but he usually doesn't like to look … weak."

Meg nodded. "Total guy thing."

Sam looked at Jade again. "If he told you, he must trust you."

Jade stared down at the countertop, avoiding Sam's gaze. This was the problem all along. Matt was willing to trust Jade, but somewhere along the way she had lost her ability to trust anyone or anything. She didn't trust men not to break her heart, and she didn't trust herself to pick a man who was reliable. She had fallen in love so easily with Nick. At least it had seemed that way at the time. Now if something was too easy, too good, that fast, she didn't quite trust it to last.

She could see her future stretched out ahead of her. A future where she jumped in and out of relationships, praying they never got too serious and nothing bad ever happened. When they did, she would undoubtedly find a way out and move on. She knew that Matt hadn't lied to her to be deceitful. In fact, if she really looked at it, she had known it even in the moment that he came clean. It just gave her the perfect excuse to run. If it hadn't been that, she would've found some other reason to run. Nick was out of her life, but Jade was still making decisions based on that relationship.

Jade knew that if she wanted something different, something more, she was going to have to do something different, risk something more. She had no idea how to make a relationship with Matt work, or if they even had a relationship anymore. But she was willing to give it a try.

Jade sighed and got up from the stool at the counter. She was suddenly restless and wanted to walk. She left the kitchen through the door to the yard without a word to either Sam or Meg.

# Chapter 18

The next morning, Matt got the envelope lying on his doorstep with a tray of scones and a large insulated carafe of coffee. There was no note or clue as to who left it. Whomever it was had simply knocked on the door and then ran. Matt smiled; it seemed like the kind of prank Sam would pull. He set the tray up on the small table in the kitchen, poured himself a cup of coffee, and brought it to the couch along with the envelope.

The papers slid out easily, and he shuffled through them. There was a cover page, some notes, and a letter. Matt felt his heart rate kick up at the salutation in the letter. It was from Adam to his mother.

On the one hand, Matt didn't believe that the treasure was still out there. Too much time had passed and from what he could glean, the chest had been wood and the metals in many of the pieces would have been delicate and susceptible to the elements. But the search for it had become a game to him, piecing together these lives from so long ago, finding clues, coming up with theories. Matt loved to win and was fascinated with putting the puzzle together.

He set aside the letter for later and looked through the notes. There were descriptions of various artifacts and pieces of jewelry. One description really caught his attention. It was a ring, a large brown diamond surrounded by marquise cut emeralds that circled the diamond like a ring of leaves. That sounded like the piece Adam Cartwright had intended for Alsoomse's wedding ring. The sources seemed to corroborate one another, lending credibility to the contents of Adam's letters. Matt smiled and flipped through some of the other pages. Nothing else seemed to jump out at him, and he was just about to dig into the letter when there was a knock at his cabin door. He had less foot traffic at his Manhattan penthouse. Of course, that building had a doorman . . .

Matt put the letter down and went to the door. Sam stood there in a pair of ratty sweat pants and a long-sleeved t-shirt printed with the words: *shirts with a haiku/ they're kind of overrated/ but I'm wearing one*. Matt wondered how a woman who looked so put together Monday through Friday could turn into such a fashion disaster on the weekend. Her hair hadn't been brushed and stuck out at crazy angles. Of course, she had the *New York Times* in her arms, so Matt let her in.

She immediately dropped the newspaper on the couch, noticed Matt's coffee and went to the kitchen to pour herself a cup. "How come you get room service, and I had to go to the main house to get my paper?"

"I don't know. I didn't even order it. I thought you might have dropped it off."

Sam walked back in from the kitchen with her mug. She was shaking her head. "Nope. If it hadn't been for the paper, I would still be in bed."

Matt sighed and moved the envelope, notes, and letter onto his desk. He could always look at them later. He started to flip through the paper section by section. "How did you get the paper out here anyway?"

Sam sat on the couch and sipped her coffee. "I have my ways. Give me entertainment."

Matt slid the section toward her and took the sports section for himself. They settled in and read in comfortable silence for a while until Sam spoke. "I think I finally have a plan."

Matt lifted his head from the paper and smiled with relief. "Oh thank god."

"Did you know that Ben is escorting Jade to a retirement dinner honoring her father?"

Matt had not known, and it didn't make him happy to find out now. He frowned at the news. Sam smiled smugly, which made Matt frown harder. She was supposed to be on his side, but seemed to relish delivering the bad news. "How do you know this?"

Sam shrugged, "I talked to him, to Ben. I was fishing for some angle, anything useful and he seems to have a lot of information about everything. He's really a pretty great guy. I kind of like him ..."

Matt's patience grew thin. "The plan?"

"Well, I did a little digging and the dinner is honoring Doctor Sawyer, but the Board of Regents also turned it into a fundraiser for Doctor Sawyer's pet project, the Library of Antiquities."

Matt's scowl turned into a look of speculation. "So, you don't have to be invited to attend?"

Sam shook her head. "No, as a matter of fact, you already purchased two tickets to attend the event."

"Two tickets, huh?"

Sam batted her lashes coquettishly at Matt and faked a pleased gasp. "Why, I'd love to go!"

Matt shot her a wide grin. This plan was starting to have potential. He was pretty sick of sitting back and playing the sensitive guy. That strategy was turning out to be extremely lame. In what he supposed was typical male fashion, he was ready to take action. Get on the court. A fundraiser was right up his alley. Thanks to his mother's training and years of dance lessons, Matt was a natural at these events. He was damned charming and looked good in a tux. Or so he'd been told.

He nodded at Sam and she waggled her eyebrows at him. Let's see if they could goad Jade into dancing with him. Or more. He leaned back into the cushions of the couch and stretched his legs out. "Of course, everyone knows how much I love books. Naturally, I would become a sponsor."

Sam smiled. "No, not a sponsor, an *angel*. The angel table is closer to Doctor Sawyer's table, and besides, you don't want to look like a cheap ass in front of her dad."

Matt laughed and wrapped Sam in a great big bear hug. "I love you so much. I don't even want to know how you paid for it."

Sam turned her head so that her cheek was smushed against Matt's chest. "I have at least three of your credit card numbers on file."

Matt laughed.

# Chapter 19

*Hudson River Valley*
*September 12, 1616*

*Dearest Mother,*

*I am so happy to tell you that Alsoomse and I are finally wed. The wedding was a breathtaking event. It was, perhaps, not the most elegant of settings, at least not by society standards. The ceremony itself was a simple one. It is her people's custom to exchange gifts with the parents of the bride, and I was so proud to be able to give them some of the beautiful golden goblets. I hope they will use them in ceremonies and pass them down to our children and our children's children.*

*They have no custom of a ring exchange, and indeed, Alsoomse rarely wears adornments, but for the wedding she had a simple beaded headdress and agreed to wear the leaf ring. It was important to me to be able to give her a gift, a small token that in no way can adequately express my feelings for her. It was important to me that she wear it, and she made the loving concession to do so.*

*She and I were in complete agreement about the wedding site. Her people have a reverence for the land, for nature, that I have come to appreciate fully. It was decided that we would hold the ceremony outdoors. We spent many days wandering hand in hand around the lake looking for just the right spot, just the right view. In the end, we both agreed on a high ledge overlooking the water. It was a favorite spot for Alsoomse to sit and dream, even as a young girl. It was her first choice and after a great deal of searching, we realized there was no better spot. The event was scheduled for sunset and, I must confess, I spent much of the day feeling restless and out-of-sorts. The day seemed to move slowly, and I felt the way a child does on the eve of Christmas.*

*Finally, the time came and we walked hand in hand to the high clearing at the edge of the lake. We were accompanied by her family and by Pierre, who stood for me as my best man. The sun sent glittering bands of light across the lake's surface as we said simple words of commitment and prayer. The last moments of the ceremony were spent watching the sun sink down below the peaks across the lake. Those final rays turned the water orange and red and glinted gold off Alsoomse's hair. In the fading light, the mountain ridge turned from deep midnight blue to black. It was a wonderful show of nature's beauty, and I am certain I will remember it with my dying breath.*

*You were missed dearly, and I wish with all of my heart that you could have been here. I'm sure that my description does not do the event justice, but hope that it gives your heart joy to hear of ours.*

*My love to you and the family,*

*Adam Cartwright*

• • •

The day of the dinner arrived and Jade was a nervous wreck. She had pretty much managed to stay as far away from the university as she could since the day she broke it off with Nick and quit attending classes. She was willing to look like a chicken if it meant being as far away from Nick and Stacy as possible. It had turned out for the best. By leaving school, she'd discovered her heart was in her art and jewelry making and not in the classroom.

Now she was going to spend an evening in the company of professors she hadn't seen in years, some of whom had known her as a child. It was probable that Nick would be there, too, kissing butt and vying for whatever accolades would guarantee him a tenured position at the university within the next fifteen years. Where there was Nick, there was Stacy, so it was inevitable that she would be in attendance. This meant that there would be questions about Matt and why Jade's "fiancé" was not her escort.

If it weren't for that, Jade wouldn't have picked the dress she did. If she was going to have to tell the truth and be humiliated, she at least wanted to look great doing it. Technically, the dress was for Stacy's benefit and not Ben's. Jade thought it might be a little shallow, but Meg insisted it was perfectly justified. She just hoped that Ben didn't get the wrong idea. It was *that* kind of dress. The kind that gave men wrong ideas.

Jade grabbed her clutch and was just about to leave her cabin when her most recently made bracelet caught her eye. It was her woven branches idea done in gold and formed into a wide, Wonder Woman style cuff. Maybe it wouldn't deflect bullets, but with Stacy there, she might need to deflect verbal barbs. Jade grabbed it and slid it onto her wrist before going out the cabin door.

•••

Matt was a bit nervous as he shot his cuff and straightened his tie. He reached up to run his hands through his hair but stopped short. Sam had spent a good twenty minutes messing it up just so and had expressly forbidden him from touching it. She hadn't let him shave either, and he had a bit of stubble that he found annoying but she insisted was very *GQ*. He was getting the idea that Sam was much more mercenary than he had thought, and that what looked like effortless seduction on her part might be more artful than he imagined. He slid a money clip into his jacket pocket and checked his watch. The limousine was scheduled to arrive in ten minutes and he still had to walk to Sam's cabin to pick her up.

Matt left his cabin and turned right down the path. He wished he were turning left, toward Jade's cabin. He wished he were picking her up, sharing the limo with her, walking into the ballroom with her, sitting next to her at dinner, holding her hand, and running the pad of his thumb across her pulse on the inside of her wrist. He felt like an idiot. Here he was, picking up a fabulously beautiful woman who was charming, witty, funny, and nice, but he couldn't be less interested. Sam was his dearest friend, and he loved her. Yet Jade took his breath away. He felt like he wouldn't breathe easy again until she was one hundred percent his.

He got to Sam's cabin and knocked. She threw open the door and flung her arm out to the side. "Ta-dah!" she shouted.

Matt looked her up and down. Her dress was a one-shouldered, sleeveless sheath with some sort of origami-like pleating and a hemline just above her knees. It was trendy and notable and would definitely turn heads. Matt smiled and nodded. "Very nice, Parker."

"Why, thank you, McLaughlin." Sam gave a little curtsy and then looked Matt over. "Good, you didn't touch your hair."

Matt slid his hands into his pockets and struck a pose. "Don't I get a compliment?"

Sam smiled devilishly. "Yeah, you look real pretty."

Matt grinned and returned the volley. "Well, at least one of us should."

Sam punched his shoulder and then turned back toward her cabin. "Just let me grab my bag and then I'm ready."

They walked back down the path and across the main lawn with Sam leaning on Matt to keep her heels from sinking into the thick grass. By the time they reached the parking area, the limousine was just pulling up. The driver got out and opened the door for Sam. Matt smiled to himself as she slid into the car. Matt was guessing that limos and evening wear were not the standard at Lakehaven.

•••

Ben and Jade arrived at the university promptly at seven. The dinner was taking place in what was once the original university library. A new, modern library had been built on the other side of campus and this one had become the antiquities library. It was a grand, old structure with a ballroom downstairs and the books housed on the second floor.

Tonight the event organizers had pulled out all the stops, so rather than making their guests park in the parking lot and enter through the front parlor, a valet had been set up at the front left corner of the building and a carpeted walkway ran along the side of the building to the patio. Ben jumped out of the car, handed his keys to the valet, and rushed around the front of his car to help Jade out. It wasn't a real date, but Ben and Jade were friends, and she was grateful for his consideration and effort. He offered his arm, and Jade took it as they made their way down the carpet.

Jade took a deep breath and forced a smile. "Well, here goes nothing."

Ben looked down at her with concern and gave her arm a squeeze with his other hand. "It'll be fine."

At the end of the walkway, a bar had been set up and students wanting to make some extra money were dressed in white shirts and black slacks to pass trays of hors d'oeuvres. Heat lamps were scattered about, and old iron streetlamps at each corner of the patio provided some light. Behind the bar, a wall of leaded glass doors and windows spilled light from the ballroom to the outside, washing the patio in a soft glow.

Jade looked around for familiar faces but didn't see any. Ben spotted the bar and asked Jade for her order before heading that way. It didn't look like Nick and Stacy had arrived yet, so she figured it was safe to be left alone. Jade found a small cocktail table and perched herself on one of the high stools around it. While she waited for Ben to return, she looked around.

This building had always been one of her father's favorites. On one side of the patio, beyond the glass doors, was the ballroom. On the other side was a wide lawn that transitioned to a traditional English garden. The ballroom was a beautiful old room with recently restored parquet flooring, intricate moldings and woodwork, as well as the original leaded glass doors and windows. There was constant arguing among the regents, alumni, and even some faculty as to whether some of the land should be used to expand the original law library, which was small and outdated but sat adjacent to the soft expanse of lawn. So far, the alumni and Professor Sawyer had prevailed, and the ballroom and its grounds were perfectly preserved. There were, of course, some minor concessions to modernity, but for the most part, the grounds remained elegant and enchanting.

Ben returned with their drinks: a dry martini for Jade and a beer for himself. They were even serving the beer in tall pilsner glasses rather than bottles. Ben raised his glass toward Jade and toasted, "Here's to averting disaster."

Jade laughed and touched the rim of her glass to Ben's. "I'll drink to that. If it all goes to hell tonight, at least I'll have a good time on the way."

Ben smiled down at her. "That's the spirit."

A waiter came by with little crab puffs and Jade took two. Ben declined, which made Jade feel like a pig. She probably was only supposed to eat carrot sticks or something. She popped one in her mouth anyway.

Ben looked around. "They did a good job."

Jade nodded but couldn't say anything. The hors d'oeuvres were bigger than they looked and her cheeks puffed out around the mouthful of food. She put her hand up in front of her mouth in what she hoped was a dainty fashion.

"I always liked this part of campus."

Jade nodded again. She finally swallowed the mouthful then sipped at her martini as she looked off at the lawn over Ben's shoulder. "It feels weird being back. It's only been three years, but seems much longer." Jade shrugged. There were things that happened to her when she was six that she could remember as if it were yesterday. Yet everything that had happened here on campus and had seemed so terrible, so dramatic at the time, now seemed like a dream. "I've got these vague memories, but it's like they aren't really mine. Like they're someone else's memories."

Ben nodded like he got it. "*Meerschaum.*"

Jade quirked an eyebrow at Ben. "*Gesundheit?*"

He waved his hand in the air in front of her. "It's German. Means sea foam. Memories are like sea foam."

"Okay, yeah, they're—"

"Elusive?"

"Foamy." Jade bit into the second crab puff.

Ben took a swig of beer. They were chewing and swallowing, respectively, when Ben's eyes latched onto something over her right shoulder.

Jade heard her before she saw her, and purposely didn't turn around. She placed the half eaten crab puff on a napkin on the table and picked up her martini. She thought about taking a swig but was worried she'd end up choking on it in front of Stacy. Things would probably be bad enough without that.

"Oh my God! Jade! I didn't know *you* would be here!"

*At my father's retirement party? Really?* Jade swiveled in her seat and glanced at Stacy. She was dressed in red and covered in sequins. It was extremely … festive. Jade deadpanned, "Surprise."

Stacy got right down to business. "Where's your fiancé?" She scoped the patio eagerly.

Ben's expression was guarded. "Hey, Stace. Where's Nicky?" Stacy hated the nicknames and Jade knew Ben used them on purpose. Jade wasn't sure if she was grateful for Ben's loyal effort, or if she wanted him to just let it go.

"*Nick,*" Stacy put extra emphasis on his name, "is parking the Benz. He'll be here in a minute. "Maybe they'll run into each other in the parking lot."

Jade's smile was tight. "Matt isn't here."

Stacy nodded. It was weird that she wasn't as hostile as Jade expected. In fact, rather than being smug, she looked sorry that he wasn't there.

"Look, Stacy, I should tell you … "

Stacy was still scanning the patio with her eyes, but finally returned her attention back to Jade. "Oh, don't worry, I already know. I should be embarrassed that I didn't recognize him at first, but when he mentioned that your wedding planner was Eve Stanford, I just knew he had to be *somebody*. I had to look up references to her and Lady Carlyle before I came across a picture of him. Honestly Jade, I can't believe you didn't tell me. Riley McLaughlin! No wonder you were both acting so strangely that night. I'm sure he has to be back and forth to Manhattan all the time. It's too bad he couldn't make tonight. When you two have time, Nick and I will have to have you over for dinner. Can you imagine?"

*Oh, yeah, I can imagine* … Jade almost shuddered at the thought, but that didn't stop Stacy who was apparently on a roll. "Dinner with *the* Riley McLaughlin?" Stacy laughed. "Well, I guess you can!"

Jade sighed and nodded. She thought about setting her straight but couldn't muster up the energy. "Yes."

Stacy was back to scanning the patio. It seemed if Matt wasn't going to be here, she had bigger fish to fry. "Oh, is that Professor Gaines? Nick and he will be working together on some research. I'd better go and say hello!" She paused for a moment, and Jade was afraid that she was going to go in for a BFF hug and cheek kiss. But apparently even Stacy saw the absurdity of that and settled for a tidy little wave and a wink as she strutted away, her next victim firmly in sight.

Ben took a sip of his beer. His eyebrows were sky high over the rim of the glass.

"Shut up." Jade glared at him.

"What? I didn't say a thing."

Jade's parents arrived shortly after that. Jade hadn't even had time to finish her martini. Jade's mother saw her immediately and headed in her direction while her father made a side trip to the bar. Her mother was wearing a loose fitting, flowing dress that looked vintage and perfectly fit her personality. Kiki Sawyer was a gentle hippie who happened to have a spine of steel, but she always dressed to suit her whimsical side.

She swept in to give Jade a kiss on the cheek and to wrap Ben in a big hug.

"Hi, Mom."

Kiki smiled as she looked Jade over. "Wow, that is quite the stunning back view!" She looked over at Ben. "Is there something you two want to tell me?"

Ben and Jade shook their heads simultaneously. "No way, Mrs. Sawyer! You scare me," Ben said. Kiki laughed, and it was a warm, rich sound that reminded Jade of chocolate chip cookies right out of the oven.

Jade sighed. "No, Mom. Nick's here, and I just wanted to be petty."

Kiki nodded. "Good girl! It's dramatic, but without causing a scene. Although sometimes a scene is just what's needed."

Jade rolled her eyes. "What, are you twelve?"

Kiki nodded. "Definitely young at heart."

Jade continued. "Anyway, Stacy has the scene thing covered."

"Well, I'm just glad you've got your spirit back. I hated to see you so … " Jade's mom waved her hand around in lieu of actually completing the sentence.

Jade nodded. *Yeah, I got my spirit back all right. Just in time to have it trampled again.*

"Here you are, one Tequila Sunrise." Jade's father handed Kiki her drink and leaned down to kiss Jade on the top of her head. "How's my Pumpkin?"

Jade smiled at her father. He was looking distinguished around the edges but still very handsome. "Good, Dad. Are you ready for your big night?"

Joel Sawyer shrugged. "Nothing to do but enjoy myself. The organizing committee did all of the hard work, setting everything up and recruiting generous benefactors."

Kiki chimed in. "You should see the ballroom! It's packed with tables, and at least half of the guests are here to support the antiquities library. You're leaving a fine legacy, Joel."

Ben raised his eyebrows. "I'm surprised that they found that many people to support the cause. Lakehaven isn't exactly populated by people in love with old books."

"Thankfully, the committee looked a little further than Lakehaven for supporters. Once Joel came up with the idea, the planning committee ran with it. They could raise money for their cause without looking like they were asking for themselves, not to mention invite the press to do a special interest story." Kiki patted Joel's hand, which rested on her shoulder. Joel was not usually someone who loved being the center of attention.

Joel smiled ruefully. "Hey, I don't mind being the poster boy for their cause. It was my idea. As long as they focus on the library and not me. The idea of an event or an article dedicated to me makes me cringe."

"Well, Dad, you are a fine looking poster boy."

Joel struck a pose. He looked like a parody of a male model, reminding Jade of the movie, *Zoolander*.

She laughed so hard that she almost snorted martini out of her nose.

Her dad grinned at her, still holding his pose. "It's the tux, isn't it?"

When she could speak again, she said, "Yeah, Dad. It's the tux."

# Chapter 20

"Okay, let's rock and roll." Sam smoothed the skirt of her dress as she slid across the seat to the door. The limo hadn't even rolled to a stop, but she was not, as a rule, a very patient person.

Her eagerness made Matt smile. He was just as impatient to get to the fundraiser, to see Jade, to dance with her, to talk with her. He just hid it better.

Sam pushed the door open just as the limo driver slid to a stop. The driver shot Matt a questioning look in the rear-view mirror. He was trained to get out and open the door for passengers, but Matt just shrugged and waved him off. Matt slid out of the car and took Sam's arm. The two were a stunning picture as they made their way down the carpet to the patio.

The evening had gone from pale blue to midnight, and glowing lamps led the way to the outdoor area where drinks were being served to a mostly older crowd. Matt's eyes scanned the guests, grouped in threes and fours and scattered among the tall cocktail tables that dotted the slate patio. He spotted Jade talking to an older couple with Ben at her side.

Her hair was swept up in an artful mess with tendrils of it brushing the nape of her neck. Her back was framed by silver stitching that trimmed the deep "V" at her waist. Thin straps tied at her neck held the top of the dress in place. In between was a breathtaking expanse of creamy skin and the delicate curve of her spine. There was no artifice or seduction in her pose, but she sat strait with her shoulders squared. The image of her sitting there, smiling up at this older man, probably her father, was so natural, simple, and real.

Matt froze. Whatever he thought he was doing here, whatever his intentions, they were suddenly swept out of his mind by a tsunami of emotion—desire, caring, and a healthy dose of lust to boot. There was love and admiration in her eyes as she looked at her father. Ridiculously, Matt felt a surge of jealousy. In that moment, he would have traded his millions if she would look at him that way. Then her father struck a silly pose and Jade threw her head back and laughed. The laugh was full of life, rich and open with no reserve. It was so purely her that he felt something tighten in his chest, in his throat.

*Love.*

He felt warmth wash over him and he swore his heart stopped beating. He suddenly understood the term heart stoppingly beautiful. She was and he wanted her, all of her, the laughter and arguing and all of it. He wanted it so powerfully, with such conviction that the whole idea of making Jade jealous and faking anything seemed ludicrous. He was sure that his feelings were all over his facc. This was not going to work.

Sam touched his arm, and he almost jumped. He had forgotten she was there. She smiled up at him, and he blinked at her.

"Uh, hello, anyone home?"

He shook his head. "This is not going to work."

Sam shrugged. "I never let the possible complete and utter failure of a project dissuade me."

"Which is why you are my manager?"

"That's right baby, and don't you forget it."

Matt managed to pull his gaze away from Jade's gorgeous back. He smiled down at Sam and took a deep breath. "Okay, let's do this."

Sam reached for his hand and gave it a friendly squeeze. "Crash and burn, baby, crash and burn."

"*Ohmigod!* Riley McLaughlin!" The dulcet tones of Stacy's shriek carried clearly across the patio to where Sam and Matt stood. Many of the guests swiveled their heads to watch as she barreled across the patio with her arms open. "It's so great to see you again!"

Sam winced and glared up at Matt. Their plan had not included being outed by a blonde bomb who was about to detonate all over them. Luckily, Matt was highly experienced at deflecting overeager females. There was nothing he could do about her announcement, though. They could already hear the murmurs traveling through the crowd.

Matt had immediately dialed in his paparazzi face, which was a dazzling smile combined with an inscrutable expression. It looked great in photos, and had the added benefit of making it impossible to tell what he was thinking.

Sam beamed up at Matt. "I know what you're thinking."

Matt turned toward Sam with a quirked brow.

Sam smiled smugly and quirked one of her own delicately shaped brows back at him.

He sighed. "Please?"

"Okay, but only because I hate to see a grown man beg."

"Liar."

Sam grinned and shot forward to intercept Stacy. She grabbed Stacy by the arm and swiveled her toward the bar, talking as she went. "Hi! I'm Samantha Parker, Mr. McLaughlin's manager. I'm afraid I don't know anyone here. You, however, seem to know just about everyone! I was hoping you could make some introductions …"

Matt smiled at Sam's retreating back and turned to find Jade.

•••

If Matthew was good looking in t-shirts and jeans, he was nothing less than devastating in a tux. A perfectly fitted, molded to his broad-shouldered, tapered waist, narrow hipped, long-legged body tux. Jade couldn't breathe. Or maybe it was just the shock of seeing him there. Standing next to Samantha Parker. Who, it was now official, was in fact a Bond Girl. As in straight out of the *007* sex kitten handbook. Or maybe she had a team of costumers, make-up artists, hair stylists, trainers, and personal chefs to get her looking that good. A good head thunk was in order here. And then Sam moved away from Matt, who was now walking straight toward Jade.

He wasn't smiling, but had honed in like a heat-seeking missile. Clearly, Jade was his target. Matthew McLaughlin in motion was pure male predator. Jade tried to keep from looking dazed at the sight of him headed in her direction. She smiled weakly and locked her feet around the rung of the stool to keep herself from falling off. Or melting in a puddle. Or throwing herself at him. Any of those reactions were possible, and each would have been bad in their own way.

Partygoers' heads swiveled to watch as Matthew crossed the patio to Jade. It made her nervous to have all those eyes directed toward her, but if it had any effect on the famous Matthew *Riley* McLaughlin, it didn't show. She was used to a quiet, simple life and didn't think she could ever get used to the idea of people watching her every move. The staring thing was particularly unnerving when her thoughts were leaning toward mentally undressing Matt.

He stepped up in front of her and slid his hands into his tuxedo pockets. It was an elegant move, calculated to charm. "I have something for you." His voice was deep, enticing.

Jade resisted the temptation to roll her eyes. She glanced where his hands had slid into his pockets. "Is it in your pants?"

Ben coughed, but it was really just an ill-disguised laugh. Jade shot him a look. Ben held up his hands in supplication. "Hey, who wants a drink? I'm headed for the bar." He made his exit.

Matt didn't bat an eye. He managed a complete poker face and shot back a response. "No, on my desk."

"Hmm … a fountain pen."

"No, guess again."

"Animal, vegetable, or mineral?"

There was a brief pause, then he said, "Vegetable."

Jade fought a smile as she thought through some of the possibilities. She wasn't really willing to voice any of them aloud. "Uhm … okay. I'm all out of guesses. You'll just have to show me."

Matt didn't even smile. "Okay, you'll have to come by my cabin."

Jade feigned indifference. "Name the time."

Matt took a step forward. "Tonight."

Jade checked her watch, which would've looked cool if she were wearing one. "I'm a bit busy this evening."

Matt stepped forward again. There was barely an inch between them. "Later."

Jade swallowed. It was amazing how much saliva one martini could produce. "I might be available then."

Whatever Matt was going to say was interrupted by a petite blonde, aggressively dressed in a black suit. "Mr. McLaughlin, may I have a word with you?"

There was a moment where Matt said nothing. He was so singularly focused on Jade, his eyes locked on hers, the heat between them smoldering. The reporter cleared her throat, and Matt turned toward her. His smile was polite, with just enough charm to make the reporter's previously serious expression break into a smile.

He nodded toward her and the young woman thrust out her hand. "Lindsay Sands, from *the Allegheny Press*. May I ask a few questions?" She pulled a small recorder from her jacket pocket and held it out.

Matt shook her hand and graciously agreed.

"Okay." The reporter checked her notebook. "You are known to be a strong supporter of the arts. What was it that drew you to tonight's cause?"

Matt's gaze slid to Jade and swept down her torso before returning to the reporter. Jade could see the impish gleam in his eye as he answered Ms. Sand's question. "I am particularly fond of books."

The reporter nodded, as if Matt's answer was expected and moved on to the next question. "You spend most of your time in Manhattan. This seems rather far to travel for a good cause. Wouldn't it have been easier to just mail a check?"

Jade started to get nervous. Despite the fact that *the Allegheny Press* was a smaller local paper, this reporter was shrewd. She didn't badger or harangue, but instead gently posed her questions. She was clearly fishing for a story but managed to do it in a manner that seemed innocuous and probably was anything but. Lindsay Sands looked young, but Jade was reassessing her capabilities. The whole thing made Jade uncomfortable. Matt's answers were being recorded, but Jade knew the reporter could take quotes out of context. If the potential minefield bothered Matt, Jade couldn't see any signs. It was just one more example of how thoroughly Matt belonged in a different league.

He smiled. "Of course, it would be easier, Ms. Sands, but then you wouldn't be here." His voice was warm and he leaned on the "you" in a way that was pure flirt, but it didn't make Jade the least bit jealous. It was too smooth and with no heat. Still, he managed to make the reporter blush. "I have a lot of respect for small academic communities and the legacy that they provide. They deserve acknowledgement for their efforts. If my attendance here tonight brings some attention to the cause of this university or any of the other groups who continue to support the ongoing existence of the arts in our society, then it is worth it to go a bit out of my way to be here tonight."

It occurred to Jade that she was not so much watching Matt answering questions, but rather watching *the* Riley McLaughlin give an interview. He was really quite good at it.

"And what about your next book? Can we expect that soon?"

"Next spring."

"What is it about?"

Matt shook his head. "When we're closer to the release date, my publisher will put out a press release with all of the relevant details. Until then, I'm afraid I really can't give you an answer. You wouldn't want the surprise spoiled, would you?"

Lindsay Sands grinned conspiratorially. "Actually, it's kind of my job to spoil the surprises."

Matt slid his hands back into his pockets and shifted his weight back onto his heels. "Ahhh, well, I'm sorry I can't help you then."

Lindsay shrugged and clicked off her recorder before slipping it back into her purse. "It's all right. I've got enough to keep my editor happy." She shook Matt's hand and turned to shake hands with Jade. "How rude of me. I didn't even introduce myself. I'm Lindsay Sands."

Jade shook hands with her. "Nice to meet you."

Lindsay tilted her head. "I'm sorry. I didn't catch your name."

"I'm Jade."

The reporter tilted her head back toward Matt and then turned to Jade again. "How do you two know each other?"

*Oh crap!* Jade had no idea how to answer. It had never occurred to her that the reporter would ask her anything. Particularly anything relating to Matt. She was terrified that she would give away some detail that Matt would rather not have published in the paper, but the truth was that she wasn't sure what information he wanted kept private. She glanced up at Matt with panic.

He quickly came to her side and took her hand, laying it on his forearm. "Jade and I are friends." Jade smiled a silent thank you up at Matt.

The reporter raised an eyebrow but didn't question him. "Well, so nice to meet you, Jade. And thank you for the interview Mr. McLaughlin."

"My pleasure."

The reporter left and Matt sighed. "I'm so sorry about that …"

Jade wasn't quite sure what he was apologizing for. The reporter? The interruption? His answers? Before she could even ask, the event coordinator swept onto the patio, announced that the ballroom was open, and invited the guests to take their seats.

As the guests filed into the room it was clear that, though everyone was decked out in their finest, not everybody had the same idea of finest. Some of the older professors had suits that looked to be forty years old. One professor, political science if Jade remembered correctly, paired suede Birkenstock clogs with his spanking new Hugo Boss suit. Which, strangely enough, kind of worked. It was the ultimate in not trying too hard.

The younger faculty candidates dressed the part, and Nick looked fresh out of a Brooks Brothers catalogue. His shirt was lightly starched and so was his hair, just enough to keep its shape but not look too done. He was tan, but not too much. Jade thought that perhaps he had a few more crinkles around his eyes, but they looked good. She wasn't sure if he would have come to talk to her on his own, but since Stacy was on his arm and tugging him straight toward Matt, it looked like he would at least have to say hello.

Stacy screeched to a stop in front of them and beamed a wide toothy smile at Matt. "Honey, you remember Riley McLaughlin, don't you?"

Nick nodded and shook hands. "I thought you were Matt."

Matt nodded. "Matthew Riley McLaughlin."

Nick smiled. "Much better than my middle name." He caught Jade's gaze and his eye crinkles deepened.

Jade smiled back.

Stacy's smile was tight. "I think it's royal."

Nick laughed. "Royally stupid."

Matt lifted his eyebrows but didn't ask.

"Romanov," Nick and Jade said at the same time. Nick continued, "My dad was a professor of Russian history. Thus … Nicholas Romanov Halloway."

Jade was still smiling at Nick. He really was nice. She started to remember all of the reasons why she had dated him in the first place. "I remember you used to joke that the only thing missing from your name was 'the third.'"

Nick nodded. "Thankfully, none of my other ancestors were crazy enough to go that route. It was bad enough we had two poodles named Alexander and Anastasia. Which, I might mention, made me the least cool kid on the block."

Stacy leaned into Nick with her chest and rubbed against him like a cat. "Well, you're the coolest kid on my block."

Nick smiled at her and slid his arm around her waist. "Thanks, honey."

Jade waited, but she didn't even have to suppress a shudder. They were smarmy and sweet, but Jade couldn't quite be as annoyed or as cynical as she wanted to be. Apart from his falling in love with her roommate, Nick was a pretty decent guy. When she looked at the Ken and Barbie pair, she actually thought they made a good couple. They both wanted the same things: he wanted a secure, tenured position in a small university town, and Stacy wanted to be a big fish in the insular community of a small pond university. Jade hated to admit it, but they were perfect for each other.

Stacy turned to Matt. "Well, I'm so glad you could make it tonight after all. Jade seemed to think you wouldn't be here."

Matt shrugged. "Last minute schedule change."

Stacy nodded knowingly. "I know how that is. Whirlwind life, huh?"

*As if.*

Matt nodded. "Mmhmm."

"Well, Nick and I would love to have you and Jade over for dinner next time you are in town. Wouldn't that be fun?"

*Uh, not.* Jade did have to suppress a shudder at that comment.

Matt raised both eyebrows at Jade before turning back to Stacy. "That is so kind of you, but we'd hate to impose on your incredibly busy schedule."

Stacy's smile widened. She was obviously not easily deterred. "Oh, nonsense. For you, we'll make time."

Nick finally saved the day. "Oh honey, I really want to make sure we get to sit next to Carl and Beverly. Could you grab us some seats at the table?"

Jade watched Stacy's indecision. To stay and schmooze with Matt or go and schmooze with Professor Paulssen and his wife? So much schmoozing, so little time. At least she utilized her skill set.

Stacy finally chose the path of least resistance and did what Nick had asked. She and Matt turned to watch Stacy's butt sway away from them.

To Jade's surprise, Nick didn't follow immediately. Instead, he turned and took both of her hands in his. "Jade, I should have said this a long time ago, but I'm sorry. I never set out to hurt you."

Jade nodded. "If you had said that a long time ago, I probably wouldn't have listened." She slipped her hands out of his and touched his face, once so familiar to her. "I'm sorry, too."

Nick nodded, his smile wistful, his eyes worried.

Jade dropped her hand. "It's really okay, Nick. It was hard at the time, but you made the right choice." Jade glanced over her shoulder at Stacy, who was enthusiastically chatting up Beverly Paulssen. When Jade turned back to Nick, he had followed her gaze and was nodding. Jade smiled at him. "You two are somehow right for each other, and I just want you to be happy."

Nick laughed. "I never thought I would hear you say that."

Jade's mouth twisted in a wry smile. "Neither did I."

Nick cleared his throat. "Well, I'd better … " He looked back at Stacy.

"Yeah."

Jade watched Nick as his broad back retreated into the ballroom, and he slipped up behind Stacy. He leaned down to say something to her and then pushed her chair in for her as she took a seat. Jade took a deep breath and blew it out. She smiled up at Matt. His expression was carefully neutral. Jade studied his face for signs of what he was thinking. "Okay, I give up. What's with the face?"

Matt blinked. "What face?"

Jade bent her arms at the elbows, rotated her torso stiffly back and forth and spoke in a monotone. "I am a robot. I have no expression."

Matt smiled at her antics. "Cute."

Jade nodded. "Sooo … ? What's with the poker face?"

Matt shrugged. "I don't know what you're talking about."

Jade narrowed her eyes at him. She took her forefinger and tapped it on her lip, considering him. Her eyes widened. "Were you jealous?"

Matt rolled his eyes. "I think we'd better take our seats now."

Jade broke into a wide grin. "You were! You, the great Riley McLaughlin, were jealous." She was practically dancing with glee.

Matt looked toward the ballroom. He didn't say a thing, but put his arm around Jade's waist and turned her toward the wide doors. He pulled her in close, plastering her to his side in a move that felt thrillingly proprietary. His hand rested in the small of her back. Her dress was low enough that his hand was warm on bare skin, and she felt heat pool low in her body at his touch. They entered the glittering ballroom, and Jade smiled. It looked like the evening might turn out fine after all.

# Chapter 21

The room was warmly lit with candlelight and softly glowing bulbs reflecting off crystal chandeliers. The chairs and tables were covered in ivory damask, which coordinated nicely with butter yellow accents. Yellow rose centerpieces and napkins complimented the pale yellow walls of the ballroom. Tables were scattered around a central dance floor, and in front was a low stage with a podium on one side, a band set up and a large screen behind.

Jade was seated at the head table with her mother and father. The dean of the School of Arts and Sciences, who was also Dr. Sawyer's boss, and the president of the university were seated there as well. Ben had already taken his seat and Matt reluctantly led Jade to her place beside him. Matt was seated at a table at the front of the ballroom, equally close to the dance floor as Jade's table, but to the left of it. Matt noted with satisfaction that Jade sat on the right side of her table, which faced his seat. When he moved to his table, he was pleased to see that Sam had chosen to sit on the left side of the round table so that Matt could see Jade without having to rubberneck. Sam was an expert strategist, which was why he loved her as a friend as well as a manager.

When Matt got to the table, Sam was already seated, so he unceremoniously plopped down next to her. She had her chin in her hand and was staring in Jade's direction.

Matt looked at her suspiciously. "I'm not going to have to compete with you for her affections am I?"

Sam jolted from her reverie and glanced up at Matt in surprise. "What?" She waved her hand around; it reminded him of a teacher wiping a chalkboard. "Oh, no … I was just thinking."

Matt nodded. "Well, don't hurt yourself."

Sam just glared at him. "How did operation Prince Charming go?"

Matt looked across to Jade's table. She was looking their way. He caught her eye and held her gaze. She didn't quite smile, but she didn't frown either. She licked her lips, maybe it was a nervous gesture, or maybe it was a conscious attempt to flirt, but it didn't matter. The end result was that Matt wanted to walk over to her table, grab her, and drag her back to his limo where he could kiss the living crap out of her. He reached for his water glass and took a sip instead. Then he turned back to Sam. "Not sure."

"Not sure?"

"Nope." Matt took another sip of water, but what he really wanted was two fingers of Glenfiddich. Maybe three.

Sam's brows pulled together. "You invited her over?"

Matt nodded.

"And she said … "

"She agreed to come later."

"Later what? Later tonight, later this month?"

"I don't know. I just said 'later,' and she said she might be available then." Matt's voice was steady but held the slightest hint of exasperation.

Sam looked incredulous. "You just said 'later'?"

"I meant later tonight, but it sounded better to just say 'later.' Less … eager."

Sam dropped her head forward and shook it. "For someone who works with words for a living, you are not good at communicating."

Matt looked around the room for a waiter. "I need a drink."

Sam put her hand on his arm. "I'm sorry. Look, it's okay; this can be fixed. You laid the groundwork, and she seemed receptive, right? She's a yes."

Matt sure as hell hoped so. What he really hoped for was a *yes, please, oh God, right now!* He looked around again. Where the hell was the waiter?

Sam continued. "So, now you'll just need to—Oh, holy hell!"

Matt had been looking over Sam's shoulder for any sign, any sign at all, of a waiter. He turned his attention back to her. "What?"

Sam swore again. "Your mother is here." Matt glowered at Sam, but she already had her hands up in surrender. "I swear, I didn't tell her about the dinner. Swear to God." She had three fingers held up in front of her.

Matt looked at her three fingers. "I think that's the Boy Scout oath."

"Fine, I swear to them, too. I had nothing to do with this. Oh, nice! Amanda Carmichael is just behind her." At that moment, they must have noticed Matt and Sam, because Sam's face suddenly broke into a wide smile, and she lifted her hand in the air and turned the three-fingered oath into an elegant little wave. "Okay, they're headed this way."

Matt muttered under his breath, "I *really* need a drink." He spotted a waiter across the room and waved him over. Unfortunately, his mother made it to their table first.

"Hello, Matthew."

Matt leaned over and kissed his mother's cheek. She was as put together as always, but Matt thought she looked a little tired.

"Hi, Mom."

"You remember Amanda, don't you?"

Matt pulled the chair out for his mother and once she was properly seated, turned to Amanda. He did, indeed, remember her. He leaned in and gave her a kiss on the cheek as well. "You've gotten taller."

She smiled up at him. "As have you."

Matt and Amanda had gone to the same private school in the city. For that matter, so had Samantha. The last time Matt had actually seen Amanda had been in high school. Back then, she had been gorgeous and popular and featured prominently in some of Matt's favorite fantasies. Some of that hadn't changed. He hadn't seen her since then, but she was still beautiful and from the updates his mother gave him, very successful. She ran an art gallery and was masterful at public relations. She had gone to Vassar and, again, according to the grapevine via Elizabeth McLaughlin, loved to read and was in a book club. He didn't remember her being a big bookworm in high school, but then he hadn't really run in the same circles as she had. Her chestnut hair was tightly coiled in a complicated knot at the nape of her neck, and her big blue eyes were framed by just the right amount of makeup to be dramatic but not overdone.

"It's been a long time. I'd ask what you've been up to, but my mom keeps me in the loop on these things." Matt shot a glance at his mother, but she just smiled up innocently at him.

"I'd ask what you've been up to, but I read the paper."

"Even the social pages?"

Matt had laced his question with a bit of disdain, but Amanda shot back a quick rejoinder. "Arts and Entertainment."

Matt smiled. Actually, he was a bit impressed. She wasn't interested in pandering to him or fawning over him. He pulled her chair out for her, and she slid into it effortlessly. He noticed that his mother had engineered it so that Amanda was in the seat next to him. Amanda had to know that his mother was manipulating everything, but her level of complicity was not clear.

Matt sat down next to her. "What brings you so far from home?"

Amanda blushed a bit but was still smiling. "Your mother invited me, and I accepted."

Elizabeth piped in. "I was worried that your social skills might shrivel and die. We haven't seen you in months."

The waiter finally arrived with a Glenfiddich for Matt and a martini for Sam. Matt took a sip of the whisky. "I thought it was like riding a bike, you never forget."

Elizabeth shook her head. "No. In your case, you become an absolute caveman. You are clearly an example of use it or lose it." She turned to the waiter. "I'll have a Pellegrino with lime."

"Champagne, please," Amanda ordered, and the waiter moved away.

Matt's smile was dry as he turned to Amanda. "Well, thank you for rescuing my imperiled social abilities."

Amanda's mouth quirked. "I consider it my civic duty."

Matt smiled at Amanda, but he thought he heard Sam mutter something under her breath.

. . .

Jade could barely follow the conversation at her table. She was focused on Matt two tables away, flanked by the most beautiful women she had ever seen. Sam looked modern in a one-shoulder dress made of satin that gleamed in the gold lights of the ballroom. The same light sent shots of caramel highlights through the chestnut hair of the woman to Matt's right. Matt said something to Sam and then turned to say something to the woman who smiled up at him in response. They had talked throughout the whole meal in a way that made Jade think that they knew each other. What she wanted to know was how and how well?

The whole tableau was out of *Lifestyles of the Rich and Famous*. Jade guessed that this wasn't the brunette's first fundraiser. Matt and the mystery woman were slick and glossy like pages of a magazine. *Fundraiser Quarterly*. Jade knew she could never be that. He had glanced in her direction several times throughout the dinner, but she had managed to look away in time to give the impression that she wasn't obsessively staring at him. Or the brunette. It was all she could do to maintain her dignity.

After dessert, her dad took the podium and gave a brief speech, which was followed by a video presentation highlighting the historical significance of the antiquities library. The president of the university thanked the generous benefactors for their support and the band started to play.

While Jade watched the stage, Sam came to their table and stood between Ben and Jade. "Are you enjoying yourselves yet?"

Ben grinned. "We are now."

Sam pressed her lips together but there was something teasing in her eyes. "So like a man, to answer for both of you."

Ben smirked. "Well, I am a man."

Sam just ignored the comment. "Jade, are you enjoying the evening?"

"I'm surviving."

Sam winced. "Ouch! That bad? Well, at least the evening's still young."

Jade looked horrified. Her hands flew up to her face. "Oh, no! You mean it could get worse?"

"I think it's about to get better." Sam noticed Jade's bracelet. "My God, that cuff is stunning."

Jade felt herself blushing. She ducked her head, pretending to glance at the object in question. It glittered in the softly lit ballroom, scattering beams of light across the white table linens. It was pretty. "Thanks," she muttered.

Ben jumped in. "It's her own design."

Sam gushed for a bit, but Jade didn't know how to respond, so she listened and smiled dumbly.

Eventually, Sam turned her attention back to Ben. She gave him a smug smile. "Dance with me."

Ben looked at Jade, then back at Sam. "Sorry, I'm already spoken for."

Jade started to protest, but Sam was already talking. "I guarantee you, she's about thirty seconds from being swept off of her feet." Sam's eyes flicked back toward the table she had come from. Jade followed the glance and could see Matt getting out of his seat.

Ben looked to Jade, who nodded. Ben narrowed his eyes. "What guarantees will you give me?"

"I guarantee you won't regret it."

"Money back guarantee?"

Sam gave a faux gasp. "What kind of girl do you think I am?"

Ben waggled his eyebrows. "I'm hoping my kind."

Sam extended her hand to him. "Just twirl me onto the dance floor, you jerk."

Ben turned to Jade. "You're sure?" Jade nodded. Ben stood and bowed to Sam. "My pleasure."

He took her hand and twirled her out onto the dance floor. What he lacked in elegance, he made up for in enthusiasm. Sam seemed to love every bit of it.

Jade watched them wistfully. There was something about Ben's face, beaming with happiness that just made her long for the same.

Just as Sam promised, Matt was walking toward her. His jacket fit him to perfection, molding to broad shoulders that tapered down to a narrow waist and hips. Perfectly fitted pants skimmed his long legs. Unfortunately, Jade had seen it all without the clothes and could vividly remember tracing most of his planes and angles with her tongue. Her pulse sped up just thinking about it. She was grateful she didn't have to think about the view of him walking away. Yet.

When Matt got there he didn't say a thing, but just extended his hand to her. She stood almost unbidden, an involuntary reaction, lured by lust and something more. She wanted to be mad at him, but for what? For talking to the woman seated next to him? He brought her out onto the dance floor and pulled her up against his chest. There was no distance between them, and she felt her body mold itself to his. Her whole being seemed to sigh, to relax into that perfect place. She was petite and felt his chin brush the top of her head as he tucked it against his shoulder. She felt the press of his hips against her stomach, moving her around the dance floor with ease. His hand on her lower back pulled her up against his strong thighs, and she flushed with want. Her back arched in response, and some primitive part of her brain begged for his hand to slide lower.

This was what good dancing felt like, his body leaning into her, each subtle move pushing her to counter. It was sex standing up, with clothes on and a bit of an audience.

Jade had trouble focusing, and it was lucky for her that he didn't try to talk at first. He just moved with her until she was breathless and sensitized from head to toe. If she had known he would be here, she might not have left so much skin bare for him to caress. Then again, maybe she would have. It was unfair because, though she could feel his muscled shoulder under her hand, there was a barrier of cloth between them. It left her feeling at a disadvantage, exposed. Her body shuddered.

Matt whispered into her ear, his breath warm there. "Cold?"

Jade's voice came out husky. "Warm."

He chuckled. It rumbled through his chest where her cheek rested, sending shivers down her spine. He moved her around the dance floor, using his body to guide hers smoothly, easily. It was a perfect moment.

Matt smiled down at her. "Jade, I … "

"Excuse me, Miss Sawyer?" a college-aged woman with a camera around her neck interrupted.

*Damn it! Jade, I … what? I want you? I have heartburn?* Jade sighed and turned to the student. "Yes?" Jade and Matt stopped moving, which was really a shame.

The photographer had the decency to look chagrined. "Sorry to interrupt. We wanted to take some pictures," she said, waving the camera around in front of her as if she needed to make it more clear, "with your father, for the alumni magazine and the local papers."

Jade looked at the woman. "Are you sure you wouldn't rather … " The media was definitely Matt's territory, and it felt odd to have to excuse herself for a photo op. Not to mention she would rather be in Matt's arms than having her picture taken.

The woman interrupted her thoughts. "Your father really wanted you in the pictures."

Jade looked up at Matt. "Sorry about this."

His look was searing, his voice deep. "You'll just have to make it up to me later."

Jade swallowed nervously and moved away with the photographer.

•••

Matt sighed as he watched Jade move away. This view of her shot a stab of longing through him. She was gorgeous in anything, but in that dress she was spectacular. It was black with silver threads forming a pattern in the material. The front was a halter, but the back view was pure hard on. She was bare from nape to the curve at the small of her back. Matt could only stare.

He didn't notice Amanda until she spoke. "You seem to be short a dance partner."

Matt turned to her slowly. She looked elegant and cool. He turned on the charm. It was a default with him at these types of events. He had been to so many of them in the past ten years that he had lost count. There were always beautiful women, one indistinguishable from another. Blonde, brunette, auburn, redhead, raven-haired, and all gorgeous, but none of them stood out. Until Jade. Still, the charm came as easily as breathing. "Are you volunteering?"

An artful smile slid across her face. "I'm quite good."

Matt's face was impassive. "No doubt." He took her into his arms and moved her around the floor.

"I wasn't sure you would say yes."

He lifted an eyebrow. "My mother taught me never to refuse a pretty woman."

Amanda grinned up at Matt. "Smart woman."

"Smart and obstinate."

Amanda winced. "I know she didn't exactly check with you when she invited me. I hope I'm not intruding on your evening."

Matt shook his head. "No harm. My mother didn't exactly know the whole situation here anyway."

"She told me she thought you were 'holing up' out here."

Matt laughed. "That's pretty accurate, actually."

Amanda's face softened. "She really cares about you, you know."

"Yeah, I know. Sometimes it's just exasperating."

Amanda tilted her face up at him and laughed. It was a charming sound that made him smile back at her. "My mother does the same stuff. There was this family dinner. It was just supposed to be family, my brother and sister and their spouses. She asked if I had a date. The answer was no. I mean, I was dating, just no one that I wanted to subject to the family dinner yet. Mother couldn't stand that I was going to show up solo and ruin the symmetry of her table, so she called up my uncle's cardiologist and invited him to dinner. She had never spoken to this man, not even once, and she invites him to eat with our family. He didn't know the first thing about us other than my uncle has a bad heart. Can you imagine?"

She was laughing throughout the story, and it was contagious. Matt laughed too. "Unfortunately, I can."

Amanda shook her head. "I can't imagine why he agreed to it."

"If your mother is anything like mine, she can probably be very … persuasive."

Amanda nodded. "I just didn't want you to think that I was part of your mother's plotting. I'm just here because I enjoy your company."

Matt returned the compliment. "Likewise."

Amanda gave him a seductive smile, heavy on the seducing. "A lot." She played her fingers lightly along his collar, occasionally brushing them against his neck. Her message was loud and clear. Now, the question was, what was he going to do about it?

# Chapter 22

"Okay Miss Sawyer, can you step a little closer to your father? Great. Now smile." The flash blinded Jade for a moment. She hoped her eyes were open for that one. "That was great. Let's get a few with Dean Cline and President Palmer, and then we're done."

Jade and her mother moved to the side while the photographers got their shots.

Kiki Sawyer sent her daughter a sidelong glance. "So … you and Riley McLaughlin … "

"He goes by Matt."

"And?"

Jade sighed. "I wish I knew. I like him. We like each other." She smiled at herself, at the gross understatement. She was head over heels in love, in over her head, out of her league, and about a hundred other clichéd phrases. She wasn't going to share any of that with her mother.

Kiki smiled. "That's nice. I understand he was looking at some of your father's papers."

Jade nodded. "Yes, the Cartwright stuff."

Kiki looked surprised. "Is he looking for the treasure?"

Jade shrugged. "Sort of. He's not all that serious about it. I mean, look at him, it's not like he needs the money." Jade gestured to where he was dancing with the brunette. She stuffed the sharp and sudden pang of jealousy down. Jade took a deep breath and turned back to her mother. "I really think it's more just research."

A small crowd had gathered around the photo op. Some were reporters waiting for their chance at an interview, others were faculty and spouses waiting for a chance to congratulate her father. One of the women standing close to Kiki and Jade smiled at them. "You must be so proud of your husband, Mrs. Sawyer."

Jade had been so intent on Matt and his dance partner that she hadn't noticed the other woman.

Kiki nodded. "I am. Not just because of tonight either. Not just his career."

The woman nodded. "I understand. He must be quite a husband."

Kiki beamed. "I can't complain."

The woman turned to Jade. "I saw you dancing with Riley McLaughlin earlier. Are you close?"

Jade shrugged. "Just friends."

The woman smiled. "Too bad. Did I hear you say he's been doing some research while he's here?"

Jade narrowed her eyes. "I'm sorry, who did you say you were?"

The woman stuck out her hand. "Mackenzie Whitman. I'm with the *Times*."

Jade took her hand and shook it. "I'm sorry; I'm not really authorized to say anything about Mr. McLaughlin."

Mackenzie nodded. "I completely understand. It's not really for a story actually. I'm just a big fan of his." The embarrassment showed in her smile. "It would be completely off the record."

Jade bit her lip and thought for a moment.

Mackenzie's eyes gleamed conspiratorially. "Did you read his last book? It was so amazing! I think I read the whole thing in two days, and that was while I was working. I just couldn't put it down. He's a remarkable writer."

Jade nodded. "When I found out who he was, I started reading some of his stuff that I hadn't read. He really knows how to keep your attention." *In more ways than one.*

Mackenzie laughed. "When you found out who he was! You mean you didn't recognize him at first?"

Jade blushed. "Yeah, I guess I don't read the society pages much."

"Or watch the entertainment shows."

Jade nodded. "That either."

Mackenzie smiled at Jade. "So, was he here long before you recognized him?"

Jade blushed. "Long enough."

Mackenzie grinned. "He must be hard at work on his next novel by now. I can't imagine what brought him out here. I guess there's a lot of history in the area. He loves to include a lot of history in his works; he's a bit of a history buff."

Jade smiled. "My dad, too."

Kiki piped in. "I remember the first summer your dad started looking into the Cartwright treasure. He was gone to the library for days at a time. He was obsessed."

Jade smiled at her mom. "I remember that, too. Matt reminds me of him."

Mackenzie raised an eyebrow. "Matt. You must be good friends."

Jade blushed again. "I don't know. We've talked a lot and his enthusiasm for the myth of the Cartwright treasure is kind of contagious. We've taken it on as a pet project together."

Mackenzie pursed her lips. "Do you think he'll use any of that in his next book?"

Jade shrugged. "It's possible."

Mackenzie smiled. "Well, I don't mean to keep you from the party. I guess I'd better go get some interviews, if I want to keep my job."

Kiki shook her hand, followed by Jade. "Nice to meet you."

"Nice to meet you," Mackenzie spoke over her shoulder as she made her way toward the crowd of VIPs.

•••

"Thank you for the dance."

The music had stopped and Amanda pulled back out of Matt's arms. Matt was surprised. "Are you stranding me up out here on the dance floor?"

Amanda laughed. "You know what they say, 'leave them wanting more.' Besides, I'm sure someone else will come along and rescue you."

Matt glanced around, dubious. "With my luck, a reporter will corner me and grill me about my latest project. He slipped his hand behind her elbow and led her back toward their table.

"You seem to handle them pretty well."

He shrugged. "A lot of practice, I guess."

Amanda nodded. "It's definitely gotten easier for me the more I do it."

There was a pause in the conversation. Matt looked down at Amanda and she smiled up at him. "Well, I've really got to get back to the city. I'm hanging a new artist and … I'd love to—" They stood by their table, and she took a moment to reach into her clutch and pull out a business card. She flipped it over; on the back was a phone number, handwritten. "Here's my home number. If you ever want to get together, I'd love to spend some time with you."

Matt took the outstretched business card and slid it into his pocket.

Amanda bowed her head. "Good night, Mr. McLaughlin."

Matthew mock saluted her. "Good night, Miss Carmichael."

• • •

Jade went to the bar for her second martini. There was a bar inside, but they had also left the one set up on the patio. She went out there for the cool air and crickets' song as much as for the drink. As the bartender mixed her martini, Jade heard a voice behind her.

"Scotch on the rocks."

His voice slid over her like velvet, thick and deep. He was right behind her, and she could almost feel his warm breath on her. She wanted to lean back into him right then and there but held herself still.

The bartender turned his back to them, and Matt took the opportunity to slide his hand across the small of her back. It was an intimate touch, whispered across her sensitive skin, and it echoed other intimate moments they had shared.

Matt took his drink off the bar and slipped his arm around her shoulder as if to lead her away. They had been interrupted earlier, and Jade could sense that Matt wanted to continue their conversation, if not their dance. She had left a lot unsaid between them. Maybe it was time to remedy that.

They moved away from the bar, but rather than lead her back into the ballroom, Matt turned toward the lawn. He stopped at a table toward the edge of the patio and pulled out a chair for her.

"Thank you for coming to support my dad."

Matt smiled. "I was worried you might be mad at me."

Jade sighed. "No." She was playing with the stem of her martini glass with one hand, fishing for the olive with the other. She stopped to look up at him. "I'm actually glad."

He raised his eyebrows. "How glad?"

She smiled tentatively. "Pretty glad."

"I'm glad you're glad."

Jade laughed.

Matt grinned. "I guess there were a lot of surprise appearances tonight. My mom was here."

Jade nodded. "Sitting at your table, next to the brunette."

"I didn't know either of them was coming."

"Who is she?"

Matt shook his head. "Not anyone I know well. She moves in my mother's circle, and my mother just thought … "

"You two looked good dancing together." There was no accusation in her tone, just a question.

"Not as good as you and I feel dancing together." Matt's eyes met Jade's and held her there. In his gaze was every moment she had spent in his arms or wrapped around his body. She felt a blush creep up her face.

He slid his hand across the table, running his thumb in little circles on the back of her hand. It reminded her of his hands on more intimate parts of her body. She shivered. This time, he didn't ask if she was cold. "Come home with me tonight, Jade."

"No." She shook her head and paused for a moment, gathering her courage. "You come home with me."

• • •

Her smile, her laugh, her body in that amazing dress, her wit, and her angel face had all bewitched him. The only thing registering in his brain was where and how soon could he get himself inside her. His eyes landed on her furniture. His brain, or parts lower, took in the vertical surfaces. The couch was ahead of him and looked incredibly soft. He considered it for a moment, but it was too short for his long frame. The coffee table was even shorter and lower. It was also cluttered with a pile of books, including, he noticed, one of his. There was a fairly good-sized dining table to the left strewn with the most beautiful pieces of jewelry.

Jade paused at the threshold to put her purse down. He rested his hands on her shoulders. He wanted to jump her then and there and struggled to keep himself reigned in. A part of him thought about the table. It was big enough to seat her up there, slide off her underwear, and if he bent his knees a bit . . .

Jade stepped away and headed for the bedroom. She was in front of him, so again, he could appreciate that amazing view of her back. His hand reached for her instinctively, and he finally did what he had longed to do all evening. A single finger started at her nape, just barely making contact with the silkiest skin on the planet. He drew the moment out, the pad of his finger skimming along her neck, down between the elegant sweep of her shoulder blades. Still, he drifted lower to where her back dipped into her waist and lower yet, to where she curved back out to the most graceful backside he had ever seen. With steely control, he stopped there. Or he meant to, but she shivered. Just the slightest tremor ran through her, and it tempted him further. He ran his fingers down, no longer on her back, but just a bit lower. His finger played along the edge of that very naughty dress. That dress was an invitation in and of itself, and he dipped the slightest bit lower, under the dress. There was a bit of a lace under-thing, and still his finger moved lower, just tracing the very top of the cleft of her bottom. She sighed and arched her back. Matt froze for a moment, fighting himself and his incredible urge to just upend her and take her. He wanted her fast and hard on the floor or against the wall, with no finesse or grace. He wanted that with her, but not tonight. Not tonight.

Tonight he wanted to make love to her, to say everything he felt for her, if not in words then at least with touches and kisses and tenderness. He pressed his hand to her back, palm flat, gently moving it north into only slightly less dangerous territory.

He pulled her back up against his front so he couldn't see all that beautiful exposed skin, and rested his chin on the top of her head while he took a few deep breaths. She leaned back into him and sighed. When he felt like he could trust himself again, he turned her in his arms. One arm held her to him, all of that softness pressed into him. With his other hand, he brought her hand to his mouth. He had meant to kiss her there but by the time he brought her hand to his mouth, he found himself running his tongue along the tender inside of her wrist. It was as if kisses weren't enough. He just needed to taste her. He licked along the inside of her arm until he reached her bracelet, the same gold weave design as the pieces on the table. He slid it off and steered them both closer to the dining table where he deposited the cuff.

He continued to taste his way up the inside of her arm to her elbow. He could feel her pulse beating there. It matched the rhythm of her breathing. She was plastered up against the front of him, and each breath pushed her breasts into him. He hoped he could wait for the bedroom. He slid his hand up her arm to her shoulder, then neck, cupping the back of her head to come in for a kiss. He tried to keep it gentle, but she took the kiss deeper. Her hands had eased into his tux jacket and were up by his shoulders, pushing the garment off of him. She wouldn't get an argument there.

In fact, the move inspired him to untie the halter of her dress, and just like that, the whole dress slid to a puddle of black on the floor. She stood in heels, stockings, a pair of lace panties, and a soft smile.

In that moment, he felt his world tilt. It wasn't just how she looked there, naked and tripping about every fantasy in his head that he had ever had. There was anticipation of what was to happen, but it was more than that. There was all the time he had already spent with her, all of the time with her in his arms feeling just right. There was the space between those moments. The time he spent waiting to hold her again. Not just today, but tomorrow and next year and forty years from now. He laughed. It was that or cry.

"God, I love you." He just barely breathed the words, but he knew she heard him. She gasped, just a small intake of breath. He knew his heart was in his eyes, because she held his gaze with a look of wonder. Her lips parted, but before she could say anything that he might not want to hear, he pulled her back up against his chest and kissed her. He put his heart and soul into that kiss. When he finally came up for air, she was breathless and laughing.

She moved her delicate hands down the front of his shirt, fumbling with buttons, laughing, pushing him backward. She was steering him down the hallway toward her bedroom. Though really, at this point he wasn't even going to be picky about needing a horizontal surface. Vertical would work. She got the buttons undone on the shirt, slipped it off, and left it on the floor of the hall before moving them through the doorway and moving her hands down to his waistband.

He barely noticed the brief walk down the hall. He was too busy enjoying her hands sliding inside the waistband of his pants, inside his boxer briefs, and along his bottom. He was kissing her the whole time too, sliding his hands down her arms, along her ribcage, and up over her breasts. He was really enjoying her breasts, the feel of them, perfect and soft except for the nipples, which had pebbled into firm little points. Her bedroom room felt dark and exotic, like some Moroccan love nest. Of course, maybe that was just his mood.

She had backed him up to the bed, where he turned her around and sat her down. He left her there for a moment. He didn't want to spoil that perfect image: her, the thong, the stockings, the high heels. He wasn't sure, but he thought he remembered seeing seams up the back of the stockings. The thought made him even harder.

Then she did the perfect thing. The thing that made him hope and wonder for his sanity. She smiled up at him and took two little pins out of her hair. Just two little pins sent the whole artful mess tumbling down around her shoulders. She sent them scattering to the floor, scooted herself back on the bed, and like an X-rated ice tea plunge, fell back into the softness of the satin comforter. Her black hair floated around her pale face. All that pale skin shone against the rich burgundy and plum of the comforter. She was laughing, but he couldn't even smile. He couldn't even breathe.

She slid one foot up onto the comforter. She was reaching for the top of the stocking to roll it down, but his hand stopped hers.

Instead, he shucked off his clothes, shoes and all, and then climbed up onto the bed. He hovered over her, leaning his head in close to kiss her again. He worked his way down her body, down every curve and inch. When he got to the lace thong, he slipped his thumbs under the waistband and inched it down over her legs and shoes. The stockings and shoes he left right where they were. The lace of the thong made a rasping noise against her stockings as he slowly slid it down her body. His body responded to the noise and he forced himself to pause a moment. He rested his head on her abdomen, breathing her in, struggling for some thread of control.

Not willing to wait, she pulled him back up to kiss her. Her hips lifted up toward him in invitation. One stiletto-clad foot wound around the back of his leg and pulled him closer. Her back arched and he thought about teasing her, moving away, making her wait, making her beg.

*Maybe next time.* He slid into her warm and wanting body and could almost hear their cooperative sigh. There was an absolute perfect moment of union, of fitting together, a pause before they started to move against each other and with each other. He glanced down to see himself pushing into her and pushed harder. He could tell he had done something right as he felt her tighten around him, so he did it again.

He was either forcing her toward the edge or she was forcing him. He couldn't tell and didn't give a damn. Her head was thrown back, and he could barely see her eyes under the brush of lashes. Her skin had a sheen to it; her mouth was damp and slightly open. Every bit of her skin felt like satin gliding across him. She filled him with sensation after sensation, flooding his circuits with overwhelming pleasure that drove him higher but still left him wanting more. He wanted more of her and wanted her to take in more of him. If he could, he would have crawled inside her. Her body, her muscles echoed the sentiment, pulling him in deeper with each thrust.

Even as her body took him in, as he pressed himself into her again and again, he bent down to taste her shoulder. Her skin was warm and sweet. He licked her and nipped at her neck. She rewarded his efforts with a little noise in the back of her throat that sounded like heaven. The sound shot straight to his groin, and he felt himself pushed to his limit. She arched toward him again, and he couldn't help but groan her name. He pushed into her one more time and felt her tighten in cascades around him. He kissed her one last time before he let go and went with her.

●●●

It was an absolutely perfect morning, with soft light seeping around the blinds in the room, a warm man spooning her from behind, and the chance to sleep in late. Jade stretched her legs and then snuggled her bottom closer to Matt. She thought about the night before. *He loved her. Her. Jade.* She pulled the comforter up to her face and smiled widely into the corner of it. She inhaled deeply and could smell him on the blankets. His smell mingled with all the familiar scents of her bed, and she smiled wider. She thought about the night before. She thought of the glitter, the orchestra, the socialites, the press, her insecurities. All of those things that seemed important the night before seemed silly now. None of that mattered to Matt. What mattered to him was her. Jade.

"God, I love you."

He had spoken the words softly, but he had meant them. Yes, she had been practically naked at the time, but somehow, she believed him. Something in his eyes, his certainty, made her believe it could work. Joy flooded her, and she felt content, peaceful, whole. She was afraid her face would split if she were any happier. She snuggled into him again, and his arm tightened around her waist. Even in sleep he pulled her closer. Somehow, this might work. She closed her eyes and slowly drifted off, the smile still on her face. The only thing that could improve this day would be coffee gnomes magically appearing with her first cup of the morning.

# Chapter 23

She had fallen back to sleep for twenty minutes, maybe more. When she woke again, the morning seemed brighter and someone was banging on the door.

"Come on, Sparky, I know you're in there." *Do I know a Sparky?* Jade tried to figure out if it was a dream. It sounded like Sam at the door. "C'mon! I need to talk to you. Kind of important!" It was definitely Sam. She was pounding on the door now and sounded … pissed. What had started out as a perfect morning was going downhill fast.

Jade rolled onto her back and glanced over at Matt out of the corner of her eye. When she moved, he rolled over on his back and threw an arm up over his eyes. Jade poked him in the shoulder. "Do you know a Sparky?"

Matt mumbled and grabbed a pillow to hide under. Jade shoved his shoulder harder in response. "Uhm, is there a reason why Sam is yelling and pounding on the door?"

The pounding got louder.

Matt rolled over on his side again and wrapped his arms around Jade's waist while he buried his face in her hair. The pillow still covered most of his head. Jade lifted the corner of the pillow. "Uh, pookie-bear-snookums? Could you pretty please get up and deal with the deranged woman at the door, since she is your best friend?"

He opened one eye and then the other. Then grunted. Jade batted her eyelashes and flashed a wicked smile. "I'll make coffee."

Matt rolled out of bed, grabbed his pants off the floor, and slid them on in one smooth motion. "Deal."

• • •

Matt yanked open the door and spoke around a stifled yawn. "This had better be good," he grumbled.

Samantha pushed the door open and stepped inside. Surprisingly, she was dressed for battle, in a suit tailored to perfection, black pumps, and a tightly pinned up-do. "If by good you mean bad, it is."

Matt sighed. It was insanely early to be doing this. He had spent far too little time actually sleeping last night to deal with whatever emergency had come up. "We need to get going." Sam glanced down at her BlackBerry, typing a text and pressing "send" before she looked back up at Matt.

He stood there trying to make sense of things. "Go?"

Sam looked up at him then glanced toward the kitchen where Jade was preparing coffee. "We need to go back into the city today to deal with some business." She reached for Matt's arm, turned him away from the kitchen, and lowered her voice. "We have a media shit storm brewing. Mackenzie Whitman from the *Times* claims that she got a quote from Jade stating that you have been researching the Cartwright treasure for your next book."

"Bullshit!" He was loud enough that Jade looked up from what she was doing. The worry was clear in her face. She flipped the switch on the coffee maker and moved toward them.

Sam shrugged. "True or not, we've got to deal with her."

Jade's brow furrowed. She looked back and forth between Sam and Matt. "What's wrong?"

Matt pulled Jade up against his side. "Don't worry." He wanted nothing more than to push Sam out the front door, lock it behind her, and crawl back into bed with Jade. Unfortunately, Sam was rock solid. If she was here telling him that there was something that needed to be dealt with, then he trusted that implicitly. What he didn't trust was a reporter's version of anything. "Did this reporter have any of this on tape?"

Sam shook her head. "No, but she found some people who were willing to go on the record."

Jade pulled her robe more tightly closed and fussed with the belt. "What reporter?"

Matt ignored her. "We can stop the story."

Sam shook her head. "Sorry, this is not exactly going to be top priority for a court to grant an injunction. You'll just piss off the judge for wasting her time. You can threaten to sue for damages after the fact, but if Mackenzie wants to run her story, the damage will already be done. A legal battle will only add to your bad press."

Jade spoke a little louder. "Um, what's going on?"

Matt waved her concern off. "It's nothing ... Just some reporter conning her way into a story." Matt turned back to Sam. "Fuck it. How much damage could it cause? Let her run whatever story she wants. People won't even remember this a day later."

Sam nodded. "Yeah, we can ignore her and let the story run, but it will do damage. Your readership will get excited about a treasure hunting story then pissed when they realize your book doesn't have anything to do with that."

"What was this reporter's name?" Jade asked.

Matt spoke over Jade's head. She was so petite than that he could rest his chin on her silky hair and still talk to Sam. "It's in there a little."

Sam shook her head. "I read your synopsis. It'll piss off the readership. I also don't want to subject Lakehaven to an incoming flood of treasure happy yahoos."

Matt agreed. "There are enough local yahoos."

Sam nodded. "This is better handled with honey. We go in, give her an exclusive, and make a friend in the process. It's a win-win."

Jade asked again. "Who?"

Sam finally took pity on Jade and answered her question. "Mackenzie Whitman."

Matt felt Jade go completely still in his arms. He pulled back and started to ask what was wrong but stopped when he saw her face. She had gone pale, and her eyes were too wide.

"Oh, God." She looked frantically up at Matt. "I did talk with her last night."

•••

Jade started to tremble. She looked back and forth between Sam and Matt and desperately tried to remember what exactly the conversation had been. She peered up at Matt. "We talked, but I didn't think … She said it was all off the record."

Matt winced and gave Sam an apologetic look. The mess had been made and now Sam was going to have to clean it up. Their heavy glances made Jade feel worse. Sam shrugged it off. "Not a problem. I've made the phone calls and set everything up. It's nothing a day or two in New York can't solve—an easy fix. It's just that we need to leave now." Sam's smile oozed bitterness. "Our new best friend Mackenzie has a deadline to meet."

Matt looked at Jade with sympathy, and she could feel tears pressing at the back of her eyes. If they had been mad or accusing, it might have been easier for her to endure. They weren't, though. They were trying to make it better, and their concern left her feeling like a small child. "She promised it was off the record. How could she lie like that?" Jade knew she sounded naïve, but she couldn't help it. The tight knit community of Lakehaven was pretty straightforward. People who had a problem dealt with you face to face rather than behind your back. She was completely out of her element.

Sam tried to help. "It's a game they play. The reporter agrees that what you say is off the record. You tell them some little detail and then they dig around, get five other people to go on the record corroborating the story. Mackenzie Whitman didn't exactly lie to you. She won't quote you. All of the quotes will be from other sources who are completely willing to go on the record."

They weren't trying to be condescending, but she could only imagine what they thought of her at that moment. She bit the inside of her mouth to keep from crying and straightened her spine. "I'll fix it. I'll make it right."

Matt's smile was sympathetic. "There's nothing you can do. Mackenzie wants Riley McLaughlin."

Jade bit her lip. "I am so sorry. I had no idea." Again, she felt like a fool.

Sam shrugged. "Don't worry about it. It was just a rookie mistake. Could have happened to anyone."

Sam's phone dinged and she glanced at it. Her expression was tight. She texted a response while cursing under her breath. She finished the text and looked at Matt. "We need to go now. I'll brief you in the car on the way. You can shower when we get there. I want to be on the road immediately so we can bypass as much traffic as possible."

He ran his hands through his hair, making it stick up. "Damn. I hate this."

Sam patted Matt on his back and shot him a dangerous grin. "Don't worry, Sparky. I've got it all under control. The big bad reporter will be eating out of my hand and owe us about a billion favors by the time I'm done with her."

Matt dropped his head forward to look at the floor. He stood there for a moment before lifting his head up. "Okay. Fine. Let's do this." He was already turning back to the bedroom, on the move. He moved quickly and confidently, but Jade could see the tension in his shoulders.

She followed him into the bedroom. "Matt, I wish there was something, anything I could do."

He shook his head but didn't make eye contact. He was looking around the room for his underwear. "Don't worry about it. Sam's handling it."

"Maybe I could talk to the reporter."

His pants were back on, and he was fastening them. "It won't matter. At this point, anything less than Riley McLaughlin won't be enough. Don't worry, Sam's good with PR. She knows what she's doing. I trust her."

Jade stood there stunned. On top of being naïve and foolish, she was incompetent and untrustworthy. She bit her lower lip.

If Matt was aware of how his words had landed, he didn't show it. He really wasn't looking at her at all. He found his shirt and threw it on, not bothering to tuck it in, and grabbed his wallet and cabin key off the dresser before moving to the foot of the bed. "I don't think this will take more than a day or two to handle." He bent to pick up his socks, which he shoved into his pockets, and then slipped his shoes on his bare feet. "I'll call you when I know for sure how long it will take and when I'll be back." He moved to the door where Jade nodded numbly at him, and bent to kiss her before he headed back to the living room.

• • •

Matt's call didn't come until twenty-four hours later. For Jade, that meant twenty-four hours of worry, obsessing over her mistake. She tried to keep busy; there were accounts to settle and supplies to order, and when she was done with her duties up at the main house, she cleaned her cabin. She straightened her living room, did the dishes, even tidied her bedroom ... which was when she found a little white business card on the floor.

It was at the foot of the bed where Matt had dropped his pants, and it didn't take much to guess where the card had come from: *Amanda Carmichael—Sutton Galleries.* It had a Hudson Street address and a 10013 postal code that Jade didn't recognize, but at least she knew that the 212 area code was New York. The font was elegant and the card stock felt expensive. She felt the jealousy bubble up in her.

Amanda Carmichael probably had no problem dealing with the press. Amanda Carmichael was in a creative industry—the art world—and no doubt she was comfortable at fundraisers and gallery openings and luncheons and film premieres and wherever else Matt might have to go. Amanda Carmichael was everything that Jade was not: polished, and if not perfect, perfect for Matt.

Jade sat hard on the end of her bed and stared blindly at the business card. She had made the mistake once before with Nick. When she had been in love with Nick, she hadn't really thought about what it would be like to be a part of his future, part of his *forever*. She had assumed that since they loved each other, it would work itself out. She was not going to make the same mistake twice. The fact of the matter was that though she was really angry at the time, she could see now why Nick would want a future with Stacy. They were right for each other. They both wanted the same future. Jade might have made it work, being the professor's wife to Nick's tenured professor, but she never would have thrived.

She had no doubt that Matt loved her, but could she make him happy? She thought about him in New York having to clean up the mess she had made. Yes, it had been an innocent mistake, but how many more of those would she commit? The reality of it was that she couldn't imagine being in his world, in his future. She could imagine Amanda Carmichael in it. Easily.

The phone jolted her out of her thoughts, and she swallowed hard around the lump in her throat. "Hello?"

Matt's voice was rough. He sounded tired. "Hey."

Jade took a steadying breath. "Hey yourself. How did it go?"

"It's gone well so far. We put out the fires, and Sam and my publicist are going over some other details. They figure if there is going to be press anyway, they might as well use that to our advantage. Turn it into a positive. So your mistake might have been for the best anyway."

*This time,* Jade thought. "That's good news."

"I'm going to wrap up here in a day or so, and then I'll come back up."

Jade bit her lip. "I don't know if that's a good idea."

Jade heard the concern in Matt's voice. "What's wrong?"

Jade felt the first tear slide down her cheek but managed to keep the quiver out of her voice. "I just think … " She swallowed and started again, this time with certainty. "I'm not right for you."

Matt laughed. "What are you talking about? You're perfect for me."

"Your life is so different from mine—the publicity, the social whirl."

Matt sighed. "That isn't even my life. That's an act for the sake of publicity. Don't you see? That's part of why you're perfect for me. I get to be myself with you. So many other people want some slick version; they want Riley McLaughlin instead of me."

"But it's your career. It's a part of your life. You're a writer, and the public you is a part of that."

There was a pause on the line and when Matt spoke again, she could hear the tension there. "Jade, God, please don't do this. We'll work this out when I get there."

Jade pleaded, hoping he would get it. "Matt, I love you. But that's not necessarily enough to make it work."

Matt interrupted, his voice low, controlled. "It *is* enough. Dammit! Just let me come up and—"

"No!" She hadn't meant to yell, but this was hard enough over the phone without seeing him. She was trying to save them both a lot of pain later on, but it was killing her now. She used the back of her hand to dash the tears from her eyes. "You have an entirely different lifestyle! This time all I did was make a little mistake and look at all the time, effort, and juggling you've had to do to fix it. Next time, it could be worse. I am not willing to do that to you. A future with me is not going to be easy."

"Fuck easy! If I wanted easy, I'd have a fucking one-night stand. I don't want easy. I want you."

She was sobbing now and knew that her voice was unsteady, but she plowed on anyway while she still had the nerve. "You know what I want? I want you to be happy. Truly happy."

He sputtered, incredulous. "But *you're* what makes me happy!"

She yelled then, hoping that it would get through. "No, Matt, just *listen*. You are having to jump through these hoops and put on the Riley McLaughlin show for the press because of *me*. I hear the strain in your voice, and I know I put it there. And it's killing me. I can't do this. I can't bear to work at it and work at it, each day falling a little more in love with you, and each day failing you. In the end, it doesn't work. It won't work."

"Goddammit, Jade! You know what, you're right. It won't work. Do you know why? Because you say so. Christ! People have overcome a helluva lot more than this to have a relationship. But you won't even try. You want to talk about failing? The only failure is quitting. If you don't quit, we can make it work." There was a pause on the line and when he spoke again his voice was low, rough. "Don't quit on us, Jade."

She was still crying but had lost her bluster. Her voice was subdued. "I'm sorry, Matt. I can't."

"Shit, you know what? I am, too. I am so fucking sorry. I'm sorry I misjudged you. I never took you for a coward. You say you love me? Love takes courage. It takes faith. No guarantees. Just courage and faith. I'm sorry that you don't seem to have either." The last thing Jade heard was the click of the phone as Matt disconnected.

# Chapter 24

Jade went through the rest of the week numb. Another hole showed up on the lawn, this time on the opposite side of the main house. Jade couldn't even get distressed about it. She had Jeff fill it in and order some sod. Other than that, who cared? It was a stupid hole. So what?

Matt sent for his duffel but left behind a large envelope. Jade's name was scrawled on the front in his distinct handwriting. She had expected a personal letter from Matt, but instead there was a personal letter of an entirely different sort. Adam Cartwright's letter to his mother captured the romantic moments of his wedding briefly but eloquently. It was a beautiful description of their love and their commitment. The concession that Alsoomse made in wearing Adam's ring made Jade feel stingy and miserable, as Matt's words echoed in her ears. *People have overcome a helluva lot more than this to have a relationship.*

A tear fell from her cheek onto the page, and she brushed it away. She looked down at the spot on the paper and read it again. *"She and I were in complete agreement about the wedding site ... In the end, we both agreed on a high ledge overlooking the water ... The sun sent glittering bands of light across the lake's surface ... The last moments of the ceremony were spent watching the sun sink down below the peaks across the lake ... In the fading light, the mountain ridge turned from deep midnight blue to black."*

Jade's pulse quickened. *A high ledge on the edge of the lake facing the setting sun and a ridge. A westward facing ledge.*

Jade knew the area by heart, and there was only one ledge like that on the entire lake. She and her sister used to jump off that high ledge into the water below. She recalled the thrill of the jump, her heart pounding as she stood on the edge ready to hurl herself into the open sky. She remembered the feel of cool water on her body as it plunged into the water. They would jump over and over again, even as the sun sank in the sky, even as twilight fell, knowing that their parents wanted them home by dark. The memory was still vivid:

*"Just once more, Jade. C'mon, just one more time," her sister begged.*

*"Okay, Lib, but then we've got to go, okay?"*

*Libby nodded vigorously in response. "Let's do it holding hands this time!"*

With the pages of Adam's letter still in hand, Jade grabbed her coat to rush out the door.

When she got there, whether it was by coincidence or providence, the sun was setting. Jade sat down and caught her breath. She had rushed the whole way, running in stretches, walking where the trail was steeper. She wasn't really sure why she wanted to see the spot so badly. She thought she wouldn't care anymore, especially now that she had alienated Matt so completely. She was surprised to find that she did. Tears sprung to her eyes. She pulled her knees up and hugged them to her chest.

The sun had begun to dip below the ridge. There was a line of molten orange rimming the silhouetted peaks, and she watched them darken in the waning light. It probably had looked just like this over 400 years ago on the eve of the Cartwright wedding. Adam and Alsoomse were dead now, but the sun still set the surrounding hills on fire every night.

Jade hugged her knees tighter, crumpling the pages still clutched in her hands. Four hundred years ago, two people from separate continents had promised one another their love. They had kept that promise until Adam fell ill and died. She sighed. It was a simpler time. There were fewer reporters then. Jade watched in silence as the sun disappeared behind the ridge, leaving her in darkness.

...

To say the call from Samantha was a surprise would be an understatement. Jade was livid. "You did *what*?"

Sam was unperturbed. "Look, *Solemain* is the most trendy boutique in the city. Jewelry on display there one month is in the pages of *Vogue* the next."

"You stole one of my bracelets?!"

"Borrowed. Come into the city with the rest of your line and Bianca will give it back."

"When did you take it?"

"When I was at your cabin, while Matt was getting dressed."

"You didn't ask!"

There was a smile in Sam's voice; she wasn't bothered in the least. In fact, if Jade had to guess by her tone, she would say that Sam was pleased with herself. "It slipped my mind."

Jade was galled. She plucked a pen out of the cup on the desk and stabbed it into the desk calendar. "You aren't even sorry!"

"Nope. Look, you won't get an apology from me. I've seen your work, and it's genius. I wasn't going to let the opportunity slip by."

"What if I don't want the opportunity?" Jade did, but that was beside the point. Sam had no right! "You had no right!"

"Again, I'm not going to apologize. You can't tell me this isn't a dream come true."

"I hate to break it to you, Sam, but not everyone wants to make it big. Some people want a peaceful, quiet, stress-free life. I was happy making jewelry for myself. No pressure, no demands, no deadlines."

Sam's laugh was skeptical. "No one to appreciate your art? It's like being Picasso and hanging your work in a closet."

"So what?!"

"Look, I get it. You're scared. Maybe you'll fail. Maybe this line won't sell. Maybe it will, and you'll have to top yourself next time. Maybe the accessories editor at some magazine will dub you a hack. You still have to take the risk."

"Why?" Jade sounded petulant, even to her own ears.

Samantha sighed heavily. "Do you know how I tell if a person is fulfilled and happy?"

"Gee, I don't know. They're smiling," Jade sneered.

"Nope. Ask them about their biggest failures. If they have some spectacular failures to share, they're fulfilled. If they can't think of a single one, then they haven't ever taken a risk. Is that really how you want to live your life?"

Jade dodged the question. "Why are you doing this for me? You're Matt's best friend and right now he hates me."

Sam was silent for a moment and Jade thought she might hang up. A moment later, she continued softly. "Jade, I saw your jewelry and it took my breath away. I didn't think or analyze; I just acted from my heart. I didn't think about the consequences. I couldn't do anything else. I didn't do it for any particular reason other than that I wanted to."

"You should've asked."

"Well, I didn't. What's done is done. Now you have to decide what you're going to do about it."

Jade took a deep breath and blew it out. She picked up a pen and started to doodle in the margins of her desk calendar. A little design started to take shape in her mind.

Sam waited. "Just think about it, okay?"

Jade's pen strokes formed a small nest with an egg in it, or maybe a pendant ... *Just think about it.*

"Jade, are you still there?"

"Yes. Okay."

Jade hung up and wandered into the kitchen for her fifth cup of coffee that morning. Meg was washing a mixing bowl and humming "Girl from Ipanema" while doing a little cha cha with her feet.

Jade poured a cup of coffee, sat at the counter, and sipped. She drummed her fingers on the counter as she thought about what Sam had said. *Think about it.* She had a lot to think about. She had tried to call Matt but he wasn't answering his phone, and now her bracelet was being held hostage in a boutique in Manhattan. Jade sighed.

Meg turned to look at Jade. "Uh oh. Is that a love-lost sigh or is there something else I should know about?"

Jade rotated her coffee cup 360 degrees and took another sip. "What would you do if your greatest dream and worst fear were the same thing?"

"Uh, that's a little vague. I can't give Yoda wisdom unless you actually tell me what you're talking about."

"Sam took my bracelet to a boutique in Manhattan, and the owner wants to see everything."

Meg squealed. "Oh my God! That's great!"

Jade shook her head. "It's like showing a complete stranger my very heart and soul. What if she hates them? What if they're terrible?"

Meg lifted her eyebrows. "What if? *If* she hates them, it's just one person's opinion." Meg turned back to the sink and put down the mixing bowl. She started gesturing. "Do you love your work? I mean the finished pieces."

Jade nodded. "That's the problem. I love them, but she might not."

Meg waved the concern away. "Who cares! I mean really, what does it matter, as long as what you create makes you happy."

Jade sighed. "And then if this line succeeds, if everyone loves them, there is the pressure to do it again. To have the next line be better and more successful. I don't know if I can deal with the stress."

Meg pursed her lips. "Yeah, well. You'd have to stop being a wuss and start believing in yourself." Meg nodded. "Yeah, you're right. Don't go. I mean, what if you fail?"

Jade laughed. "Okay, Captain Reverse Psychology."

Meg laughed with her. "It worked for Tom Sawyer. It might as well work on Jade Sawyer. Look, life isn't perfect. There are risks and stuff can, does, and will go wrong. But even if you lock yourself in a room, an airplane could fall out of the sky and kill you. So you have a choice: wait in that room for the airplane to get you, or have the airplane get you while you're skydiving naked with the US water polo team."

Jade looked concerned. "Do I have my art supplies locked in the room?"

Meg walked around the counter and smacked Jade on the back of the head. "Have you seen the water polo team? Seriously hot bodies."

Jade sipped her coffee. "Okay. I'll do it."

The Kent sisters choose that moment to make an entrance. They had apparently been listening at the door. Adele spoke first. "Ooooh! You're going to skydive naked? I think I'd like to do that as well."

Jade tried to deny it, but Beatrice spoke right over her. "I dated a water polo player once. Athletes are so adept at pleasuring women."

Adele and Beatrice went right for the iced tea pitcher in the refrigerator. Adele turned to her sister. "Did you ever skydive naked with him?" Before Bea could open her mouth to respond, Adele turned to Jade. "When are we going?"

Jade shot Meg an accusing look. This was clearly her fault. "Well . . ."

Adele barreled on. "Bea, are you going to go with us?"

Bea shot her sister a truculent look. "What about the water polo players?"

Adele ignored her sister's response. She gasped and clapped her hands in delight. "Do you think they would let us do a naked tandem jump? We could find a good looking instructor and ... "

Bea and Adele poured their tea and turned to head out of the kitchen. Their conversation flowed on without any input from Meg or

Jade. The sisters had seemingly forgotten them. As they left, Bea mused, "The university might have a water polo team. I'll check the intercom."

"Isn't it the Internet?"

"Why do you always have to be right about everything?" Like an afternoon thunderstorm, the sisters were gone as quickly as they had arrived.

The kitchen was silent for a moment. Jade sipped her coffee and leaned in toward Meg. "Can I tell you a secret?"

Meg's eyebrows jumped toward her hairline. "Does it have anything to do with naked skydiving?"

Jade lifted a bar towel off the counter and threw it at Meg. "No!" She leaned in, her eyes glittering. "I found the site where Adam Cartwright married the princess."

Meg looked doubtful. "How do you know?"

"Matt left me some of Adam Cartwright's letters to his mother. He has a research assistant in London who dug them up. There's a description of the wedding, and there was only one site that matches it! I went up there, and it was exactly like he described in the letter. Over four-hundred years, and it's virtually the same."

"So? Did you look for the treasure?"

Jade shrugged. "Honestly, I didn't even think of it. I … " Jade sighed. "I just kept thinking about the wedding. Their commitment. They were from such different worlds. It was so unlikely that they would ever find each other across the world in a time without airplanes, but they did."

"Yeah, and now, with the world shrinking, we sometimes don't even see what's there in our own backyard."

Jade sipped her coffee and considered Meg's words. In the silence of the moment, she thought she heard the kitchen door gently swinging shut. She turned to look, but if anyone had been at the door, they were already gone.

# Chapter 25

Matt sat in his mother's living room waiting for her to come out of the kitchen. She was fixing him a sandwich despite the fact that he had asked her not to. He really didn't have much of an appetite lately, but Elizabeth was determined to feed him. Among other things. He looked around the room, familiar but a bit more sparse than he remembered from his adolescence.

"All right, Matthew. Since I know you didn't come over for chit chat, to what do I owe the pleasure of your company?"

Matt ran his hand through his hair. His mother winced, which probably meant his hair looked even messier than it had before. "Look, Mom. You know I love you."

"Oh, God. This cannot be good. Should I pour myself a drink now?"

Matt laughed. "I'm not dying or anything."

"Well, that's a relief. Though, may I say, you look terrible. You haven't been sleeping."

Matt's response was dry. "Thank you."

His mother shrugged. "Sorry, but it's true."

"Mom, you have to stop meddling."

Elizabeth's right eyebrow shot sky high. "Impossible. I'm your mother."

Matt tried but failed to keep the sarcasm out of his voice. "Well, try."

"Matthew, you are so unhappy, and I see it. You need people in your life, people to share it with. It's not enough to gallivant about."

"I agree. Did you say gallivant? I don't gallivant."

"Did you just agree with me?"

Matt sighed. "I agree that I want someone special in my life. I want someone to share all of it with, the good and the bad … " His mother was nodding emphatically, which was not a good sign. Matt wondered if maybe he had made a terrible mistake. In general, he didn't agree with much of what his mother thought or did, but he plowed on anyway. "I just want you to stay out of it. If I want to date Amanda Carmichael, I'm perfectly capable of finding the woman's phone number myself."

Elizabeth gave him a smile that lit up her whole face, and then she did something that stunned Matthew. "You're right, dear. I should've stayed out of it. I'm sorry." Matthew was speechless, but unfortunately, Elizabeth was not. "Now, tell me why you look like hell."

• • •

Jade's heart was pounding and her palms were sweaty on the handset. "Okay, great. Tuesday, then. I look forward to seeing you." Jade hung up the phone. She couldn't believe she had done it. It was so out of character for her to forge ahead recklessly. In fact, she had spent the past three years backing away from her life, from her dreams, from risk, from men. She stared at the phone handset and laughed giddily. She had done it. She had thought about Alsoomse and Adam forging ahead through whatever life had to dish out, and she had called Bianca to schedule a meeting at Solemain. She had e-mailed photos of her jewelry to Meg's friend who owned a smaller shop and scheduled a meeting there as well. If the meetings didn't go well … Jade laughed again. *Okay. If you're going to fail, fail big.*

She dialed Samantha's number. She felt a little off-kilter. She listened to the phone ring and waited for Samantha to pick up, half hoping for a voice message. *Breathe in, breathe out.* Okay, good, still alive. The phone rang one more time, and Jade was just about to hang up when Sam's smooth voice sounded on the other end.

"Samantha Parker."

"Hi, Sam? It's Jade. Jade Sawyer."

There was a pause on the other end of the line, then Sam responded, "Oh."

"Look, I wanted to tell you that you were right. I was afraid to fail, but I went ahead and called your contact at the boutique. I'm sorry I yelled at you, and I wanted to thank you."

Sam laughed. "Apology accepted, and you're welcome."

Jade felt herself stop. When she and her sister Libby would jump off the ledge, Alsoomse's ledge, into the lake, they started just by standing on the edge. As they got more confident, they would back up and take a running start. Once, holding hands, they had started running, and Libby had stopped suddenly at the edge, practically pulling Jade's arm out of its socket. Jade flashed on that image and knew she was standing on that ledge right now. She took a deep breath and did what she always told Libby to do. *Jump!*

"Sam, I have a huge favor to ask you."

•••

One week later, Jade was in Manhattan, standing on the sidewalk outside the boutique. She had purchased a rolling case and spent the week filling it with polished pieces of jewelry. She had a new haircut, a blowout, a new suit, and wore makeup. She had thought she would feel like a kid playing dress up. Surprisingly, she didn't feel like an imposter at all. She felt like herself. A kickin'-butt-and-takin'-names self, but still herself. She tried to imagine Samantha or Amanda Carmichael at Lakehaven chopping wood and couldn't do it. She glanced down at her new suit and heels and imagined herself splitting a log cleanly wearing this outfit. The image popped in her head easily, and she laughed. She was still laughing as she pushed through the door of Solemain.

The boutique had a downtown feel to it: open space, concrete floors finished with a high gloss, antique mixed with modern. It managed to seem haphazard, but Jade was sure it was staged down to the last detail. A woman, who Jade assumed was Bianca, stood behind a display case and was showing a svelte young woman a pair of earrings. The young woman held them up to her lobes and turned her head from side to side. Jade admired the earrings. Their simple sculptural lines swayed prettily with the customer's movements, but the brushed silver finish gave them edge. Contrast. Jade felt her heartbeat quicken and wondered that such simple beauty could give her such joy. She smiled at the earrings, at the customer, at Bianca.

Bianca nodded to Jade over the customer's shoulder then leaned down to speak to the woman. Jade watched as Bianca listened to the customer and then moved away, giving the woman space to make a decision. Then Bianca waved Jade over. Jade's heart was pounding, but she smiled through her nervousness. She was getting used to feeling her heart beat hard and decided that it was a good thing rather than a sign of an impending heart attack.

"Hi, I'm Jade Sawyer."

Bianca smiled back. She was older than Jade, but not old. Beautiful and exotic looking, she reminded Jade of a well-mannered gypsy. A gypsy in a four thousand dollar suit. Jade extended her hand for a handshake, but Bianca took Jade's hand in both of her own. Each movement was measured, nothing rushed. "So pleased to finally meet you." Bianca looked Jade in the eyes. She examined Jade's face and smiled, seeming pleased with what she saw. "I have something that belongs to you." She turned back to the display case behind her, opened a panel, and pulled out the cuff that Samantha had pilfered. There was a tray lined in black velvet, and Bianca set the piece there. "You have more like it?"

Jade was about to respond, but the client looking at the earrings had shifted her attention to Jade's cuff and the interaction with Bianca. She interrupted. "Do you have earrings?"

Jade resisted wiping her hands on her skirt. *Here goes nothing.* She unzipped the case and started to pull out the pieces. By the time Jade was done, the young woman had purchased a pair of earrings, a necklace, and two rings.

• • •

Her next meeting was scheduled for two. Jade arrived at the restaurant at a bit past two o'clock and glanced around. It was a small Italian place with dark wood paneling and low lights. She took a deep breath. She had made it through one meeting. Bianca had liked her jewelry, and when Jade had shown her some sketches of the nest series, she had liked those, too. If it continued to sell well, she would take more. Jade grinned to herself. It was worth the risk. She knew that even if Bianca hadn't loved the designs, she would feel ten feet tall. Her blood pumped through her veins, and she felt bold and alive. Jade took another deep breath, being careful not to hyperventilate. She was going to need some of that courage now.

The maître d' was a young man with olive skin and dark hair. "Can I help you ma'am?"

"I'm meeting someone here. A man … " She looked beyond the maître d's shoulder and saw him sitting alone at a quiet table in the back. He hadn't noticed her yet.

Jade's heart thudded in her chest. She took one look at his so familiar profile and thought, *How could I throw that away?* She wouldn't make that mistake twice. She squared her shoulders and headed toward the back of the restaurant.

Matt froze when he saw her. His gaze had lifted as she approached but then froze as she stood there at the table. He pushed away from the table and stood. Whether it was to be polite or to leave, Jade couldn't be sure.

Jade held her hands out in surrender. "I'm not who you were expecting."

Matt's jaw tightened. "Did you talk Sam into this or was it the other way around?"

Matt sounded angry. Jade had imagined this being easier, Matt being kinder. Jade looked at the floor and gathered her courage. Then she looked Matt squarely in the eyes. "It was me. You wouldn't answer my calls and I … I owe you an apology. I'm so sorry."

Matt nodded tersely. "Okay, great. Feel better now?"

Jade sat down at the table and gestured for Matt to sit with her. He didn't move. She felt the press of tears. "Please."

For a moment it looked like Matt would leave. He glanced toward the door, then up at the ceiling for a moment, then suddenly jerked the chair back and sat.

Jade could breathe again. She looked at him. Really looked. It had been weeks since they had seen each other, and she could see the strain on his face. She had done that to him. Her tears tracked down her cheek. "God, Matt. I am so sorry. You have to know that I thought … " She shook her head and started over. "I love you. I love you so much that I freaked out. I said I was protecting you from me, but the fact was, I was so happy and that terrified me. If I let you matter that much, you could hurt me that much. You were right. I didn't have the courage or the faith. Not in us, but in me."

Matt wore his poker face, his writer face, but Jade just barreled on. She met Matt's gaze, letting him see her whole heart in her eyes. "I can't promise I won't make mistakes, or that I'll be perfect, or even that I won't get scared from time to time. What I can promise you with every bit of my heart is that I won't quit. I won't quit loving you with everything I've got. No matter what life throws our way, I won't quit. On you, on me, on us."

Jade paused for a reaction, any reaction. What she got was stony silence.

"I've spent these last weeks being safe but numb. It was horrible. I've never been so miserable in my life. Today I took a huge risk, and I've never felt so alive." She paused to see if Matt had any response; there was still nothing.

She swallowed hard, reached into her purse, and pulled out a pen. "Here." She started to draw. "I reread the Cartwright letter you left, and I found it, Matt. The wedding site. I sat there in the waning light and thought about those two people from completely different worlds. It was so unlikely that they would ever find each other, and even more unlikely that they would ever make it work." She continued to draw on the napkin. "But they did. They went for it anyway, in the face of much larger obstacles. If Alsoomse could do it, so can I. I can do anything, because I say I can." She wrote a date on the napkin and slid it across to Matt. "You said it to me once: don't quit. I'm asking the same from you. Don't quit. If you're willing to take a chance on me, meet me here at sunset." Jade marked an *X* on the napkin. It was a map of Lakehaven with the cabins and main house at the bottom. The *X* marked the Cartwright wedding site.

Matt looked down at the map and then back up at Jade, but he didn't pick it up.

Jade stood and backed away from the table, leaving the napkin where it lay. She tried to think of something else to say, something that would change Matt's mind, something that would touch his heart. She couldn't think of a thing, so she just repeated something Samantha had said to her. "Just think about it, okay?" She had to swallow around the tightness in her throat. Squaring her shoulders, she turned to leave and did the one thing that took more courage than anything she had ever done. *Trust.*

# Chapter 26

Jade sat alone on the bluff, watching the sunset shimmer off the surface of the lake. She hugged her knees to her chest and wondered for the hundredth time whether Matt would show. She desperately hoped that he would, but whether he did or not, she had given it everything she had. This was what it was to be alive. She rested her cheek on her knee and tried to appreciate the beauty and peace of the moment.

A twig cracked behind her, and she swiveled around. Her heart raced in anticipation. She smiled and scanned the woods behind her for movement in the branches. It took every ounce of patience not to jump up and race toward the noise. Then she heard the beep. She tried to make sense of the electronic noise out in the woods. *Cell phone?* The trees parted and Jeff stepped into the clearing, swinging a metal detector around.

Jade's hopes plummeted. "What are you doing here?"

Jeff's look was sheepish. "I … ah … " Jeff scratched his neck. "I found some papers in your office and copied them. Plus … I maybe overheard you speaking with Meg a few days ago, and I followed you up here." Jeff gestured with the metal detector. "You don't mind if I … "

Jade took a deep breath and, staring at the ground, shrugged. She was afraid if she spoke she would scream.

Jeff started to move off to her left but turned at a sound behind him. Jade lifted her head, her spirits restored as quickly as they had fallen. She beamed with joy. Except that it was Stu and Maddie, the Lakehaven cleaning crew, emerging from the woods and not Matt. Stu carried a shovel with the word *Lakehaven* stenciled on the wooden handle and Maddie had another metal detector. Jade's jaw dropped. "I don't believe this! What are you doing here? You stole the shovel? We've been looking for that for weeks!"

Stu wouldn't meet Jade's eyes but Maddie was downright chipper. "That writer fellow just left the letters on his desk right under our noses. What do you expect? I could hardly clean his room with my eyes closed! You don't mind, do you sweetie?" She and Stu moved off to the right, scanning the ground with their detector.

Jade sighed in frustration. "I guess not."

Another noise came from the woods, and Jade looked toward the sound with renewed hope. *This has to be Matt.* She waited for his broad shoulders and sandy, sun-tipped hair. What she got was stooped shoulders and white hair as Mr. Boyle entered the clearing, followed by the Kent sisters. *Of course.* Jade gritted her teeth. The sisters argued about where to dig. Mr. Boyle hefted a pickaxe over his shoulder and waited for directions.

Jade couldn't stop herself from asking, "What are you doing here?"

The Kent sisters looked surprised at the question. Bea started. "Helping you, of course. We saw everyone else coming to help you, and we wanted to help too."

Adele nodded in agreement. "After all, we love you!"

Jade flapped her arms. "But I'm not searching for the treasure!"

The sisters ignored Jade and picked a spot to the left, beyond where Jeff was scanning with his detector.

Jade was about to argue further when the branches parted and Ben and Meg arrived. She threw her arms up in the air. "Oh, for God's sake! What are you doing here? No, forget I asked. I don't want to know!"

Just then, Jeff's metal detector began to beep wildly and everyone but Jade swarmed the spot. Jade just sat down and hugged her knees again. *Well, at least I have friends … crazy friends, but friends.*

Mr. Boyle hacked at the dirt, Stu tried to muscle his way in closer, and for a while it was pure chaos. Mr. Boyle's pick hit something metallic, and the crowd pushed in closer. Jeff bent down and brushed away the loosened soil to reveal ... a bottle cap. The group let out a collective sigh, which was followed by grumbling.

The beautiful, peaceful scene had been turned into a farce, and when the bushes behind her rustled, she lost her patience. *"Oh, for crying out loud! Now what!"*

Matt raised his eyebrows at her, the slightest trace of a smile playing around his mouth. At first, neither of them spoke. Her eyes met his and for a moment, the world stood still. She smiled up at him. He moved toward her, opening his arms as he got closer, and she stepped into his embrace. They stood, body to body, breathing. Everything fell away but her love for him and his for her. She could smell his warm scent and thought, *home*.

Finally, he spoke into her hair. "Hey you."

"Hey." Jade pulled away and took his hand, leading him to the edge of the bluff. She sat, and he sat next to her.

She swept her arm in an arc in front of them. "Here it is."

He nodded. "Beautiful."

She bit her lip. "I think I want to get married here."

Matt leaned back and looked down at her. "Do you have a specific groom in mind?"

She shrugged. "Someone willing to take a chance." His gaze shifted to some point beyond her. He squinted into the dropping sun, but said nothing. She gathered her courage and continued on. "Matt, I ... " She had intended to tell him everything she felt for him, but he still was looking at some point over her shoulder. He leaned forward oddly, then suddenly stood and walked away, leaving her with her mouth hanging open.

She watched as he walked past her to a small bush. He lifted its lowest branches and dug around a little until Jade could see what he had: a tiny piece of metal glinting out at her from the ground under the bush. He pulled the small object out. The object was covered in dirt, but even so, parts of it shone in the fading sunlight. It was silver and hammered and had an arch to it like the top of a little jewelry box. Jade just stared, mesmerized. Matt brushed away some more dirt and dug out a few pieces of rotted wood. Then he reached down into a depression in the earth and pulled something else out of the ground. He turned it one way then the other and Jade gasped. It caught the light and sent out little beams of green and gold. Matt wiped it off on his jeans, looked at it carefully, and walked back to Jade. He looked down at her and back at the object in his hand. He shook his head but she couldn't tell what he was thinking. Then he got down on one knee in front of her and held out the object.

There in his hand was the most perfect ring Jade had ever seen. It was gold with a chocolate diamond, flanked by smaller leaf-shaped emeralds. Matt took her hand and brought the ring toward it. His eyes met hers. "I was going to wait. Now that just seems ridiculous. I have no idea why I thought I should wait … but I … Jade, I love you. Will you marry me?"

Her heart was pounding, which she knew now was a good thing. She laughed and nodded and felt tears well up as he slipped the ring on her finger. The squabbling had stopped, and all of Jade's friends watched as Matt pulled her into his arms and kissed her. She was so happy that she didn't even mind when their audience responded with a simultaneous, "*Awwww!*"

Matt pulled out of the kiss and spoke to Jade, not caring who could hear. "I said that relationships aren't complicated unless you make them that way, but maybe that isn't quite true. Life is sometimes complicated. Maybe that's just part of the deal. The real treasure is knowing that and forging ahead anyway."

Jade kissed Matt again. She couldn't have agreed with him more.

Her eyes were closed, and she couldn't see who spoke. "I think he found the ring over here." She just kept kissing him, and he kissed her.

"Bring the detectors over here."

Still they kissed.

"Bring that shovel, too."

"We should work in sectors … "

Matt and Jade pulled apart as the sun fell behind the mountains. Arm in arm they made their way to the path.

The voices of treasure hunters faded in the distance. "Here, let me take that! You're doing it wrong!"

Other than the ring, none of the Cartwright treasure was ever found. Not that Jade or Matt really cared. They had both found what they had been looking for all along.

# About the Author

Ana Krista Johnson lives in Southern California with her husband, two kids, a dog, and a fish named Frothy. She loves books, a good cup of coffee, a day at the beach, and all things quirky.

# A Sneak Peek from Crimson Romance
### (From *Baby by Design* by Elley Arden)

"My God, he cleans up nice." Trish DeVign said the words around a mouthful of anise-flavored birthday cake while she stared at a suit-and-tie clad Tony Corcarelli. His colorful tattoos were covered by the sleeves of a fitted single-breasted jacket and navy dress shirt. His pitch-black hair was combed away from his face. And he'd shaved, leaving a slight contrast of color on his cheeks and chin, drawing her eyes straight to his unblemished lips.

"Too bad he's such a screw up."

Trish tore her gaze from Tony to level her best friend with the stink eye. "That's not a nice thing to say about your brother."

"It's true. Look at him playing paper football with the kids while he's dressed in an $800 suit. He should try spending less on clothes, keeping more of that money in the bank, and acting like a grown-up once in a while."

Trish sighed as the sinfully handsome man flicked a white triangle across the table to the tune of children's cackles. "I think it's cute."

"You would. Shoot. Aunt Helen's got a slice of cake big enough to prompt diabetic shock. Where's my mother?" Angie whipped her head in all directions and growled. "I'll be back."

Alone in the midst of familial chaos, Trish tapped her nails on the bottom of her plate and looked around the banquet room of Cestone's Italian Restaurant. Four generations of Corcarellis were a sight to be seen; a sight that made her smile even though it made her heart hurt. In the corner of the room, middle-aged women fussed over the food tables, directing servers, corralling cookies, and spearing meatballs, while in the center of the room, middle-aged men ate until their belt buckles popped. All around, the older generation talked…and talked…and talked, punctuating every sentence with nodding heads and waving hands. She loved them all, but it was the children that tethered her heart, tugging her toward their joyful noises.

"Tony, me next. I'll kick your as…"

Trish surmised the kid to be about twelve, and when he noticed her approaching, he bit off his last word amid oohs and ahhs from other kids around the table.

With sheepish eyes he looked from her to his cousin. "I'll beat you is all. That's what I was gonna say, Tony. Honestly."

"Sure you were," Tony said with a grin that tightened the tether on Trish's heart. "Just gimme ten minutes to throw some cake down my throat and I'm all yours." He stood, smoothed a hand down the button line of his suit coat, and blinded her with the full power of his male magnetism. All it took was a crooked smile, one that created a dark dip in his left cheek, not quite a dimple—no, dimples were too cute for a man this…edgy. "Hey, Boss Lady. I'd ask you to join me for cake, but I see you beat me to it."

Trish looked down at her empty plate and swallowed the ridiculous butterflies that escaped their netting whenever Tony came around. "What can I say? It was delicious."

He grinned again. "In that case, you should have another."

She'd been raised by a bone-skinny woman who espoused never eating a second serving of anything. Despite the doctrine being tattooed on Trish's brain, Tony Corcarelli was the kind of guy who could convince a girl to splurge. A classic bad boy, he was capable of more harm than good. But the good… *Mmm. Mmm. Mmm.*

Trish shook her head, scattering the thoughts that had her wallowing in adolescent purgatory, and reached for a more comfortable, competent topic. "How's the Jorgen's sofa coming along?"

"Should be done tomorrow. I can have the wingbacks ready next week." There wasn't a wrinkle on or around his lips, just smooth, perfectly puffed skin that circled a mouth decorated with teeth so white they were a sin on a man that dark.

"That's fine. I'm still waiting on the completion of a couple inlaid rugs, but the sooner the better. I want to keep this project on time." She sounded professional…and uptight, which was out of place for their surroundings but so much better than sounding like a crushing teen.

"So don't go changing the fabric on me again." He dropped his chin to his chest and regarded her through wide, smoky eyes. "Ya hear?" And then he winked.

Her stomach tumbled, churning the cake she'd eaten into cream.

"There you are." Jackson wrapped a sweaty hand around her bicep. "I have to go."

Tony lifted his full brows. "Duty calls, Doc?"

"Something like that."

But Trish knew better. Jackson wasn't on-call. He simply wasn't fond of the Corcarellis, something she'd learned on the car ride to the restaurant when he called them "Jersey Shore without the booze." The comment nagged Trish until she couldn't dismiss it as a poor attempt at humor, so she added it to the mental column of negatives vs. positives she kept for all her dates.

"Enjoy the rest of your evening, kids," Tony said with another crooked grin and a bob of his brows as he maneuvered around them. It was the kind of look that insinuated the rest of Trish's evening would be filled with hot, sticky, adventurous sex.

Trish would be lucky if she got a goodnight kiss. Looking up at prune-faced Jackson, she sighed. Three dates in, and already the negatives assigned to his list dipped perilously close to the kiss-off line.

"Tony, wait." A frilly-dressed, raven-haired girl shoved between Trish and Jackson to scurry after Tony.

Trish watched Tony turn and catch his little cousin as she leapt into his arms. The heartfelt, unscripted gesture made her smile, but when she turned back to Jackson he was scowling.

"These people have no manners," he grumbled. "And too many kids."

Thirty minutes later, after enough goodbyes, *arrivedercis*, and double-cheek kisses, Trish tucked inside Jackson's Porsche and listened to his continued complaints.

"That was a waste of three hours."

"I disagree. Nonna turning eighty-five is a big deal."

He rolled his eyes. "She's not *your* grandmother. None of those people are related to you—thank God. You could've sent a card and some flowers. Why subject yourself to that circus?"

*That circus* was all Trish wanted from life—not that specific circus, but a circus of her own. Loud, brash, unconditional love, not the kind of love that was earned by good behavior and hefty bankrolls. She sighed, because this part of getting to know someone in order to ascertain compatibility was always the most uncomfortable. "I'm adopted."

"Oh." He glanced at her as he adjusted his grip on the steering wheel. "I didn't know that."

Considering how much Jackson adored her surgeon father and socialite mother, she couldn't help but wonder if he was disappointed she didn't share the sacred DeVign genes.

"It's not really a big deal until I'm around a family like the Corcarellis," Trish continued. "Then I start to wonder what my biological family is like."

Road noise swirled between them as she waited patiently for his reaction.

He snorted. "If you ask me, that's dangerous thinking. I mean obviously you're better off now. Look how lucky you are. Hell, I'd stand in line to be adopted by the DeVigns."

She bet he would. "Yes, well, there's something to be said for knowing where you came from. Don't you think?"

"If I came from a family like the Corcarellis, I'd never want to know. Somebody needs to gift them with a lifetime supply of birth control so they stop polluting the gene pool." He laughed.

She clenched her hands in her lap and stared out the window at the shadowy shapes and lighted signs flying by. "I'll skip the nightcap, Jackson. Just drop me off at home."

"Oh. Hey." He slowed at a stoplight and stretched an arm across the top of her headrest. "I was kidding. I mean, they're accommodating enough. They're just rough around the edges, and it takes some getting used to." He smiled as he leaned closer, and for a second, hope bubbled in Trish's chest. "For a guy like me who'd rather have non-anesthetized surgery than kids, it's a real stretch to relate."

Every one of those stupid, hope-filled bubbles popped. "The light is green," she said, redirecting his attention to the road and her attention to the nauseous pit in her stomach.

She was tired of this; tired of getting her hopes up only to have them trashed. At thirty-two, according to her calculations, eight good baby-making years remained. She'd spent the last two years methodically dating, hoping for a ring and white dress. But when she imagined a lifetime with each prospect, and concluded it was more like a life sentence, she lowered her standards. After all, she was an independent woman who didn't need a man to help her raise a child. But she did need a man to help her make one…and for more than his sperm. She wanted his family history, too. The impersonal, anonymity of creating a baby with a bodiless stranger from a donor clinic wouldn't work. She wanted her baby to have a complete medical history, intergenerational stories, and at least a quarterly look at his or her dad.

"Are you sure you don't want that nightcap?" He parked in front of her house and flashed a suggestive grin.

"I'm sure." She'd rather have a baby. "My stomach isn't feeling right."

"Maybe it was the cake," he said as she opened the car door. "Who likes anise birthday cake anyway?"

She stood up and spun around. "I like anise birthday cake." And with that, she slammed the car door on his bewildered face.

"I'll call you tomorrow," he sputtered out his open window as she clip-clopped around the front of the car to her stone walk.

*Don't bother*, she thought.

Talk about a disappointing night. She should've had a second piece of cake.

•••

Tony pulled the burlap tight around the wingchair's retied springs and fired staples from his gun into the wooden frame. He could tell a lot about a person by the condition of their furniture. This particular piece belonged to a newly minted chief of radiology and his wife, a friend of Trish. Before Tony could repair the split and crumbling frame, he'd had to remove three layers of dollar-table, outdated fabric, foul-smelling Dacron, and way too much foam rubber. The haphazard upholsteries told a rags-to-riches tale. When Tony was done, these once sad and neglected chairs would flank the finest fireplace in a Trish DeVign-decorated home. Something that didn't come cheap.

"Why don't you ever answer your freaking phone? Ma's been trying to get ahold of us all day." Angie barged into the garage like she owned the place… Well, technically she did. It was attached to her house, but Tony paid rent to use the space as his sometimes-upholstery shop. He couldn't very well upholster sofa-sized items in his downtown efficiency.

He kept his eyes on the staple line. "What's wrong with your phone?"

"My phone? I was onsite all day. You expect me to hear a phone ringing over a floor sander? You weren't here, were you? You were out on your bike."

"Maybe. What's it matter to you?"

"It matters, Tony. It matters."

That's what the women in his life—and there were a lot of them—were always telling him. Nonna, Ma, Angie, and his aunts were forever pressing him to sell the bike, cover the tattoos, and quit playing with furniture so he could take his place at the helm of Pop's carpentry company.

*No, thank you.*

Becoming a carpenter and taking over the business hadn't done Angie any good. The responsibility robbed her of free time and fun. Besides, Tony already owned his own business, contracting out his upholstery services. The business was small and nondescript, which left his freedom intact.

"What'd Ma want?" he asked, rather than stoke his sister's perennially pissy mood by defending his life's direction.

"I don't know. I can't reach her now. The line's busy. How hard is it to get call waiting and caller ID?"

For a woman who still couldn't figure out the TV remote? Hard.

Strains of "Born to Be Wild" echoed above the air compressor.

"That's her," Angie yelled, pointing in the direction of his phone.

"You answer it," Tony said, preferring to spare himself the gory details of which cousin said what, more than a week ago at Nonna's birthday party, and why aunts X, Y, and Z were no longer speaking.

Angie kicked his thigh with her steel-toed boot as she walked by on her way to answer his phone. "Why is nothing ever important to you?"

As he listened to his sister answer their mother's call, he winced at his stinging thigh and traded the staple gun for an old-fashioned hammer and tacks. Wailing on the metal wedges would help. He had news for his too-serious-for-her-own-good sister, lots of things were important to him. Fun topped the list, with happiness running a close second, followed by friends who fed the fun and happiness.

"Oh God, no," Angie sobbed, and then wailed. "Tony, Nonna has ovarian cancer."

The mallet slipped from his hand.

As much as they drove him crazy, family was important, too.

An hour later, Tony was packed like a sardine into Nonna's galley kitchen with a collection of aunts and uncles who watched the stricken woman stir sauce despite the horrible news.

"I give it to God," she announced, raising one palm to the ceiling. "I no take it back."

There were a few amens, but as Tony looked around the room, he was struck by the paleness of the usually olive faces. And there were tears, but only when Nonna wasn't looking. And there were whispers of sentences he couldn't quite catch.

*Stage IV. Too late for surgery. Chemo. Radiation. Prayers.*

He felt sick, like he swallowed a jar of lug nuts and couldn't cough them up, let alone crap them out. And when the bowls of food started around the table, he couldn't eat.

He pushed away his chair, knowing the bathroom was the only rational escape. If he left the house, someone was bound to snitch, and once again he'd be a disappointment; the Corcarelli son not man enough to face the truth. Away from the heavy emotions, he flipped the lid down on the toilet and pulled his cell phone from his pocket. Rather than dwell on the turmoil twisting his guts in knots, he'd dwell on his fantasy football team's lousy performance. His wide receivers tanked, and there were never any good ones available after the draft.

*Tap. Tap. Tap.*

Tony looked at the door. "Occupied." And yet he couldn't stay much longer, knowing someone waited, unless he wanted to look like an inconsiderate pig. So he hurried up and dropped a running back, picked up a defense, and took a deep breath before he opened the bathroom door.

Nonna stood on the other side. "Antonio." She smooshed his cheeks in her scratchy, onion-scented hands and smiled the saddest smile he'd ever seen.

All he could do was hug her, squish her weathered body against him and wish he were strong enough to expunge the cancer with one good squeeze. "Love you, Nonna."

She pushed out of the hug and patted his cheek. "Why you want to be alone?"

Of all things…she was bringing up his marital status today. "I'm not alone, Nonna. I have all of you."

Both of her hands patted his face. "Life should be shared."

"And I *am* sharing my life." He slid his hands around her wrists and held them in his.

"No wife. No *bebe*." She nodded. "You make a good priest."

He bit back a laugh. A tattooed, Harley-riding priest. Come to think of it, he'd like to see that. But not him. No way. He was pretty sure celibacy was bad for his health.

"I'm fine, Nonna."

But she wasn't.

She nodded and shuffled past him to the bathroom. He wondered if she was going in to get away—like him. But if losing Pops taught him anything, it was that cancer left nowhere to hide.

"Tony, you need to be out here for this." Ma poked her head into the hallway and flagged him back into the dining room.

Aunt Josie was speed talking in a whisper when he walked into the room. "How do you know she can fly?"

"I'll check with the doctor," Aunt Carmella said.

"I think it's a wonderful idea," Ma added.

"Aunt Carmella and Uncle Gene have offered to take Nonna back to Lucca for a couple weeks," Angie explained in Tony's ear. "And when she gets back from Italy, Aunt Jo and Uncle Mike are going to surprise her by flying her brother in from California. Sort of like a surprise bucket list."

Tony nodded. A lot could happen during ten minutes holed up in a bathroom.

"I'm going to become Catholic," Ma announced. Her sisters-in-law gasped.

Angie flashed a look at Tony. Even Dad's illness hadn't prompted a gesture like that. But in the years after his death, Ma and Nonna had grown close, close enough that Ma declared her the mother she'd never had. And now this? Talk about grand gestures.

Tony watched as Angie wrapped her arms around their mother's neck and squeezed. "I want to do something, too," Angie said. "I'll have to think about it though. Tony, what about you?"

If the burn from the air hitting his wide eyes was any indication, he looked like a deer in headlights. His family stared back at him.

"Take your time, Tony. Something will come to you."

But all around him, they didn't look convinced.

Nonna shuffled into the kitchen. "*Mangia. Mangia.*" She pointed at the table full of food.

With the conversation stalled, everyone took their seats and ate—everyone except for Tony. He stared at his pasta, in between glances at Nonna. His family was united in giving her months—hopefully years—to remember. They expected him to join in. He'd ignored their expectations without a care before, but this time was different.

*Something will come to you.*

Nonna slurped a noodle into her mouth and offered him a small smile. She wanted him to join the priesthood or fall in love.

Anyway Tony looked at it, he was screwed.

In the mood for more Crimson Romance?
Check out *Simple Gone South* by Alicia Hunter Pace at
*CrimsonRomance.com.*

9 781440 571756